In the latest thriller from #1 *New York Times*–bestselling author Stuart Woods, Stone Barrington's newest foe has a short fuse . . . and it's just been lit.

Stone Barrington is enjoying a boating excursion off the Maine coast when a chance encounter leaves him somewhat the worse for wear. Always able to find the silver lining in even the unhappiest circumstances, Stone is pleased to discover that the authors of his misfortune are, in fact, members of a prestigious family who present a unique business opportunity, and who require a man of Stone's skills to overcome a sticky situation of their own.

The acquaintance is fortuitous indeed, for as it turns out, Stone and his new friends have an enemy in common. He's the sort of man who prefers force to finesse, and who regards any professional defeat as a personal and intolerable insult. And when Stone's sly cunning collides with his adversary's hair-trigger temper, the results are sure to be explosive . . .

Praise for the Stone Barrington Novels

Below the Belt

"Woods is a formidable storyteller who knows the art of monopolizing your attention."
—*Washington Book Review*

Sex, Lies & Serious Money

"[An] irresistible, luxury-soaked soap opera."
—*Publishers Weekly*

Dishonorable Intentions

"Diverting." —*Publishers Weekly*

Family Jewels

"Mr. Woods knows how to portray the beautiful people, their manners and mores, their fluid and sparkling conversation, their easy expectations and all the glitter that surrounds and defines them. A master of dialogue, action and atmosphere, [Woods] has added one more jewel of a thriller-mystery to his ever-growing collection."

—*Fort Myers Florida Weekly*

Scandalous Behavior

"Addictive . . . Pick [*Scandalous Behavior*] up at your peril. You can get hooked." —*Lincoln Journal Star*

Foreign Affairs

"Purrs like a well-tuned dream machine . . . Mr. Woods knows how to set up scenes and link them to keep the action, emotion, and information moving. He presents the places he takes us to vividly and convincingly. . . . Enjoy this slick thriller by a thoroughly satisfying professional." —*Fort Myers Florida Weekly*

Hot Pursuit

"Fans will enjoy the vicarious luxury ride as usual."

—*Publishers Weekly*

Insatiable Appetites

"Multiple exciting storylines . . . Readers of the series will enjoy the return of the dangerous Dolce." —*Booklist*

Paris Match

"Plenty of fast-paced action and deluxe experiences that keep the pages turning. Woods is masterful with his use of dialogue and creates natural and vivid scenes for his readers to enjoy." —*Myrtle Beach Sun News*

Cut and Thrust

"This installment goes down as smoothly as a glass of Knob Creek." —*Publishers Weekly*

Carnal Curiosity

"Stone Barrington shows he's one of the smoothest operators around . . . Entertaining." —*Publishers Weekly*

Standup Guy

"Stuart Woods still owns an imagination that simply won't quit. . . . This is yet another edge-of-your-seat adventure." —*Suspense Magazine*

Doing Hard Time

"Longtime Woods fans who have seen Teddy [Fay] evolve from a villain to something of a lovable antihero will enjoy watching the former enemies work together in this exciting yarn. Is this the beginning of a beautiful partnership? Let's hope so." —*Booklist*

Unintended Consequences

"Since 1981, readers have not been able to get their fill of Stuart Woods' *New York Times* best-selling novels of suspense."

—*Orlando Sentinel*

Collateral Damage

"High-octane . . . Woods's blend of exciting action, sophisticated gadgetry, and last-minute heroics doesn't disappoint." —*Publishers Weekly*

Severe Clear

"Stuart Woods has proven time and time again that he's a master of suspense who keeps his readers frantically turning the pages." —Bookreporter.com

BOOKS BY STUART WOODS

FICTION

Quick & Dirty[†]
Indecent Exposure[†]
Fast & Loose[†]
Below the Belt[†]
Sex, Lies & Serious Money[†]
Dishonorable Intentions[†]
Family Jewels[†]
Scandalous Behavior[†]
Foreign Affairs[†]
Naked Greed[†]
Hot Pursuit[†]
Insatiable Appetites[†]
Paris Match[†]
Cut and Thrust[†]
Carnal Curiosity[†]
Standup Guy[†]
Doing Hard Time[†]
Unintended Consequences[†]
Collateral Damage[†]
Severe Clear[†]
Unnatural Acts[†]

D.C. Dead[†]
Son of Stone[†]
Bel-Air Dead[†]
Strategic Moves[†]
Santa Fe Edge[§]
Lucid Intervals[†]
Kisser[†]
Hothouse Orchid[*]
Loitering with Intent[†]
Mounting Fears[‡]
Hot Mahogany[†]
Santa Fe Dead[§]
Beverly Hills Dead
Shoot Him If He Runs[†]
Fresh Disasters[†]
Short Straw[§]
Dark Harbor[†]
Iron Orchid[*]
Two-Dollar Bill[†]
The Prince of Beverly Hills
Reckless Abandon[†]
Capital Crimes[‡]
Dirty Work[†]
Blood Orchid[*]
The Short Forever[†]

Orchid Blues[*]
Cold Paradise[†]
L.A. Dead[†]
The Run[‡]
Worst Fears Realized[†]
Orchid Beach[*]
Swimming to Catalina[†]
Dead in the Water[†]
Dirt[†]
Choke
Imperfect Strangers
Heat
Dead Eyes
L.A. Times
Santa Fe Rules[§]
New York Dead[†]
Palindrome
Grass Roots[‡]
White Cargo
Deep Lie[‡]
Under the Lake
Run Before the Wind[‡]
Chiefs[‡]

COAUTHORED BOOKS

Smooth Operator[**]
(with Parnell Hall)

Barely Legal[††]
(with Parnell Hall)

TRAVEL

A Romantic's Guide to the Country Inns of Britain and Ireland (1979)

MEMOIR

Blue Water, Green Skipper

[*]A Holly Barker Novel
[†]A Stone Barrington Novel
[‡]A Will Lee Novel

[§]An Ed Eagle Novel
[**]A Teddy Fay Novel
[††]A Herbie Fisher Novel

FAST & LOOSE

STUART WOODS

G. P. PUTNAM'S SONS

New York

PUTNAM

G. P. PUTNAM'S SONS
Publishers Since 1838
An imprint of Penguin Random House LLC
375 Hudson Street
New York, New York 10014

Copyright © 2017 by Stuart Woods
Excerpt from *Indecent Exposure* copyright © 2017 by Stuart Woods
Penguin supports copyright. Copyright fuels creativity, encourages diverse
voices, promotes free speech, and creates a vibrant culture. Thank you for buy-
ing an authorized edition of this book and for complying with copyright laws
by not reproducing, scanning, or distributing any part of it in any form without
permission. You are supporting writers and allowing Penguin to continue to
publish books for every reader.

The Library of Congress has catalogued the G. P. Putnam's Sons hardcover
edition as follows:

Names: Woods, Stuart, author.
Title: Fast & loose / Stuart Woods.
Other titles: Fast and loose
Description: New York : G. P. Putnam's Sons, 2017. |
Series: A Stone Barrington novel ; 41
Identifiers: LCCN 2017003230 (print) | LCCN 2017008147 (ebook) |
ISBN 9780399574191 (hardback) | ISBN 9780399574214 (EPub)
Subjects: LCSH: Barrington, Stone (Fictitious character)—Fiction. |
BISAC: FICTION / Action & Adventure. | FICTION / Suspense. |
FICTION / Thrillers. | GSAFD: Suspense fiction.
Classification: LCC PS3573.O642 F37 2017 (print) | LCC PS3573.O642
(ebook) |
DDC 813/.54—dc23
LC record available at https://lccn.loc.gov/2017003230
p. cm.

First G. P. Putnam's Sons hardcover edition / April 2017
First G. P. Putnam's Sons premium edition / November 2017
G. P. Putnam's Sons premium edition ISBN: 9780399574207

Printed in the United States of America
1 3 5 7 9 10 8 6 4 2

FAST & LOOSE

1

Stone Barrington lay back in the cockpit of the Concordia 40, a small cruising yawl built by Abeking & Rasmussen, a German yard, in 1938, and let the light breeze take him back toward Dark Harbor. The sails were nicely balanced as he sailed up Maine's Penobscot Bay, and he lashed the helm while he looked around, then peed overboard. Thus relieved, he settled back into the cockpit and tucked a cushion behind him, relaxed and happy.

He dozed off.

The yacht jerked a bit, waking him, and he found himself in the thickest fog he had ever experienced. He could barely make out the stem of the boat, and he was uncertain about his course. He had been headed for the Tarratine Yacht Club moorings, and his own dock beyond, but he didn't know how long he had been asleep or whether the wind had changed and put him off course. He checked the depth sounder: 55 feet of water—too deep to anchor with the rode he had aboard. He stood up and dropped the mainsail to slow the boat to a crawl, continuing with the jib and the mizzen. He went back to his cockpit seat and resumed his position, but left the helm lashed. They were making only three knots in the light breeze, and he reckoned he couldn't get into too much trouble at that speed. The depth was now 70 feet.

He heard a voice from somewhere in the fog saying, "Start the engines and drop the sails," but he couldn't figure out the direction from which it had come. Then there was the sound of water moving past a hull, but he was still unable to determine the direction. He rummaged in a cockpit locker for the air horn and pressed the button. The noise shocked him, and it was followed by shouting from the fog.

Then he saw a shape to port and grabbed for the helm. It took a moment to throw off the lashings, and in that time there was a terrible noise, and his world turned upside down. The boom swung across the cockpit and caught him on the side of his head, and darkness fell.

HE FELT THE PAIN before he felt his surroundings, and he feared that if he opened his eyes it might make things worse. He allowed some light past his eyelids, then quickly shut them again, groaning loudly at the pain. He heard a rustle beside him, and felt a cool hand on his forehead.

"He's awake," a low female voice said. "Get Father."

Stone tried to speak, but his mouth was too dry. A glass brushed his lips, and he took in a sip of water.

"Is that better? Can you speak?"

"I'm sorry to open with a cliché," he said, "but where am I?"

She chuckled. "You're in bed. You had an accident."

He got his eyes all the way open this time, and there was an arm attached to the cool hand, and a woman attached to the other end of the arm—very blond, almost white hair. "What kind of an accident?"

"What's the last thing you remember?" she asked.

He thought about that. "Fog," he said. "Lots of fog. There was a noise."

"Your foghorn?"

"Yes."

"That was the first we knew of your presence."

"I didn't hear yours."

"I'm sorry about that. The crew was busy getting the sails down."

He struggled to sit up, but she pushed him back. "Not yet," she said. She lifted his head and tucked another pillow under it, enabling him to look around—first, at the woman. Very nice. He was in a cozy cabin of beautifully varnished mahogany.

"My father will be here in a moment to take a look at you," she said. "Your name is Stone Barrington, is it not?"

"It is."

"My name is Marisa Carlsson, with a cee and two esses."

"How did you know my name?"

"You had a wallet with business cards inside. It's drying out, while your clothes are being laundered."

He realized he was naked under the covers. "Who undressed me?" he asked.

She laughed. "The pleasure was mine."

"I'm glad you see it that way."

"Well," a man's voice said, "is our patient awake?" He stepped into the cabin, an older male version of his daughter.

"More or less," Stone said.

"This is my father, Dr. Paul Carlsson," she said.

"You've had a thump on your head," the doctor said.

"I noticed that."

Carlsson laughed. "He's well enough to have a sense of humor."

"Where is my boat?" Stone asked.

"I'm afraid it's at the bottom of Penobscot Bay. There was nothing we could do—it sank very quickly after the collision."

"I'm sorry to hear it. It was an old boat that had made people happy for a long time."

"What boat was it?"

"A Concordia 40 yawl, built in 1938, at Abeking and Rasmussen."

"Funny, that's where this yacht was built," the doctor said.

"What is she?"

"A ninety-foot ketch, designed by Ron Holland, built the year before last."

"Well, I suppose the better yacht won the battle."

"Don't worry about your boat, we'll deal with that later. You've had a concussion, but your vital signs are strong and you're making good conversation, so I don't think we'll have to hospitalize you. We'll get you some soup, to keep your strength up, but then you must rest. You should be fine in the morning."

A uniformed steward came in with a steaming mug of

something on a tray. Stone sipped it. "Chicken soup," he said.

"The cure for everything," the doctor replied.

"Except my headache. Do you have any aspirin?"

"We do. Marisa?"

She left the cabin and returned with three pills. Stone washed them down with the soup. "One of them will help you sleep."

THE NEXT TIME he woke up sun was streaming through the port over his head, and his clothes, laundered and ironed, were neatly stacked on the bed. He found a razor and a new toothbrush in the head, then had a hot shower and dressed. He stepped out of his cabin into a hallway and followed that to the saloon, then he walked up some stairs to the deck and found Dr. Carlsson and his daughter having breakfast on the afterdeck.

They waved him to a seat, and the steward took his order.

"How are you feeling?" Carlsson asked.

"Almost like new—perhaps a little fuzzy around the edges."

"That's the last of your sleeping pill."

Stone looked around; they were anchored in the harbor not far from the Tarratine. "I live right over there," he said, pointing at his house. "Just down from the yacht club."

"What a lovely house," Marisa said. "Is it old?"

"Only a few years. I inherited it from a cousin, Dick Stone, who built it."

"We'll get you ashore after breakfast," Carlsson said, "and then we'll talk about your yacht, see what we can do."

"Are there just the two of you aboard?" Stone asked.

"Yes, my wife died some years ago," Carlsson said.

"Why don't you come for dinner this evening?" Stone asked.

"That's very kind of you," Carlsson said. "We'd like that very much."

"Are you Dr. Carlsson of the Carlsson Clinic?" Stone asked.

"I am one of the Dr. Carlssons," he replied, "the elder one. Marisa and my two sons are all Dr. Carlssons, as well."

The Carlsson Clinic was a famous hospital, with locations in several cities, on a par with the Mayo Clinic. "Well," Stone said, "I have not lacked for medical attention. If you say I'm all right, then I must be."

2

The tender from the big yacht dropped Stone at his dock, and he walked up to the house. The door opened, and Bob, his yellow Labrador retriever, bounded out to greet him, carrying a ratty stuffed raccoon that was his favorite toy.

Stone knelt and petted him, scratched his back, then took the raccoon and tossed it into the house. Bob followed closely.

Mary, his housekeeper, was dusting the living room. "We were worried," she said, "when you didn't come home last night."

"I had an accident," Stone said.

Mary's husband, Seth Hotchkiss, came into the room. "What kind of accident?"

"I got run down by a much larger yacht in the fog."

"Any damage?"

"Total loss. She's at the bottom of the bay."

"Such a beautiful boat," Seth said. "Very sad. You all right?"

"A slight headache is all. By the way, there'll be two guests for dinner tonight. They're coming at six for drinks. Two Dr. Carlssons, father and daughter."

"Lobster?" Mary asked.

"Just fine." She would boil it, shell it, and toss the meat in butter.

"Mr. Rawls moved out and into his place this morning," Seth said. "I drove the stuff he'd bought over there."

Stone's neighbor, Ed Rawls, had had his house destroyed by fire a couple of months ago and had rebuilt. "I'm happy for him," he said.

"Joan called already this morning."

"I'll call her back now." He sat down on the sofa and picked up the phone.

"The Barrington Practice at Woodman & Weld."

"I'm alive."

"Mary said you didn't come home last night. Anybody I know?"

"An accident—collision with a much larger yacht. I lost the boat."

"Ooh! I'll keep my picture of it as a memento."

"Anything going on?"

"You're still getting calls about the business with Christian St. Clair and Nelson Knott. What should I tell them?"

Christian St. Clair was a multibillionaire who had been running a TV pitchman, Nelson Knott, for President, putting lots of money behind him.

"Tell them they're both dead, and I don't speak for them. Tell them to call that guy, what's his name?"

"Erik Macher."

"That's the one. He was St. Clair's right-hand man in all this. They should speak to him, if he hasn't been arrested."

"It's been weeks. Why don't they leave you alone?"

"Beats me. If I talk to the media I'll find myself in the spin zone—they'll distort whatever I say."

"This morning's *Times* had the medical examiner's report on St. Clair. Cause of death was a bomb in a piece of luggage that he opened. Would that be your strong case?"

"Not my strong case, Ed Rawls's. It was taken from him at gunpoint, and he didn't have time to tell them how to open it safely."

"So Ed's not to blame?"

"I would defend him on the available evidence."

"When are you coming home? You're due for your physical first of the week."

"I'm dining with two eminent physicians tonight. Will that do?"

"It's your FAA flight physical, to keep your medical certificate valid. You can't fly without it."

"I know, I know. I hate to come back just for that. The weather up here is gorgeous—autumn comes earlier here than in New York."

"Lucky you. It's like a steam bath on the streets here."

"No calls?"

"Dino called to find out when you're coming back. He couldn't reach you there."

"I'll call him this morning. Nothing else?"

"Nope. Apparently everyone has forgotten about you."

"Everyone but the bloody media. Don't give them this number or my cell number."

"Gotcha."

"See you later." Stone hung up and wondered what to do next. He and his clothes were already clean, so he didn't need to bathe and dress. He called Dino.

"Bacchetti."

"It's Stone."

"Where the hell have you been?"

"I'll tell you, but you're not going to believe me."

"Try me."

"I was sailing late yesterday afternoon, when I encountered a fog bank—couldn't see a thing."

"Let me guess—you were run down by a beautiful yacht sailed by a beautiful woman who rescued you and nursed you back to health."

"That's pretty much what happened."

"You're kidding. I made that up."

"You must be psychic. The owner of the yacht is Dr. Paul Carlsson, of the Carlsson Clinic—and his daughter."

"What happened to your yacht?"

"She lies in a watery grave at the bottom of Penobscot Bay."

"That's sad—pretty boat."

"Listen, can you still hijack that police helicopter whenever you like?"

"Whenever I like, sometimes."

"Why don't you do that this afternoon and get them to drop you here? Weekend's coming up, and it's nice and cool here."

"Put me down for a yes. I'll check with Viv and confirm, if you'll hang on for a moment." He put Stone on hold, then came back. "I talked her into it, and the chopper's available. We'll aim for five o'clock."

"I'll meet you at the airstrip. The Carlssons are coming to dinner. They're nice folks."

"We'll look forward to it. Bye." Dino hung up.

Stone told Mary to order more lobsters.

STONE STOOD BY the lovely old 1938 Ford station wagon that was the house car and watched the NYPD helicopter settle onto the runway. The copilot got out and dumped the Bacchettis' luggage onto the tarmac, then got back in and the chopper lifted off and turned southwest, toward New York.

Stone kissed Viv, shook Dino's hand, and the three of them loaded the bags into the wagon. As they drove away, another helicopter, one Stone recognized from a charter service at Rockland airport, set down on the runway. He didn't see who got out.

"I hear Paul Carlsson is coming to dinner," Viv said. "I met him at some event last year. He was charming, and he has a charming daughter, too."

"They're both coming," Stone said.

"It's about time. You've been without female companionship for too long."

"You're not going to get an argument from me about that."

3

Erik Macher marched himself into the late Christian St. Clair's library/office, which was undergoing the final touches of repair, and sat down at a leather-topped library table already occupied by four serious-looking men.

"Good morning, gentlemen," Macher said, careful to speak respectfully.

The four nodded and mumbled something. They were the chairman of the board, two directors, and the corporate counsel of St. Clair Enterprises, and Macher was there to let them know, as gently as possible, that he would be running things from now on. Their agreement was crucial to him.

"I assume you all received the documents I sent you." They all nodded.

"And I assume you read Mr. St. Clair's will, which was

prepared by the law firm of Mr. Berenson, our corporate counsel."

"That is so," Berenson said, "and it was signed and witnessed in my presence." The others merely nodded.

"Mr. Berenson, was I a party to drawing up the will, and did I discuss it at any time with you or any of your people?"

"No, and no," Berenson replied. "I am satisfied that the will is authentic and correctly represents the wishes of Mr. St. Clair."

"Thank you," Macher said. "Do any of you have any questions about the preparation and intent of the will?"

Heads were shaken.

"Thank you."

"Mr. Macher," the chairman said, "I have a question."

"Please ask it, sir."

"What is the purpose of this meeting?"

Macher took a document from his briefcase and distributed copies to the four men. "The purpose is to pass this motion, appointing me as permanent chief executive officer of St. Clair Enterprises. Do I hear a second?"

The chairman looked up from the document. "This gives you extraordinarily broad and deep powers in the operation of the various companies and us very little oversight."

"That is quite true," Macher said, "and that is in line with the way Mr. St. Clair ran the enterprises and wished to have them run in the event of his death, is it not, Mr. Berenson?" Macher had met with Berenson earlier and acquired his cooperation, in return for the continuation of his firm's handling of all the enterprises' legal work.

"It is entirely in line with both Mr. St. Clair's past practices and his wishes for the enterprises to continue to be operated," Berenson said.

The chairman shifted in his seat. "It also says that the board will serve at the pleasure of the CEO and that he will appoint replacements as necessary."

"It does," Macher replied. "I would like to mention that I have no plans to change the way the board is presently made up or has operated in the past."

That caused a few wrinkles to disappear from the chairman's forehead.

"Or in the board's compensation," Macher added. He could see on their faces that that had done the trick.

"I second the motion," the chairman said, "and I call for it to be passed by acclamation."

"Hear! Hear!" the four said in unison.

"Thank you for your expression of confidence, gentlemen," Macher said. "There is no further business at this time, but we will meet again in accordance with the existing schedule of board meetings." That was annually. "I should tell you that, in the interests of efficiency, I shall be occupying this house and conducting business from this room, when I am in New York. Since Mr. St. Clair's will left all his residences and other possessions to St. Clair Enterprises, I shall also be using them as necessary." This, of course, included the yacht, but he didn't mention it. "Is there any further business, gentlemen?"

"There is the question of your own compensation and benefits package," the chairman said.

"Mr. Berenson's firm is working on that as we speak, and he will see that you are notified when the work is complete."

"That is so," Berenson said.

"Then if there are no other matters before us, this meeting is concluded. Thank you for your continued work and cooperation, gentlemen." He stood, causing them to stand as well, and after shaking hands, they filed out. Berenson, as previously agreed, remained.

"Thank you, Tommy," Macher said. "I thought that went very well."

"So did I, Erik."

"You may now send the prepared letters to all the operating officers of the various enterprises, and the general letter to all employees, including the staffs of the properties, and the crews of the yacht, the helicopter, and the fleet of aircraft. I think it's important that everyone understand that, for purposes of continuity and morale, a new regime is now in place."

"I agree entirely, Erik," Berenson said. "They will all go out by FedEx within the hour."

"Incidentally, Tommy, you may prepare a letter from me doubling your personal salary as counsel with immediate effect, and I will sign it upon receipt."

"Thank you for that expression of your confidence, Erik."

Macher handed him a sheet of paper. "Here is a list of all credit accounts previously available only to Christian, which should be notified that I am now the sole signatory. There is also my bank account number, to which my signing bonus and my first year's salary should be deposited, and a list of credit cards for the bank to issue to me and my secretary."

"Of course. I'll see that the signing bonus is deposited today."

The signing bonus was twenty-five million dollars, and Macher's salary was ten million dollars a year, plus an unlimited expense account. "Thank you, and I expect we'll talk soon."

The two men shook hands, and Berenson departed.

Macher walked to the new desk that had replaced the previous one destroyed in the explosion and began unpacking the boxes that he had had sent from his office in D.C., which included his files and personal photographs. He placed his belongings in the appropriate drawers and arrayed the sterling-silver-framed photographs on the new credenza behind him.

There was a knock on the door.

"Come in!"

His secretary entered the room. "I saw that the board had left," she said. "Is there anything I can do for you?"

"Are you quite comfortable in your new rooms upstairs, Hilda?"

"Yes, sir, they are very nice."

"Your salary increase will be in effect from this day, and new credit cards have been ordered for you. You may open an account with the company's bank today."

"Thank you, Mr. Macher. I'm very pleased to be working with you in New York."

"I am pleased, too, Hilda."

She left, and Macher leaned back in his new chair and placed his feet on his desk. He had never felt so good. Things could not have gone better if he had planned St. Clair's death himself.

4

Stone called Ed Rawls and invited him to dinner.

"Thanks, I could use the break," Ed replied. "Unpacking is a bitch."

"See you at six?"

"You're on."

STONE LET HIMSELF into Dick Stone's secret office, behind a panel, and checked for messages and faxes. He had just come out and locked the door behind him when the front doorbell rang. He went to answer it and found a small woman wearing a headset and carrying a microphone. Behind her stood a man carrying a portable TV camera.

"Good afternoon, Mr. Barrington. I'm Tina Charles from NBC news. You're a hard man to find—we've been driving all over the island looking for your house."

"I must remember to conceal it better," Stone said.

"May I come in for a moment? I have just a few questions for you."

"You may not. I have no wish to be interviewed."

"May I point out that, if you speak to me exclusively that will greatly lessen the curiosity of other media outlets, and there are many who wish to speak with you."

"How did you get to the island?"

"The station has a helicopter. We landed right after the NYPD chopper, but we didn't have a car and lost you while we were arranging for one."

"I'll give you five minutes," Stone said.

The woman came in and briefly surveyed the room. "You'll sit there," she said, pointing at a chair, "and I'll sit opposite you in the other chair." She began moving the two chairs to positions she liked. "Okay, Bernie?" she asked the cameraman.

"Aces," the man replied. "Light is good."

She clipped a tiny wireless microphone to Stone's shirt collar. "Give me a level," she ordered.

Stone counted slowly to five.

"Level is good," the cameraman said.

"And sit." She took his wrist and towed him to the chair, and they both sat down. She took off her headset and dropped it beside the chair, then fluffed her hair with both hands and freshened her lipstick.

Stone watched, increasingly bored. Then it occurred to him that he should seem alert on camera and, if possible, engaged. He made an effort to brighten his mien.

"Now," Tina said. "Title. This is Tina Charles at the Maine home of Mr. Stone Barrington. We're on." She stated the date and time. "Mr. Barrington, there have been many rumors floating around about your involvement in the deaths of the billionaire Christian St. Clair and his political protégé, Nelson Knott."

"Hold it right there," Stone said, raising a hand. "I had no involvement whatever in their deaths. I met them only once each."

"Let's start with Mr. St. Clair. Where did you meet him?"

"About a mile from here in that direction," he said, pointing toward the water. "He was aboard his yacht with some people, and he called and invited me and a friend to dinner. I accepted."

"Who was your friend?"

"Irrelevant. Next question?"

"Did you also meet Nelson Knott on Mr. St. Clair's yacht?"

"Yes, but not until the following day. I spent one night aboard the yacht and then, at my request, was put ashore."

"Did you know at that time that Mr. Knott was going to run for President?"

"He alluded to the possibility, and he seemed very interested in extracting campaign donations from two other guests aboard."

"And who were they?"

"You'd have to ask them."

Tina was looking a bit frustrated now. "All right, let's turn to this strong box thing."

"It's called a strong case."

"What is it?"

"A sort of large, very secure briefcase."

"And it passed through your hands on its way to Mr. St. Clair?"

"It spent a night or two in my safe, then my client removed it to his home."

"Then how did it get to Mr. St. Clair?"

"Two gentlemen visited my client's home, pointed a gun at him, and demanded he give them the strong case or be shot. He complied."

"And did he explain that it had to be opened in a certain way or it would explode?"

"If he knew that, he was not given an opportunity to explain it. The two men left hurriedly."

"And where did the case go then?"

"Eventually, to Mr. St. Clair, it would seem. I don't know how many stops it made along the way."

"And Mr. St. Clair tried to open the strong case, then it exploded?"

"I believe that was the testimony of a witness who was with him at the time."

"And that would be Mr. Erik Macher?"

"According to the *New York Times*," he said. "That is my source of information. Didn't you read it?"

"Well, yes. Why did the strong case explode?"

"If you read the *Times*, you know what I know."

"Who owned the strong case?"

"I don't know."

"But it was in your client's possession?"

"For a brief time. Two attempts were made to steal it, the last successful."

"And who was your client?"

"I'm sorry, that's privileged information."

"You're not being very helpful, Mr. Barrington."

Stone smiled slightly. "I'm not trying to be."

"Don't you think the viewing public is entitled to know everything about this event?"

"I'm not at all sure that they are," Stone replied. "It might be best if you consulted the authority investigating the event, instead of me. I'm just a bystander."

"But you're a witness."

"That is incorrect. I was not present when these events occurred."

"Are you aware that Nelson Knott took his own life?"

"Again, I read it in the *Times*. I wasn't a witness to that, either."

"All right, one last question."

"Promise?"

"Yes. What was in the strong case?"

"It was never opened in my presence."

"Is it true that there was nothing inside?"

"No. All indications point to a bomb inside."

"Well, we know that, don't we?"

"Then why are you asking me?"

"Thank you, Mr. Barrington. Now back to the studio. And . . . cut." She stood up. "Well, that was exasperating."

"Is it usually satisfying to chase people all around the northeastern United States and ask them questions to which they don't have the answers?"

"Could I have a glass of water, please?"

Stone went to the bar, retrieved a bottle of water, and handed it to her. "Good day," he said.

"May I sit down and drink it?"

"Certainly, but not in my house. Kindly go away."

She gathered up her belongings, including her headset, and bustled out of the house, followed by her technician.

Dino came down the stairs. "I heard all that from up there," he said.

"Good. I'm glad I don't have to re-create the event for you."

"Why are all these people wanting to interview you?"

"Beats me. I guess they can't think of anybody else to interview."

The doorbell rang again, and Stone got up. "Do you have your gun with you, Dino?"

"It's upstairs. Why?"

"If it's that young woman again, I'd like you to shoot her." He opened the door and found Ed Rawls standing there.

5

Rawls stepped inside; he seemed a little out of breath.

"Sorry if I'm early," he said. "I walked over here, and it took less time than I thought."

"That's fine, Ed. Come in. You know Dino."

"Hi, Ed."

"Evening." He accepted a large Talisker from Stone. "Have you heard the news?"

"What news?"

"Of course you haven't. What am I thinking?"

"Hard to tell, Ed. Spit it out."

"Oh. You remember one Erik Macher?"

"I do."

"I've had news that he has taken over Christian St. Clair's holdings, personal and business—everything except what St. Clair left his wife."

"How could he do that?"

"He met with the board and, with the support of the corporate counsel, Thomas Berenson, who drew the will and had it witnessed, he got himself appointed CEO, with power to replace board members at will, and he is heir to St. Clair's personal property that wasn't left to his wife, including the yacht."

Stone poured drinks for himself and Dino while he thought about that, then he sat down. "I know a little about Tommy Berenson's reputation, and it isn't all good. If I were a board member, I'd put that will through the wringer."

"And you'd be fired and replaced in the blink of an eye. Anyway, with Tommy Berenson backing him, he's in an impossibly strong position."

"Well," Stone said, "I'm glad I don't own stock in any of St. Clair's ventures."

"Not even the yacht?"

"Well, there is that," Stone admitted.

"Anyway, none of St. Clair's businesses are publicly owned. He started with a large fortune from his father and built his empire out of profits."

"How do you know so much about St. Clair?"

"When I was in prison it was sort of my hobby to follow the careers and lives of a number of people," Ed said. "St. Clair was one of them, and apart from the Internet, I had my own sources with good information to impart."

"You must be the most successful prisoner in the history of the federal system," Stone observed.

"Don't you believe it. I was just looking for information, while others were establishing fortunes and others were conducting criminal enterprises."

"Was prison security that loose, that these things could go on?"

"You have to remember that the Atlanta Federal Prison was closed, then later reopened in a small way, to contain special prisoners, and employing a very small staff. None of the inmates had histories of violence—they were mostly white-collar thieves and a few other, special cons, like me, who were put there to keep prisoners in other jails from killing them. A few people had cell phones and laptops, though they weren't used openly, but communication with the outside was fairly easy."

"I must remember, if I ever commit a crime, to get sent to Atlanta," Stone said.

"I'll note that preference in your file," Dino said.

"Stone," Rawls said, "you don't seem to be getting what this means."

Stone blinked. "Should I be?"

"You remember I told you that St. Clair had his own police force?"

"I do remember."

"Well, Erik Macher was its chief, and he still is. Except now he has complete power. He doesn't have to wait for St. Clair to tell him to remove somebody from living, he can just issue the order himself."

"Now, why would he do that and jeopardize his newly found position?"

"Because he is a revenge freak, and he's going to get drunk with power very quickly."

"I don't think I've ever encountered anybody quite like that," Stone said. "How would you define a revenge freak?"

"Someone who, when slighted—however slightly—

extracts a price from the slighter, usually one all out of proportion to the seriousness of the slight."

"Even unto death?"

"Death was Macher's work when he was at the CIA. I mean, he always had a title as a cover, and he did carry out covert operations for the Agency, but they usually revolved around the removal of one or more of the opposition. He was instrumental in the establishment of the Agency's drone program, which has carried assassination to new and exotic heights."

"Yes, I've seen the pictures of the firing of Hellfire missiles through windows, exploding entire houses."

"Oh, now it's much more refined than that," Ed said. "Now some of them are equipped with silenced .50 caliber sniper rifles that can, remotely, put a round into the ear of an opponent and not make a sound heard on the ground. Heads just suddenly explode, alarming others nearby."

"Please tell me that St. Clair did not have a fleet of those standing by."

"Not a fleet, but Macher, through his connections with Agency suppliers, managed to corral a couple. But I digress, I don't mean necessarily that Macher is going to hunt any of us down with drones."

"I'm relieved to hear it, and I'm glad that I hardly ever came to Macher's attention."

"Don't you believe it," Rawls said.

"Huh?"

"St. Clair knew everything about you and me that could be known, and it was Macher who gathered the intelligence on us and anyone else St. Clair dealt with. He was an information freak. He had to know everything about everybody."

"Then he would have known he was backing a political candidate, Nelson Knott, who had a proclivity for raping and sometimes impregnating women who worked for him."

"Of course he did, and he took the greatest precautions to see that that news never came out. He took the view that if there was no evidence and no witnesses, it never happened."

"But his precautions were not successful."

"Right. You managed to hide one of the women and her family at your home in England, and that recording she made blew the lid off Knott's candidacy and, incidentally, off the candidate, as well."

"How colorfully you put it."

"That's the sort of interference that Macher would take personally."

"Oh, he's thin-skinned, is he?"

"Thin-skinned and hard-shelled. Simultaneously. You must remember that most of the work St. Clair put into creating Knott as a candidate was actually performed by Macher and his wide-ranging PD."

Stone took a swig of his bourbon and let it find its way down. "Oh, shit," he said.

6

The Carlssons, father and daughter, arrived on time for drinks, and after Stone had served everybody, Dr. Paul handed Stone a brown envelope.

"What's this?" Stone asked.

"Some photographs. Take a look at them."

Stone opened the envelope and removed half a dozen color photographs of a Concordia 40. "This is gorgeous," Stone said. "Better equipped and newer-looking than mine."

"It was one of the original Concordias, the ones built in Germany, like yours," Carlsson said. "Would you consider it an adequate replacement for your yacht?"

"More than adequate," Stone said. "Superior, I would say."

"Then if you will accept it as a fair replacement, it's yours, and I will deal with my insurance company for the cost."

"Then I accept. Where is she?"

"She's out of the water in Rockland, but ready to launch after an extensive refit. One of my crew knew somebody who knew somebody, and there she was. She'll be at your dock tomorrow."

"You take my breath away," Stone said, handing them to Dino to see.

"We very nearly took your breath away permanently, and I'm relieved that you like the replacement Concordia."

Ed Rawls looked at the photos and raised his glass. "To new old boats," he said, and everybody drank.

OVER DINNER Paul Carlsson was very quiet, and his daughter noticed. "Dad, is something wrong?"

"Not wrong, exactly," Carlsson said, "just a little worrying."

"Anything an attorney and a policeman and a retired spy can help with?" Stone asked.

"I don't think so, it's a business thing."

"The Carlsson Clinic is your family business, isn't it?" Dino asked.

"Yes, it is."

"The city sent me there for my last physical."

"I hope it was performed to your satisfaction."

"Well, the city was satisfied, and that's all I cared about."

Carlsson sighed. "I'm not sure it will be the same clinic this time next year."

"Oh, Dad," Marisa said, "this isn't about that thing with that man St. Clair, is it?"

"Yes, it is."

"But he died—surely he's not a problem anymore."

"May I ask," Stone said, "are you referring to Christian St. Clair?"

"I am," Carlsson replied. "Shortly before his death, he made a takeover offer for the Carlsson clinics. I, my daughter, and my two sons own forty percent of the stock, but over the years we've awarded shares to many of our employees, mostly doctors and nurses, who were valuable to our work. They've formed an association, and St. Clair made an offer—an inadequate one, which was apparently his practice—for the stock held by the association members."

"Did they accept?"

"They voted to accept in principle, dependent on a much better offer. Selling their shares would make many of them wealthy, some of them *very* wealthy, so the prospect is tempting to them. And now I've heard that St. Clair's business interests will be run by a man named Macher, who apparently has a reputation that is something less than savory."

"Who is representing you in this matter?"

"We have a competent firm who represents us in our normal operations and who has defended us in malpractice matters, though very few of them, but I don't believe they are equipped to take on this challenge, and we're faced with a deadline. St. Clair's offer is to expire in about three weeks."

"I see," Stone replied. "If I can be of help, please let me know." That was as far as he was prepared to go without encouragement from Carlsson.

"Well, Dr. Carlsson," Dino said, "since this transaction involves a hospital, you should know that our friend Stone is a well-known ambulance . . . chaser, and very good at it."

"Thank you for your confidence, Dino," Stone said wryly, "but I'm sure Dr. Carlsson can address his problem without it."

"I confess that the matter crossed my mind when I saw your business card, while we were drying you out."

"And drying out is one of the things Stone does best," Dino said. Everyone laughed. "Sorry, bad joke, but I couldn't resist."

"I've heard of Woodman & Weld," Carlsson said, "and after making a few calls to friends more knowledgeable than I in these matters, I must say I am impressed with what I've heard. Would your firm consider taking us on, Stone?"

"I think we'd both benefit from sobriety before going into that, Dr. Carlsson, and we have taken drink this evening. May we discuss it tomorrow, in the cold light of day?"

"Of course."

"I will say that I'm optimistic that we can find a solution to your problem."

"Thank you, I feel better already."

AFTER COFFEE, THE Carlssons excused themselves, and Stone walked them down to his dock, where their launch awaited. Carlsson extended his hand. "Thank you for dinner, Stone, and I'll look forward to seeing you tomorrow."

"Would ten o'clock here be convenient, Dr. Carlsson?"

"Certainly, and you must call me Paul—everyone but my children does."

"Of course, Paul. See you tomorrow." He waved them off, then walked back to the house. Dino and Ed Rawls had disappeared. Stone sat down and made a phone call to Arthur Steele, chairman and CEO of the Steele Insurance Group, a client, and on whose board he sat.

"Good evening, Stone, is everything all right?"

"I'm sorry to call so late, Art, but something has come up that I think might be of interest to you, and there are time constraints, so I thought I shouldn't wait until tomorrow."

"That's quite all right. How can I be of help?"

Stone told him about being run down by the Carlssons' yacht. "Paul Carlsson and his daughter came to dinner tonight, and he told me that Christian St. Clair, before his death, had made an offer for the Carlsson clinics. An association of stockholders who are current and former employees own sixty percent of the company, and apparently many of them are willing to cash out."

"I see," Steele said. "And since it's St. Clair, I'm sure the offer was inadequate."

"That was my view, as well. Perhaps you've heard that St. Clair's enterprises are now in the hands of one Erik Macher."

"That came in on the grapevine this afternoon. What I know of him isn't good."

"What would you think of the Carlsson Clinic as an investment?"

"I've had many dealings with the Carlssons over the

years, and I can tell you that it is a very well-run company, both medically and business-wise."

"I had thought that the case."

"Would you like me to investigate putting together a counteroffer for the clinic?"

"I think Paul Carlsson might be receptive to that, if he could be assured of his family continuing to operate as they have in the past."

"Certainly. I think the family is one of the clinic's greatest assets. They are very profitable and operate with little or no debt, and they own the real estate on which their branches sit."

"I'm meeting with Carlsson tomorrow morning, and I'll pass on your interest and ask him for the documentation you'll need to put together an offer."

"Does the St. Clair bid have a deadline?"

"It does—it expires in three weeks."

"Then we'll want to see that the association knows a better offer is in the wings. We don't want them to cave in while we're thinking about it."

"Good. Also, as you know, I sit on the board of Strategic Services, Mike Freeman's security company, so I know that Mike is interested in acquisitions."

"Mike would make an excellent partner."

"I'm glad you think so."

"Very good, Stone. Get back to me at the office after you and Carlsson have talked further."

"I'll do that. Good night, Art."

"Good night."

Dino came into the house. "I drove Ed home," he said. "He was a little worse for the wear, and it's a dark night."

"Thank you, Dino."

"I'll bet you've already called Art Steele," Dino said.

"Ah, you know me too well. And thank you so much for those remarks about ambulance chasing and drying out."

"Anytime, pal, anytime."

7

The following morning Stone called his old friend Bill Eggers, who was the managing partner of Woodman & Weld.

"Where are you?" Eggers asked.

"In Maine."

"It's very hot here."

"It's very cool in Maine."

Eggers made a groaning noise.

"Bill, I've recently met Dr. Paul Carlsson—"

"Of the Carlsson Clinic?"

"The same." Stone explained the circumstances of the clinic's ownership and the offer from St. Clair Enterprises. "Paul has asked me if the firm would represent him in dealing with this matter."

"Of course we would. I'd be delighted to add the Carlsson Clinic to our client roster."

"I'm glad to hear it. I have another meeting with Paul

this morning at ten, and I think it might be a good idea if you would e-mail me a representation contract for him to sign, and a fee schedule."

"Certainly."

"Have you heard about Erik Macher's taking over at St. Clair?"

"Yes, and I was stunned. Christian was a very elegant fellow, if ethically challenged at times, but Macher is a thug, by all accounts."

"He has Tommy Berenson on his side, and from what I hear, Berenson drew and witnessed the will."

"And I'm sure he was paid very handsomely to do so."

"Who would you have expected to succeed St. Clair in the event of his death?"

"I should have thought one of his division heads, or a CEO at one of his companies."

"Not Macher?"

"I'm sure Christian found him very useful, but not presentable. If this takeover bid should turn into a fight, you should expect him to fight dirty."

"I'll keep that in mind."

"I'll have my secretary e-mail you those documents immediately."

"Thanks, Bill."

Stone hung up and made some notes to himself for his meeting with Carlsson. Dino came down to breakfast and ordered bacon and eggs.

"Dino, could you run a check on Erik Macher for me?" Stone asked.

"Sure. What do you expect to find?"

"I have no expectations, I just want to know what there is."

Dino made the call to his assistant, then hung up. "A few minutes," he said.

Stone had a thought; he called Billy Barnett, who worked as a producer in Stone's son Peter's film production company at Centurion Studios in L.A. Billy had once been known as Teddy Fay and had been a twenty-year employee of the CIA, rising to deputy head of the technical services division, which equipped intelligence operatives for their missions.

"Stone, how are you?"

"Very well, Billy, and you?"

"Couldn't be better. What can I do for you?"

"I'm just looking for information about somebody who was a covert operative at the Agency. His time there should have overlapped yours."

"And who would that be?"

"One Erik Macher." Stone spelled it for him.

"Sure, I knew him—I probably outfitted him for a dozen or more missions."

"What was your general impression of him?"

"The man was an assassin. Oh, he was a good officer overall and had a successful career at the Agency, but he had the reputation of being too ready to kill at the drop of a hat. I wouldn't want to meet him in a dark alley."

"Anything else?"

"Very bright and adaptable—if one thing didn't work, he'd find another way. I think management was always a little leery of him."

"That's very interesting," Stone said. "Thank you, Billy."

"Are you having dealings with Macher, Stone?"

"I expect I will be." Stone explained the situation.

"I see. May I make a suggestion?"

"Of course."

"Will you be having face-to-face meetings with him?"

"Possibly. Certainly someone on our side will."

"I think that it might be a good idea for me to attend a meeting or two with him—not to say anything, just to let him know that I'm involved with his opposition. It might make him more careful in his dealings with you. I expect to be in New York for a few days soon."

"That sounds like a very good idea. I'd be interested in your assessment of the man."

"Let me know when you'd like me to be there. I can arrange my schedule accordingly."

"I'll do that, Billy. How are my boys doing out there?" He referred to Peter and to Dino Bacchetti's son, Ben, who was head of production at the studio.

"Thriving," Billy said. "You'd be proud."

"Well, I have to run. I'll speak to you soon." They said goodbye and hung up.

PAUL AND MARISA Carlsson arrived, and they sat down at the dining table to talk. Stone presented the representation agreement and the fee schedule. "Look these over and have anyone else you rely on for advice do so, too. Sign them at your leisure, and keep a copy for your records. I'd be happy to go through them with you."

"This morning," Carlsson said, "I spoke to Dr. Willie Keeling, who is representing the stockholders' association in the negotiations. I let him know that there would likely be a better offer coming and not to do anything rash. He said he'd check with me before taking any further action."

"Good idea," Stone said. "We wouldn't want them to

rush into anything. Paul, I believe you know Arthur Steele, at Steele Insurance Group."

"Of course—we've met a number of times. Good man."

"Art would like to put together an offer from Steele Insurance Group for the association's stock, and he, as well as people from our firm, would like to go to your head office in New York and be taken through the clinic's operations and to collect the necessary supporting documentation."

"Certainly. My younger son, Nihls, is the chief financial officer of the company, and I'll instruct him to give them whatever they need. When would they visit?"

"Tomorrow morning. There may also be some people along from a security company called Strategic Services, who may be participating in the deal."

"I know of them. I'll have our head of security meet with them, and my elder son, Sven, who is chief operating officer, will be available to meet with whomever you wish."

"What is your position at the clinic?" Stone asked.

"I am chief executive officer and chief of medicine. Marisa is my deputy chief of medicine. Tell me, Stone, how is your health?"

"Very good, thanks. I'm due for my biennial FAA medical exam next week."

"Well, Marisa is a designated medical examiner for the FAA, in addition to being a pilot. She could administer the exam, if you wish."

"What a good idea," Stone said. "I'll make an appointment."

"You know the drill about filling out the application online before your visit?" Marisa asked.

"I do."

She handed him a card. "You may list me as your examiner on the form."

They talked for a few more minutes, then the Carlssons stood to go.

"Your new yacht will be delivered this afternoon," Carlsson said. "I'm informed that it was launched this morning and is being sailed over here."

"I'll look for it."

"And I'll look for you next week," Marisa said.

8

Erik Macher spent his day going through every business file of Christian St. Clair's business dealings, then his own files. In St. Clair's he found the offer for the Carlsson Clinic buyout and its deadline. He read it carefully, then called Dr. Willie Keeling, the head of the stockholders' association.

"Good morning, Dr. Keeling."

"Good morning, and who might this be?"

"I am Erik Macher." He spelled the name slowly. "Does that ring a bell?"

"I'm afraid not, and I don't have time to talk right now."

"This is about the buyout offer from St. Clair Enterprises. I believe you have that in hand. And I am the successor of Christian St. Clair."

"Ah, yes, I heard of his death and thought that might be an end to this business."

"Certainly not. The offer is still a valid one, and you have three weeks to state your intentions."

"And what will happen if we do not accept the offer by that time?"

"Then the offer will be withdrawn, and another made, but at a lower price."

"Mr. Maker—"

"Macher."

"Mr. Macher, I must tell you that I expect another offer—a better one—by that time."

"From whom, may I ask?"

"You may not. Good day, sir." Keeling hung up.

Of all the occasional irritants in Macher's life, which he fought every day to remove, being hung up on by someone who didn't know him was right at the top. He felt his gorge rising and fought to keep it down, taking deep breaths.

"I BELIEVE HE was getting angry," Keeling said to his companion, Herbert Fisher, an attorney with Woodman & Weld.

"You handled him perfectly," Herbie said. "First, by not acknowledging him, then by continuing not to acknowledge him, then by disclosing that you could do better, and finally, by hanging up on him. Just perfect. Now he knows he has a fight on his hands."

"I don't like having someone, even someone I don't know, angry with me," Keeling said, wiping his glasses with a tissue, then patting his forehead and under his eyes.

"That is because you are a professional man and not a businessman. Businessmen are accustomed to dealing with people who are displeased with them and often use that to their advantage."

"And how do I do that?"

"First, wait for his response."

"How do you know he will respond?"

"Because he wants the Carlsson Clinic—perhaps even more than St. Clair himself wanted it, because it is probably the first business transaction he will carry out in his new position of authority."

"Will he want to hurt me?" Keeling asked.

"No. Oh, he may be angry enough to do so, but he is businessman enough to know that violence would damage his position and thus cost him money and prestige with his board. He will be scrupulously polite, until he isn't, and that will let you know that it is time to deal with him."

"When will he call again?"

"Perhaps soon, perhaps later—it doesn't matter. When he calls, ask your secretary to say that you are unavailable, and she doesn't know when you will be."

"I don't have a secretary."

"Dr. Keeling, do you have a telephone answering machine?"

"No."

"I will send one over to you and have it set up. After that, never answer the phone, unless you recognize the calling number as being someone you wish to speak to."

Herbie used his cell to ask his secretary to send over a machine pronto. "It should be only a few minutes."

The phone rang again, and Herbie held up a hand when Keeling started to answer. On the sixth ring, he picked it up himself.

"Hello," he said, sounding bored.

"May I speak to Dr. Keeling, please."

"Who's calling?"

"Erik Macher."

"Can you spell that?"

Macher spelled it slowly and carefully.

"Is that Eric with a cee?"

"No, with a kay."

"And Maker with a kay, too?"

"It's Macher with a cee aitch."

"Who are you?"

"I am the chief executive officer of St. Clair Enterprises," Macher said through gritted teeth.

"What is that?"

"It is a very large business conglomerate."

"What kind of business?"

"Financial."

"Does Dr. Keeling know you?"

"I spoke to him five minutes ago."

"What is this about?"

"It's a business matter."

"What sort of business?"

"Extremely important business."

"Just a minute, I'll get him." Herbie pressed the hold button.

"If it were me calling," Keeling said, "*I* would want to kill you by now."

"Oh, good," Herbie said. He waited for about a count of ten, then pressed the line button. "Hello?"

"Hello."

"Is that Mr. Maker?"

"This is Mr. Macher. May I speak to Dr. Keeling, please?"

"He just left."

"What do you mean?"

"I mean he just went out."

"How long ago?"

"Just a second."

"Did you tell him I was calling?"

"I called after him, but I think that, what with the sound of the car starting, he may not have heard me."

"When will he be back?"

"I don't know—sometimes he's gone for hours, even days."

"Who is this speaking?"

"This is his nephew, Herbert."

"May I leave a message for Dr. Keeling?"

"Just a second, I'll have to find a pencil." Herbie pressed the hold button.

Keeling burst out laughing. "You should take all my calls."

Herbie pressed the button again. "I'm sorry, I can't find a pencil, you'll have to call back later." He hung up.

MACHER THREW THE telephone across the room.

9

Stone landed at Teterboro, and he was halfway back to the city when his cell phone rang. "Hello?"

"Stone, it's Herb Fisher. Are you back yet?"

"Almost. I'll be home in half an hour."

"Good. I've got a team ransacking the books and files at the Carlsson Clinic, and they should have everything we need by the end of the day."

"Good."

"Oh, and Dr. Keeling heard from Erik Macher."

"And how did that go?"

Herbie gave him an account of the conversations. "I've got an answering machine installed at his place now, so he won't have to talk to Macher."

"Good. Let's keep the guy guessing."

"I wouldn't be surprised if he makes another offer before the deadline."

"You think we're driving him that crazy?" Stone asked.

"Yes, I think we are."

"There's something I'd like for you to do as soon as your people are finished at the clinic. I'd like to know how much cash the Carlssons have on hand or can borrow on short notice."

"Ah, I think I see your point—you want them to make an offer to buy the non-family shareholders' stock."

"Right. If I'm guessing correctly, some will tender their shares, others won't," Stone said, "and it may be possible for the Carlssons to regain a majority of the shares without using Steele to effect a buyout. I want you to figure out how much the family can afford to offer the shareholders."

"And you want them to make an offer big enough to be off-putting to Macher."

"Absolutely right."

"And how will Bill Eggers feel about all the billable hours the firm will lose by not going the Steele route?"

"He can console himself knowing that he's done the right thing for his clients."

"I'll be sure to mention that to him when he blows his stack."

"Don't worry, your position will be unassailable. Call me when you have the numbers in order." They hung up.

Fred dropped Stone at home, then continued uptown to the Bacchettis' apartment house.

Stone entered the house through the office door and found Joan looking bored. "Obviously I'm not keeping you busy enough," he said.

"Yes, I just love being overworked when you're here. Your mail and messages are on your desk. Welcome home!"

Stone ran through the messages and found one from Marisa Carlsson, confirming his appointment for his flight physical, and he asked Joan to cancel his earlier appointment with his old FAA doctor.

"So, who's this Dr. Carlsson?" Joan asked.

"It's a name you will hear often for the next few days or weeks. New client."

"The Carlsson Clinic?"

"Correct."

"Very tony."

"Yes, indeed."

STONE SHOWED UP on time at the Carlsson Clinic for his medical exam. The clinic was housed in a large, limestone-faced building—not as large as other New York hospitals, but imposing. He checked in at the front desk and was immediately sent to the fourteenth floor.

Marisa Carlsson's office was a combination of an examination room, with the required table, scale, and drawers and cupboards for supplies, and a modern and very personal office, with bookcases, comfortable furniture, and a door that led somewhere.

He had been there for about a minute when she walked in and closed the reception-area door behind her. "Good morning, Stone," she said.

"Good morning, Marisa."

"I've got your application on my computer," she said, "and we sent the blood sample you left to our lab, and we have the results. So why don't we get started by reviewing your listed medications?"

"All right."

"That won't take long because you're taking only a statin and a daily aspirin."

"Correct."

She consulted a sheet of paper. "And your cholesterol is at one-fifty. What was it before the statin?"

"Two-forty."

"So it's working."

"Yep."

"All your blood work is in the normal range, so strip down to your shorts and have a seat on the table."

She began running through her checklist, chatting as she did so. "What do you fly?"

"A Citation CJ3 Plus. You?"

"A Citation—2. It's our family airplane—my father and my brothers also fly it."

"I flew an M-2, before the CJ3."

"Why did you move up?"

"Someone accelerated the decision process by placing a bomb in the M-2. I ordered the CJ3 the same day."

"Does that sort of thing often happen to you?"

"Not all that often, but more often than I'd like."

"Where do you fly it?"

"Among my several houses, here and there. I have a place in England, so I can fly the CJ3 nonstop from Newfoundland to Shannon, with a decent tailwind, although I have to return via the Azores. You?"

"We fly to the yacht, wherever it is, and on vacations and business trips, and among our five branches."

She continued moving down the checklist, then stopped and pulled on a latex glove and grabbed a tube of lubricant. "Okay, shorts down, please, and on your knees on the step."

"Well," he said, complying, "you've already seen me naked." He flinched a little as the exam continued, then she handed him a tissue.

"Let's do the eye exam," she said, pointing at the chart. "Read me the lowest line you can manage." He did so, then she checked his peripheral vision. "That's it, you pass. You can get dressed."

He did so. "Marisa, now that we're on intimate terms, do you think we could have dinner one night soon?"

She laughed, then signed his certificate and handed it to him. "What a nice idea."

"Tomorrow evening?"

"Perfect."

"Where do you live?"

"One floor up," she said. "You'll need to take the elevator to this floor, then ring the bell on the elevator with the mahogany door, then it will open. I'm in apartment three."

"How convenient."

"Why don't we have a drink at my place, then continue. Say, seven o'clock?"

"You're on."

10

Stone had a message waiting from Herbie Fisher when he returned to his office.

"What's up, Herb?"

"The Carlssons have the wherewithal and the borrowing power to buy out the non-family stockholders. Once they've got a line of credit with their bankers, all we need do is to draft a letter and some forms, telling the stockholders that they're offering fifty percent more than St. Clair, and if they want to sell, to sign the documents, have them notarized, and a check will be on the way."

"Fifty percent more?"

"That's my recommendation. It's enough to impress the stockholders and to simultaneously warn Macher that he's in a bidding war. If we can get this done in a hurry, they can make it a fait accompli before the St. Clair time limit is up."

"Then set up a meeting with the Carlssons as soon as possible, and let's outline it for them."

"I can do it late tomorrow afternoon."

"That's good for me."

"I'll make the call."

Five minutes later, Herbie called back. "Five-thirty tomorrow in the elder Dr. Carlsson's office."

"You're on." They hung up. A convenient time, Stone thought.

Joan buzzed him. "Dino on one."

Stone pressed the button. "Dino?"

"None other. I ran Erik Macher through the computer. Ready?"

"Ready."

"He's forty-nine years old, born in Queens, educated in the public schools, four years at Fordham, where he was introduced by a priest to a CIA recruiter. He vanished into the Agency, did his twenty years, took his government pension, and fled the premises. I don't know what he did while he was there."

"I know—he was in covert ops and had a reputation as an assassin."

"Training he put to use, if what we already know about him is true."

"Right."

"He had a couple of brushes with the law along the way—a barroom fight that he won all too handily, charges dismissed when his victim refused to testify against him. The other was more serious—a woman accused him of rape, and the DA had a good case, but the victim left town before they could haul Macher into court. The case just sat there, until the statute of limitations ran out."

"Anybody ever hear from the woman again?"

"Nope."

"You think he used his Agency-acquired skills to make sure she didn't show up?"

"Would you be surprised?" Dino asked.

"Nope."

"Me neither. He would have done serious time if it had gone to trial."

"So he's clean."

"Yep. I'm sure St. Clair would have checked before he hired him."

"I'm sure he did," Stone replied, "and I'll bet St. Clair was attracted by both charges. He wouldn't have wanted a squeaky-clean character for the job he had in mind."

"Have you talked to Mike Freeman at Strategic Services about him?"

"No, but that's a good idea."

"Dinner tomorrow?"

"I'm booked, how about the evening after?"

"Done." They hung up.

Stone called Mike Freeman and was connected immediately.

"How are you, Stone?"

"Pretty good. I want to pick your brain."

"Shoot."

"What do you know about somebody called Erik Macher?"

"St. Clair's muscle?"

"That's the one."

"You know he was Agency."

"That, I know."

"He applied for a job here when he left the Agency, so we did a pretty good work-up on him."

"And what did you find?"

"Hang on, let me fire up the computer." Stone could hear the clicking of a keyboard. "A couple of blots on his copybook—the first, a fight in a pub, during which he nearly disabled the other guy, who wouldn't testify. The second, a murder."

"The woman he raped? That turned up on his rap sheet."

"We concluded that he murdered the woman."

"But you couldn't prove it?"

"Nope. A female body turned up four months later in a fifty-five-gallon drum that washed up on a beach in Jersey. Cause of death was a shattered vertebra that could have resulted from a hanging or the attentions of somebody who was trained in the art of assisting a person to break his neck. A positive identification couldn't be made."

"Uh-oh."

"Yeah, that certainly put us off. We never made him an offer."

"How'd he take it?"

"I don't know, we just wrote him a turn-down letter and never heard from him again. Later, I heard he had been hired by Christian St. Clair to assemble a private security group, with him as its only client. Frankly, I suspect that Macher had a hand in every shady thing we heard about St. Clair in subsequent years. And now he's running the company."

"So I hear."

"You know, if he hadn't been sitting a few feet from St. Clair when the explosion happened, he would have been the prime suspect."

"I can't argue with that," Stone said. "Thanks, Mike, this is all good to know." The two men hung up.

Stone called Dino.

"Yeah?"

"I thought you might like to update your file on Macher."

"You got more info?"

"Mike Freeman had some."

"Shoot."

"Four months after Macher's rape charge, the body of a woman turned up in an industrial drum on the Jersey shore, with a broken neck as the cause of death. It was too far gone for identification."

"Not even teeth? The teeth never go away."

"Beats me. Macher had applied for a job at Strategic Services at the time, and Mike figured the body was that of Macher's accuser, though he couldn't ID her."

"Well, that was more than twenty years ago, probably when you and I were sharing a squad car. The news never filtered down, not that I knew anything about it at the time, anyway. See you soon."

They both hung up.

Stone wondered where the remains in the steel drum had ended up.

11

Stone went to his meeting with the Carlssons the next day. The two young men, Nihls and Sven, looked enough like their father to have been him at an earlier age—handsome, fit, and comfortable in their skins. Marisa was the female version.

They all sat down, and coffee was served.

"What have you got for us, Stone?" Paul Carlsson asked.

"Essentially, your clinic back," Stone said. "And without doing a deal with the Steele Insurance Group."

"How do we do that?" Sven asked.

"Your books and collective financial statements show enough liquidity to make an offer to the non-family stockholders fifty percent larger than the St. Clair offer. If they all want to sell, then you might need to borrow some of the necessary funds, but probably some of them will feel comfortable with the long run."

"Dad," Sven said, "I should speak to our bankers, in case we need to increase our line of credit."

"Do that," Paul said.

"We think it should be done quickly," Stone said, distributing a package of documents. "Here is a letter to have printed on your letterhead, Paul, and for you to sign. There's also a letter for those wishing to sell to sign, have notarized, and return to receive their money. You should print this as soon as possible and FedEx it to all the shareholders, with a return FedEx envelope enclosed. You might be able to get enough of them to agree before St. Clair's deadline expires, when Macher would probably make a higher offer."

"Is our offer too high?" Nihls asked. "Maybe twenty-five percent more than St. Clair's might do the trick."

"We think that's what Macher would offer," Stone said, "and it would be quicker and cleaner to make it fifty percent—it would be better not to get into a bidding war. The stock's value is probably greater than that."

"What do you say?" Carlsson asked his children.

They all responded affirmatively.

"Then let's do it," he said, handing the documents to Sven. "Ask somebody to stay tonight and make the copies. We'll get the packages off tomorrow morning."

Marisa stood up. "If you will excuse me, I have something I must do." She shook Stone's hand and left the room.

"Stone," Paul Carlsson said, "I want to thank you and tell you how impressed we all are with how quickly you put this plan together."

"I was very happy to help," Stone said.

"I believe we can find some more work for your firm,"

Carlsson said. "We have discussed opening a new division devoted to executive physical exams. Most companies today ask their executives to undergo them, and we think our reputation will serve us well. We have a floor downstairs that we can devote to the operation."

"What a good idea," Stone said. "We'd be glad to help. Why don't I get you together with our managing partner, Bill Eggers, as soon as the stock buyout is resolved, and we'll see how to proceed."

"Wonderful," Paul said. They all stood and shook hands and went their separate ways. In the outside hallway, Stone found the mahogany elevator door and pressed the button.

"Yes?" Marisa's voice said on the intercom.

"It's Stone."

The elevator door opened, and Stone got on. Upstairs, the door opened into a vestibule, where Marisa was waiting. "Good meeting!" she said. "Perhaps Scandinavians are not so demonstrative, but I could tell that Papa was thrilled, and so were the boys."

"I'm glad I could help."

"Come in and let me get you a drink." She led him into a large living room, paneled in a light wood and hung with many pictures, with marvelous city views to the south. She went to a bar. "What would you like?"

"Knob Creek bourbon, if you have it."

She looked. "I'm sorry, no. I'll have it next time. May I interest you in an Akvavit?" she asked.

"Wonderful idea."

She opened a freezer and came out with a bottle frozen in a block of ice, found two small glasses, and poured for them.

"Skoal," she said. They raised their glasses and tossed back the icy liquid.

"What a beautiful finish," Stone said, tasting the afterglow.

"It's a special Akvavit that we have sent over," she said, pouring them another.

Stone felt the warmth spreading up from his belly.

"Where do you live?" she asked.

"In Turtle Bay Gardens," he replied.

"Oh, good," she said. "Within crawling distance." They tossed back another.

"I think I will hold at this altitude for a while," Stone said.

"Look, I know you've booked a table, but downstairs we have a very fine chef. Why don't I have a smorgasbord sent up?"

"What a good idea." While she was calling down, he phoned the restaurant and canceled.

She came back and nestled beside him on the sofa. "You know," she said, "I should ask our crew to run down yachts more often."

"I'm quite happy to have undergone the experience, given its results."

"A good business move?"

"An even better personal one."

She smiled and poured them another Akvavit. Stone thought that, from here in, he should sip and not chugalug.

DINNER ARRIVED IN due course, and the waiter placed the large tray on the dining table, set it with china and silverware, and left.

They took their seats, and Stone surveyed the array of smoked fishes, sliced meats, hot dishes, breads, and other comestibles. Marisa opened a chilled bottle of Bâtard-Montrachet and poured them glasses.

"You have good taste in wines," Stone said, sipping his approvingly.

"Papa is the wine collector," she said. "I steal from his cellar."

"Well stolen—this is one of my favorites."

"Now," she said, joining him, "I want to hear all about you. Google did not produce sufficient results."

"The short version—born, Greenwich Village, attended public schools, NYU, and NYU law school. Became infatuated with police work and joined the force, ending up as a longtime homicide detective. Dino, whom you have met, was my partner. Took a bullet in the knee, and the NYPD took the opportunity to unload me. An old law-school buddy, who was with Woodman & Weld, advised me to take a cram course, take the bar, and come to work for them. I did so."

"Ever married?"

"Yes, she died not long afterward, murdered by a former suitor."

"Oh, I'm sorry. Children?"

"One son, Peter, now a film director in Los Angeles. One Labrador retriever, Bob. Your turn."

"Mine is more boring. Born just down the street, attended Spence, summered in Sweden with my mother—they were divorced when I was ten. Columbia, master's in biology, and Harvard Medical School. Did my internship and residency in internal medicine at New York Hospital, right over there, and since then I've never strayed far from this building."

"I hope you're getting out more these days."

"Every chance I get."

"We must contrive some things to do with your spare time."

She pushed back from the table. "Perhaps you're aware of the Swedish attitude toward sex?"

"I've heard rumors," Stone replied.

"They are all true," she said, taking his hand. "Come with me."

And he did.

12

Stone awoke alone in a large bed in a darkened room. "Oh, you're awake," Marisa said from across the room, raising a blind partway to admit a stream of bright sunlight. "Breakfast in half an hour." She slipped off her robe, giving him a large, Swedish dose of the full-frontal view. "We have time to do it again."

He raised his arms, and she came into them. Half an hour later he heard the doorbell.

"Breakfast," she said, grabbing her robe, and headed for the front door. "Join me."

Stone found a robe for himself draped over a chair, slipped into it, and went into the living/dining room. Another smorgasbord, this one with eggs, cheese, smoked salmon, and toasted muffins. They dug in.

"You are an excellent lover," she said, "gentle, kind, but assertive and willing to experiment."

"I don't believe I've ever been rated that way before," he said.

"You have been, you just weren't told. And what about me?"

"Enthusiastic, affectionate, skillful, and welcoming," he replied. "Highest marks. Oh, and I give the Swedish attitude toward sex equally high marks."

She laughed. "When will I see you again?"

"Is this evening too soon? I'm having dinner with Dino and Viv. Will you join us?"

"Of course. I'll be working a little late—may I meet you at the restaurant?"

"Eight o'clock at Patroon—160 East Forty-sixth Street."

"Agreed. How late will we be?"

"Bring a toothbrush," he replied, "and a change of socks."

STONE WAS BACK at his desk in time to receive a phone call from Ed Rawls.

"Good morning, Ed."

"Good morning. You left too soon—the Maine weather is glorious. It's getting to be autumn."

Stone groaned. "And I'm stuck here, doing business."

"It's business I called about—yours, not mine. I've heard that Erik Macher is planning to increase his offer for the Carlsson Clinic."

"You astonish me, Ed. How do you do it?"

"Intelligence is my chosen craft. I'll give you a hint. There are Agency alumni at St. Clair other than Macher."

"I should have guessed. Did you hear a number mentioned?"

"An increase of twenty-five percent," Rawls said.

"That's good to know. How about when?"

"As soon as his earlier offer expires."

"So he'll wait to see how many bites he gets."

"It would make him look too eager to do it now. I should think he's likely to pick up quite a few shares," Ed said, "though maybe not enough for a majority."

"So he'll up the ante to corral some more."

"Macher didn't even know about the offer until after St. Clair's death, but I'm told he's *very* caught up in it now. He wants the clinic badly, I'm not sure why."

"Well," Stone said, "it's probably his first deal since taking control."

"He has several left over from St. Clair, but this is the biggest one. He badly wants to see the headline in the *Wall Street Journal*."

"I'll see what I can do about getting him a headline," Stone said, "though perhaps not the one he'd like."

"For Macher, that would amount to a public shaming. He cares desperately about achieving a business reputation for himself."

"I don't have a problem with that."

"You need to think about this, Stone."

"You're against the deal?"

"No, no, I don't give a shit either way, except for the fun of embarrassing Macher. You just have to understand that if you win, you'll be making a dangerous enemy."

"Well, I suppose you don't win many friends resisting hostile takeovers."

"Of course not, but this will be of a different order of

magnitude, given Macher's background and, above all, his nature. You had better be ready for a hostile reaction."

"That's good advice, Ed, thank you."

"The least I can do," Ed said. "See ya." He hung up.

Stone hung up, too. It occurred to him that, given Ed's information, it might be better to reconsider how to handle St. Clair's offer. He called Paul Carlsson.

"Good morning, Stone," the physician said. "Did you and Marisa enjoy your evening?"

"Very much indeed," Stone replied.

"I'm so glad. I hope you will forgive her Swedish forthrightness. It has sometimes been a problem for her."

"Ah, no problem. Paul, I've had some new information about the St. Clair offer."

"Then I'm anxious to hear it. Federal Express picked up the stockholder documents twenty minutes ago. Several of my staff were up most of the night getting them ready to ship, in light of your concern for quick action."

Stone's shoulders sagged; too late for restraint. "Paul, my new information is that Erik Macher is personally, deeply invested in his offer for the clinic, and he will be very upset when he hears that he has lost it."

"Do we care?" Paul asked.

"Not really, but I've been advised that we should be prepared for a very strong reaction, possibly a dangerous one."

Carlsson was quiet for a moment. "I had not anticipated such a thing."

"Neither had I, though perhaps I should have."

"Do you have some notion of how we should proceed, given this new information?"

"I believe that for a time, we should hire security professionals to ensure the safety of you and your family."

"Do you mean bodyguards?"

"Perhaps more subtle than that. I serve on the board of Strategic Services, a large part of whose business is personal protection, and they are very, very good at what they do."

"What, exactly, will this mean?" Paul asked.

"They will want to install people at the clinic, perhaps under the guise of providing some other business service—computer evaluations, perhaps—something that will give them an excuse to be close to you, then they'll blend in. Also, it would be best if you all travel in vehicles supplied and driven by them. They will endeavor to be as unobtrusive as possible."

"All right, I'll let the kids know. When will this start?"

"Before the day is out. I just have to make the phone call to put everything in place."

"Then proceed, and thank you for your attention to this."

"I will do so immediately," Stone said. He hung up and called Mike Freeman.

13

Mike listened while Stone outlined the problem. "I'll put two people with each of them, one to watch the scene, the other to stick close."

"Uh, Mike, there will be times when the daughter won't need that coverage."

"What sort of times?"

"The times when she's with me."

"Are you prepared to go armed at those times and explain to her why you're carrying?"

"It would be better than having a strange man in my bedroom," Stone replied.

"As you wish. I'll put Viv Bacchetti in charge of getting a team together. I'll send a team to the clinic to survey the strengths and weaknesses of the place, and I'll have personal protection in place by five o'clock today."

"Make that ten tomorrow morning for Marisa," Stone said.

"Gotcha. Anything else?"

"It might be a good idea to put one of your shrinks to the task of disassembling Erik Macher's psyche, with an eye toward predicting his moves."

"A thoughtful suggestion. They sometimes complain about not being given enough work. Talk to you later."

Both men hung up.

Joan buzzed. "A Dr. Carlsson on one," she said.

Stone picked up the phone. "Paul?"

"Not the first time I've been mistaken for my father," Marisa said.

"I was under-informed. I'm sorry."

"My late appointment has been canceled. May I come to you for a drink before dinner? I want to see how you live."

"I'd be delighted. Seven o'clock, if Swedes are congenitally punctual, six-thirty if they tend to run late."

"See you at seven. I have the address." She hung up.

Stone buzzed Joan. "Next time tell me *which* Dr. Carlsson," he said, then hung up before she could come back with a snappy reply.

MARISA WAS PUNCTUAL; the bell rang as the second hand reached the top of the clock. Stone let her in the front door, and they kissed lightly.

"So far, so good," she said. "I like the flowers planted outside—not what you'd expect from a born-again bachelor."

He led her into the living room, where she stopped and performed a slow 360-degree turn. "This is you, but not entirely you," she said. "I see a little of an older person. How did you come by this house?"

"I think perhaps I'd better get us a drink before I tell you that story because it's a few paragraphs long."

She followed him into the study, looking carefully around.

"What would you like to drink?"

"What was that stuff you asked me for last evening?"

"Knob Creek bourbon."

"Some of that, please, and put this in your freezer." She reached into one of her two commodious handbags and extracted a bottle of Akvavit. "For future occasions."

"Certainly," he said, opening the door and inserting it, then he poured them both a Knob Creek.

She sniffed it, then had a taste, smacking her lips. "Not as bad as I thought it would be," she said.

"I'll let Kentucky know you said so. In addition to being sexually liberated, Swedes are also frank."

"Germans are frank," she said. "Swedes are candid."

"I see."

"Are these your mother's paintings?"

"They are. You're very well informed."

"I am a researcher by nature."

"Is that a Swedish trait?"

She took a chair. "More a personal one."

Stone sat beside her. "You were born and raised in New York, right?"

"Yes."

"How did you get to be so Swedish?"

"By way of genetics, since both my parents are Swedish, and by nature, acquired in my summers in that country as a girl. I had many opportunities to compare, and I found Swedes to be better role models than Americans."

"In what ways?"

"First, you were going to tell me the story of how you acquired this house."

"Ah. By a rather torturous route. My parents were natives of western Massachusetts, where their own parents were engaged in the weaving of woolen cloth, on rather a large scale. The two families were close, and by the time they were teenagers, my father and mother were deeply in love, somewhat to the alarm of their respective parents."

"Too young?"

"That, and my father's ambitions. He was destined for the law at Yale, where generations of Barringtons had matriculated, but he wanted more than anything to be a carpenter and a maker of furniture, which they considered to be beneath their station in life. Then there was the subject of his social and political views."

"Which were?"

"Probably more Swedish than American—very left-leaning. The two young people were forbidden to marry. By this time my father was professing communism, in its purer form. This caused my father's parents to disown him."

"How harsh!"

"It was. Then they eloped, and my mother was disowned by her parents for marrying my father, and the schism was complete. They moved to Greenwich Village, where my mother's gift for painting blossomed, and my father became a handyman, calling door-to-door at people's houses, toting his toolbox, seeking work and finding enough to allow him to, eventually, acquire his own woodworking shop and to begin thinking about having me. During those early years they were secretly helped along by my maternal grandmother's widowed sister, her aunt Eloise, who owned and lived in this house.

"Eloise helped them most by commissioning my father to make all the doors, bookcases, and wood furniture for the house, over a period of years. It became a showcase for him and allowed him to add the word 'designer' to his job title. When Aunt Eloise died, in her nineties, she willed the house to me."

"How lovely!"

"It was lovely, but in her later years the infrastructure had aged along with her, so a very thorough renovation was required, and having trained at my father's knee, I did much of the work myself, getting into considerable debt along the way.

"Then, when I was rescued from the NYPD by Woodman & Weld, I earned enough to pay off the debt and complete the job. Recently, the smaller house next door was for sale, and I bought it to house my secretary, housekeeper, and butler."

"You have a *butler*?"

"Yes, he was originally a gift from a French friend of mine, who sent him to me for a year, then I hired him. His name is Fred, and you'll meet him when he drives us to dinner."

"This bourbon drink is getting better," she said, glancing at her watch, "but I think we should have our second one at the restaurant."

"Ever punctual," Stone said, ringing for Fred.

14

Fred dropped them at Patroon, and they found Dino and Viv waiting for them. "Marisa, you remember Dino and Viv from our dinner in Maine."

"Of course," Marisa replied, shaking their hands and sitting.

"I ordered you both a Knob Creek," Dino said.

"Then it's a good thing that Marisa is a new convert to bourbon, or I'd have to drink it myself."

"You'll get around to it anyway."

"Marisa," Viv said, "you spoke so little at our introductory dinner that we hardly got to know you. I'm glad you're here tonight, so we can make up for that."

"You are very kind," Marisa replied.

Their drinks arrived.

"Skoal," Dino said, and they raised their glasses.

"By the way," Viv said to Marisa, "I'm personally handling your security, so please call me if there's something you'd like changed." She pushed her business card across the table. "Our company name is Strategic Services."

"Security?" Marisa asked. "What does that mean?"

"People with guns," Viv replied, "except when you're with Stone."

"Do you have a gun?" Marisa asked Stone.

"I do."

"I don't see it."

"It's cleverly concealed."

"This is all very un-Swedish," she replied.

"You're in New York, not Stockholm," Viv said. "Sometimes we have to take precautions."

Stone pushed her drink at her. "It will be easier to tolerate once you've had a drink."

She laughed and took a big swig of the bourbon.

"You see?" Stone said. "She's thoroughly acclimated."

"What does this 'security' entail, besides men with guns?"

"You, your father and two brothers will have two people each," Viv said. "I've arranged for both of yours to be women—it makes things less tense in the ladies' room."

"Also," Stone said, "except when Fred is driving us, when you leave the clinic you will always travel in a Strategic Services car."

"Is all this really necessary?"

"We very much hope not," Viv said, "but we must, in the circumstances, be prepared should it become necessary."

"For how long?"

"At least until the stock buyout is complete," Stone said. "Perhaps a bit longer."

"Is doing business always this dangerous?"

"It's not about business," Stone said, "it's about the ego of one man, a fellow called Erik Macher, who recently took charge of St. Clair Enterprises after the untimely death of Christian St. Clair."

"Untimely? Does that mean violent?"

"Unfortunately, yes. He opened a package that contained a bomb."

"Who sent the bomb?"

"It was an integral part of the package and would have been safe, if he had known the procedure for opening it."

"I'm sorry, none of this makes any sense at all," Marisa said. "Perhaps we should change the subject."

"Willingly," Stone said. "Marisa was brought up in both New York and in Sweden, and she takes the Swedish part to heart, especially about being candid."

"Are the rumors true about Swedish women?" Dino asked.

Viv kicked him under the table.

"What? I'm just curious."

"The rumors are all true, Dino," Marisa said. "But Stone and I have already got over that hump." She caught herself. "So to speak."

Everybody laughed, and what with the drinks, all tensions disappeared.

FRED DROVE THEM HOME, and Stone took Marisa up in the elevator to the master suite. "The intervening floors are guest quarters," Stone explained.

"I hope I'm not being relegated to a guest room."

"Certainly not!" The elevator door opened and he led her to the master suite.

"Oh, this is very nice! And I get my own dressing room and bath?"

"You do," Stone said, placing her bag inside.

"Does this mean we can't undress together?" she asked. "I like watching you undress."

"You are welcome in my dressing room anytime," Stone said. "It's right over there." He pointed.

She stepped inside her dressing room and undressed, emerging quite naked. "I didn't bring a nightgown," she said.

"That's just fine. I would only have to remove it, anyway." He stepped into his dressing room and took his clothes off, while she watched approvingly.

"I think we are a good match," she said. "Everything is the right size—you, me, everything."

Stone led her to the bed and pulled back the covers. "Let's see how we fit together."

And they did.

THE FOLLOWING MORNING she woke him, and they made love before breakfast, then again, afterward.

They lay on their backs, panting and perspiring.

"It's a good thing you have to go to work," Stone said. "I'm not sure I could survive your day off."

She laughed. "You underestimate yourself."

"You may overestimate me."

"We shall see."

WHEN THEY HAD dressed, he walked her downstairs and had a good look around the neighborhood, then put her into the waiting Bentley, and Fred drove off with her.

Stone went to his office, through the outside entrance, passing Joan's desk on the way. "For future reference," he said, "there are four Dr. Carlssons—Paul, the father; Nihls and Sven, the brothers; and Marisa."

"I'll make a note of that," she said. "I suppose we'll be seeing a lot of Marisa."

"We will," Stone said, then went to his desk and pretended to be an attorney for the rest of the morning.

SHORTLY BEFORE LUNCH, he got a call from Ed Rawls. "Good morning, Stone."

"Good morning, Ed."

"I am reliably informed that news of the counter offer for the stock has reached the ears of Erik Macher—almost as soon as it reached the stockholders."

"I believe we are ready for him," Stone said.

"I hope to God you're right," Ed said, then hung up.

15

Erik Macher read the note on his desk. He hammered his fist on the buttons before him, and people appeared from everywhere.

"What the hell is this?" he demanded of them.

Glances were exchanged, then a young man got brave. "It's in this morning's *Wall Street Journal*," he said.

Macher grabbed the unread paper on his desk and saw the front-page headline. "Someone has offered fifty percent more than our offer?"

"The Carlsson family has made the offer," the young man said.

"What is your name?"

"Charles Fox," he replied.

"How can we stop this?"

"We can't stop it," Fox said, "we can only outbid them."

"I had figured on a twenty-five percent increase, if

we encountered opposition among the stockholders," Macher said, "but *fifty* percent?"

"You could offer seventy-five percent more."

"Not a chance!"

"Well, the article does quote an unnamed source as saying that they are likely to get enough shares from this offer for the family to hold a majority, as they once did."

"Is the clinic worth seventy-five percent more?"

"Perhaps," Fox said, "but if you offer that, the clinic could still top it. It's probably worth more to the family than to St. Clair."

"Such a prestigious name, though."

"The article says that stockholders will receive the offer this morning, and that the Carlssons have included a FedEx return envelope, so if they respond quickly, there may not even be time to increase our offer."

"But our offer doesn't expire for, what, another two or three weeks?"

"It doesn't matter, they don't have to respond. They can just take the Carlssons' offer."

Macher was visibly fuming. "What should I do?"

Fox kept quiet.

"Well?"

"Perhaps look for another investment," Fox said at last.

"How long have you been here, Fox?"

"Mr. St. Clair hired me two weeks before he . . . left us."

"Why shouldn't I bid higher?"

"Mr. St. Clair acted unilaterally," Fox said, "as I'm told he often did. I've checked, and we don't have any documents that would substantiate what the clinic is worth. Either he had inside information, or he just made a guess.

An increase in your offer might do it, or it might not—it's a toss-up."

Macher thought about it; he did not relish telling the board that he had gambled on a guess about the value of the clinic.

"In the circumstances, it's possible," Fox said, "that the clinic isn't worth what Mr. St. Clair bid for it. We have no way of knowing."

"What did St. Clair hire you to do?" Macher asked.

"I think just as a general executive. I've been working at Goldman Sachs since college."

"Were you a partner?"

"Yes, but his offer was so good, I took it."

"What are we paying you?"

Fox told him.

Macher was impressed; this kid was earning almost as much as he was before his ascension to CEO. "Well," he said, "you'd better earn it. Get out of here, Fox."

CHARLES FOX left the room and returned to his office next door. He was glad Macher had not grilled him on his job before Goldman Sachs. He closed his office door, sat down at his desk, removed a burner cell phone from a desk drawer, and pressed a button.

"I'm here," Ed Rawls said.

"I thought you'd like to know that Macher read the *Journal* piece and hit the roof."

"What do you think he'll do?"

"I'm not sure, but he may just drop out. In any case, by tomorrow the Carlssons could have a majority again. I did what I could to discourage a better offer, but he could jump either way. I don't know him well enough to predict his actions."

"Thanks, kid. Keep in touch."

"Sure." Fox hung up. Christian St. Clair had promised him the moon to get him away from Goldman Sachs, but as far as he could tell, St. Clair had not mentioned his hiring to anyone else, let alone told them about the promises he had made to him. Fox had expected to be running the place in a year or two, but now Macher sat where he wanted to sit, and he was going to have to get the man out before he could advance.

ED RAWLS IMMEDIATELY called Stone Barrington and told him what he'd learned.

"That's good news," Stone said. "I'm glad we rushed the offer. This guy of yours must be very well placed."

"He is very well placed, indeed," Ed said.

"Come on, Ed, tell me his name. If you walk in front of a bus I don't want to lose the guy."

"I don't want you communicating with him directly," Rawls said.

"I promise not to without your permission, or until you turn up your toes."

"I'll think about it," Ed said.

"Is your line of communication two-way?"

"It is. Either of us can communicate at will. I should also mention that he has an 'in' at the *Wall Street Journal*. That's how the story got on the front page this morning."

"What story?" Stone asked.

"Read the paper." Rawls hung up.

Stone found his copy and read the story. Oh, this was

good; Macher must have choked on his breakfast when he saw this. He called Paul Carlsson.

"Good morning, Stone."

"Good morning, Paul. Have you read the *Wall Street Journal* this morning?"

"I have. I assume you planted the story."

"I wish I'd thought of it, but I didn't."

"Then who did?"

"An acquaintance of an acquaintance of mine."

"I take it you don't want to tell me who."

"It's not someone you know in any case. Suffice it to say he has at least one friend at St. Clair Enterprises."

"Do you know him?"

"No, it's all third party."

"I must admit, Stone, I'm anxious about the counter offer."

"We should have some idea of how we're doing when FedEx delivers tomorrow morning," Stone replied.

"I'll try and be patient," Paul said.

"So will I." They said goodbye and hung up.

16

Stone was at his desk the following morning when Joan buzzed. "The elder, male Dr. Carlsson on one."

He pressed the button. "Yes, Paul?"

"Good morning, Stone."

"Good morning."

"FedEx delivered half an hour ago, and about half the stockholders have accepted. Their checks are being written as we speak. We now own fifty-three percent of the clinic, and of course there could be more tomorrow."

"Congratulations, Paul."

"Thank you. May we now dispense with the armed guards?"

"No, you may not. This may set Macher off. Let's look at it again in a week."

"Thank you again, Stone."

"You are entirely welcome."

"I promise you, the family will never again own less than fifty percent of the stock."

"I'm delighted to hear it. Paul, I'd like to invite you and your tribe, and their wives or girlfriends, to dinner one night soon. Would Friday evening be convenient for all of you?"

"I'll take a vote and call you back."

"Good." They hung up. Twenty minutes later Paul called back. "This Friday is good for all of us. The boys will bring their wives."

"Will you bring a lady?" Stone asked.

"Well, one of Marisa's security guards is very attractive. Shall I ask her?"

"Please do. Seven o'clock for drinks?"

"Perfect." They hung up and Stone called Dino.

"Bacchetti."

"Good news—the Carlssons are majority owners of their clinic again."

"Great news."

"They're all coming for dinner on Friday evening. Will you and Viv join us?"

"Sure we will. She'll actually be in town."

"Drinks at seven." They hung up. Stone called Ed Rawls.

"Yeah?"

"It's Stone. Will you, by any chance, be in New York the day after tomorrow?"

"Give me an excuse."

"The Carlssons are owners of their clinic again, and we're celebrating. Dinner Friday evening?"

"That's a good excuse."

"How's the widow hunting in Islesboro?"

"They're thick on the ground."

"Would you like to bring one? I'll put you both up, together or separately."

"Yes, I would. If we fly from our little airport directly to Teterboro, we could arrive late afternoon."

"Excellent. See you then." He hung up and buzzed Joan.

"Yes, sir?"

"Will you let Helene and Fred know that we'll be twelve for dinner at eight, on Friday? Drinks at seven."

"Certainly."

"Ask her to get back to me with a menu."

"Certainly."

ON THURSDAY MORNING, Erik Macher picked up his *Wall Street Journal.* There it was, on page one again: MACHER AT ST. CLAIR LOSES BID FOR THE CARLSSON CLINIC.

He wanted to throw up on his desk. He started to ring for Fox, but he wasn't the go-to guy for where Macher wanted to go. He picked up the phone and dialed an extension in a basement office. The man was standing before him in less than a minute.

Jake Herman was ex-FBI, having been asked to leave in the wake of an unnecessarily violent incident some years before. He was smart, in a feral sort of way, and entirely without scruples of any kind—a classic sociopath. He was also inordinately fond of money.

Macher explained what had just happened. "Jake, I want retribution," he said.

"I suppose you want them all dead?" Jake asked with a look of distaste.

"Not necessarily. In fact, it would be better to avoid killing. The police work too hard at solving murders."

"How about if I do something to the clinic?"

"What did you have in mind?"

"Maybe some Legionnaires' disease in their air-conditioning system?" Jake suggested.

Macher thought about it. "Too likely to kill a patient or two."

"Then how about a *rumor* of Legionnaires' disease in their air-conditioning system?"

"Where could you plant such a rumor?"

"It would make it more credible if it were in two or three publications on the same day."

"Can you do that?"

"I know a guy who knows a guy—a failed publicist who writes a gossip blog. If he got it out late this afternoon, it could hit the papers tomorrow morning—they read all the blogs. It'll have to be a little on the subtle side—the guy isn't interested in lawsuits."

"Do it," Macher said, "for tomorrow's papers."

"I'm on it," Jake replied. He left the room.

ON FRIDAY MORNING, Paul Carlsson's son Sven came into his office with a newspaper. "Look at this," he said, placing the paper on his father's desk.

A circle had been drawn around a headline: AT SWANK CLINIC: LEGIONNAIRES' DISEASE?

Paul read on: "'An anonymous report has come in that

two, possibly three, patients at a swanky Upper East Side
private hospital with Scandinavian connections have presented with symptoms of an often-fatal respiratory illness.
Their air-conditioning system is suspected, and the New
York City Department of Health is descending on the
clinic with swarms of inspectors.'"

"Do we have patients with any such symptoms, Sven?"

"No, sir. I checked, and our air-conditioning system
was checked and disinfected the day before yesterday, as
it is monthly."

Paul buzzed his secretary. "Get me the head of the
New York City Department of Health."

A moment later, she came back. "Mr. Swanson on line
one."

Paul picked up the phone. "Mr. Swanson, are you
aware of a report in a morning newspaper that a clinic on
the Upper East Side may have patients with Legionnaires'
disease?"

"That has just come to my attention, Dr. Carlsson."

"I believe this to be a malicious rumor aimed at our
facility, and I want you to know that we have checked,
and we have no patients exhibiting symptoms of anything
they didn't arrive with, especially not Legionnaires' disease. Also, our air-conditioning system was checked and
disinfected two days ago, as part of our monthly inspection routine. If you wish to send inspectors here to confirm this, we will welcome their attention."

"Dr. Carlsson, I think it would be to the benefit of
both of us if I send a team over there this morning."

"We will give them full cooperation. Tell them to ask
for me, personally." He hung up. "Sven, thank you for
bringing this to my attention. The health department will

deal with this immediately, and I want to issue a press release when they are done." Sven returned to his office.

Paul called Stone Barrington.

"Yes, Paul?"

"Stone, I believe we have now heard from Mr. Macher."

17

Stone's fax machine cranked out a sheet of paper early in the afternoon; it was printed on the letter-head of the Carlsson Clinic and he read it with interest.

THE CARLSSON CLINIC DENIES
LIBELOUS NEWS REPORT

This morning's papers printed a report implying that the Carlsson Clinic, one of America's foremost medical institutions, had patients exhibiting signs of an infectious lung disorder that was being spread by its air-conditioning system.

This report is false and malicious. After a thorough check of each resident patient, it has been determined that not one harbors these symptoms. The clinic summoned the New York City Department of Health

*inspectors and asked them to inspect the air-
conditioning system, and they reported that no trace
of a microbe or virus was detected.*

*The Carlsson Clinic demands that an abject re-
traction by these publications appear in Saturday's
and Monday's editions in the same front-page space
occupied by the false report. The clinic has instructed
its attorneys to immediately bring a libel action
against any publication that does not meet this demand.*

It was signed by Paul Carlsson.

STONE CALLED Dr. Carlsson.

"Yes, Stone?"

"I want to compliment you on your deft handling of
this Legionnaires' nonsense. I'm confident you will get
your retractions."

"Thank you, Stone. The part about having instructed
our attorneys was a little inaccurate, so I will instruct you
now. If these retractions are not satisfactory or are printed
anywhere else in the papers than the front page, file an
immediate action for libel, slander, and anything else you
can think of."

"I acknowledge your instructions," Stone replied.

"Thank you. We'll all see you at dinner."

STONE FOUND THE evening's menu on his desk:
seared foie gras, crown roast of lamb, risotto, haricots
verts, and a dessert of crème brûlée with fresh Maine blue-

berries. He approved it, then went to his cellar with Fred and chose the wines.

SHORTLY AFTER FIVE, Ed Rawls arrived with a handsome woman of about fifty in tow, whom Ed introduced as Emma Harrison, and Stone showed them to the same bedroom, at Ed's request.

AT THE STROKE of seven o'clock the front doorbell rang, and Fred escorted a gaggle of Carlssons into the living room. The boys' wives, Greta and Inge, were introduced, and Paul introduced his date for the evening, Cara Neilsen. While Stone was welcoming them, the Bacchettis arrived and Ed and Emma emerged from the elevator.

Marisa whispered to Stone, "What do you think of Papa's new girlfriend?"

"Very nice."

"She is the first armed woman he has ever taken out. Can you guess where her gun is?"

"No."

"Good."

FRED SERVED COCKTAILS in the living room, as the study would have been cramped with so many people, and piano music wafted over the invisible sound system.

"I like the music," Marisa said after a few minutes. "Who is the pianist?"

"I fear it is I," Stone replied.

"Have no fear, it's lovely. A secret talent?"

"Fairly secret." He warmed to the praise.

FRED CAME TO him after a few minutes: "There is a phone call for you."

"Who is it?"

"He won't say, but he says it's very urgent."

Stone went into the study and picked up a phone. "This is Stone Barrington. Get it off your chest."

"Mr. Barrington," a man's gruff voice said, "there is a bomb planted in your house that will detonate in exactly three minutes." There was a click, and Stone could hear the ticking of a stopwatch.

Stone thought about it for about ten seconds and decided it was impossible that anyone could have planted a bomb in his house. "Please give Mr. Macher a message from me," he said. "Tell him that if anything like that occurs, I will shoot or have him shot before tomorrow passes." He hung up and returned to his guests.

"Anything wrong?" Marisa asked when he returned.

"Not a thing," Stone said, looking at his watch. When a little more time had passed, he clinked his signet ring on his glass to get attention. "Ladies and gentlemen, I would like you to know that I have received an anonymous phone call saying that a bomb would explode in this house in three minutes. That was five minutes ago, so you need not stop drinking."

There was a deep silence for about five seconds, then everyone put down his drink and applauded.

"Thank you for your confidence," he said, and they continued drinking.

*   *   *

THEY DINED CONVIVIALLY, and after dessert, a
port, Quinta do Noval 1960, was served with Stilton and
biscuits. When they were back in the living room on coffee and cognac, Dino came and sat down next to Stone.

"I could have had the bomb squad here, you know."

"In three minutes? Just in time to pick up the pieces?"

"How did you respond to the call?"

"I told the man to tell Macher that if it went off, I'd
shoot or have him shot before tomorrow is out."

"That was an extremely stupid thing to do," Dino said.

"If I had taken any other step it would have ruined my
dinner party," Stone said. "Nobody would have been able
to relax."

"I had a thought," Dino said.

"Did you, now?"

"How about if I call a full-scale bomb alert at the St.
Clair mansion in the middle of the night? You know,
break down the door, flood the house with men in bomb
suits and sniffer dogs, turn Macher out in his skivvies—
like that."

"Dino, my friend, that is a charming notion and one
you should hold in reserve, in case this thing escalates."

"It could very well escalate, you know."

"I know, and I expect it to, until Macher really tries to
hurt somebody. But we've taken all the proper precautions. And if we should decide to execute your excellent
plan, I'd like for everybody here to be out of town when
it happens."

"Just let me know when," Dino replied.

18

E rik Macher had just boarded what was now, effectively, his yacht when his cell phone rang.

"Macher," he said into it. "This better be good."

"It's Jake," the caller said, "and it's not good."

Macher listened as Jake played the recording of his telephone conversation with Stone Barrington the evening before. "Shit!" he screamed, alarming the two crew who were bringing his luggage aboard.

"This is what happens when we make empty threats," Jake said.

"Are you saying that we're going to have to up our offer by seventy-five percent?"

"It's too late for that," Jake said. "I'm informed that as of this morning, the Carlssons have accumulated about sixty-five percent of the stock in the clinic, and they'll probably get more. And your secretary said to tell you that the board of directors has requested a meeting Monday morning at nine AM."

Macher sat down and began taking deep breaths, trying to get his pulse and his blood pressure down.

"Erik, are you all right?"

"Not exactly," Macher said.

"Tell me what you want to do."

"Take out one of the Carlssons," he said.

"Which one?"

"I don't care, just make it look accidental."

"Erik, they've got Strategic Services protection, every one of them, and I don't have to tell you how good that outfit is. Now, I can probably get a shot at one of them, but the police will be all over us—make that all over you."

"All right, what do you suggest?"

"I suggest we lie low for a few days, wait for them to pull their guards off, then reassess. Or maybe, a more serious shot across their bows."

"That's good advice, Jake. Do the second one. Have my secretary call the board members and tell them I'm out of town, and I'll meet with them Wednesday morning at ten."

"Got it," Jake replied, then hung up.

One of the crewmen was standing by, looking concerned.

"Bring me a drink," Macher said.

"Certainly, sir. What would you like?"

"A great big single malt scotch."

"Right away, sir." The man was back in a flash with a double old-fashioned glass filled with scotch on a silver tray and an ice bucket. "Would you like ice, sir?"

"No."

The man extended the tray. "There you are, sir. Would you like me to tell the captain he can get under way?"

Macher grabbed the glass and took a big swig. "Do it."

"Yes, sir, and the chef would like to know what time you'd like lunch served."

"One o'clock sharp. We'll be four—the chopper has gone for the others."

"Yes, sir." The man dematerialized.

Macher took one more gulp of the scotch; he tossed the rest overboard and set down the glass. He couldn't be drunk when his guests arrived; for one thing, he wanted to get laid this afternoon, and he couldn't manage that with a load on.

JAKE WAS HAVING a sandwich for lunch when his phone rang. "Please, God," he said, "not Macher." It was not, it was one of his platoon of ex-FBI men. "Yeah?"

"Jake, I'm with Barrington and the Carlsson woman. You'll never guess where they are."

"Tell me."

"They've just finished lunch at the Central Park Boathouse, and they're getting into a rowboat."

Jake brightened. "What's the opposition like?"

"As far as I can tell, there isn't any, but I think Barrington is packing."

"Where are you, exactly?"

"At a table in the Boathouse. Zelda is with me."

"I'll be there shortly. Don't lose sight of the boat." He hung up, rang for a car, got a briefcase from his coat closet, and beat it out of the house.

*   *   *

STONE ROWED SLOWLY and reluctantly. "I feel like an idiot," he said to Marisa. "I haven't done this since I was in college."

"Actually, I would never have known that—you seem quite good at it."

"It's like roller skating—I haven't forgotten how, but I'd like to."

She looked at him appraisingly. "Have you ever made love in a rowboat?"

"Maybe, but not in one in Central Park on a Saturday afternoon."

"There are some bushes over there," she said playfully, pointing.

"Oh, no you don't," Stone said, steering away from the bushes.

"Oh, come on."

"I am unaccustomed to self-induced discomfort," Stone said. "That's why I gave up camping."

"What do you have against camping?" she asked.

"I don't like sleeping on the hard ground in a tent, and mosquitoes carry disease."

"You don't like the outdoors?"

"Not for some things. Think of me as a great indoorsman."

JAKE ARRIVED AT the Boathouse and found his two operatives there, lingering over coffee. "Where's the boat?" he asked.

"Two o'clock and a hundred meters," the man said.

Jake surveyed the scene. "See that clump of bushes, about thirty yards from the stern of the boat?"

"Got it."

"Pick up the briefcase and get over there. Assemble the rifle and silencer inside and put a round into the boat."

"Where into the boat?"

"Below the waterline," Jake said, "and near the stern. Don't hit anybody."

The man picked up the briefcase and hurried from the restaurant.

"You want to sink them?" Zelda asked.

"Humiliation is almost as good as a gunshot wound," Jake said.

Five minutes passed, and Jake saw the bushes move. Another two minutes, and he saw a splash near the stern of the boat.

"STONE," MARISA SAID.

"What?"

"My shoes are getting wet."

"Look around—do you see any waves breaking over the boat?"

"I'm not kidding."

Stone looked down at the space between them and found that his own shoes were getting wet. "We seem to have sprung a leak," he said, heading for the dock.

By the time he reached it and got Marisa out of the boat, Stone was ankle deep in lake water. With the help of the dockmaster, he wrestled the boat onto the pontoon and tipped it over enough to empty out most of the water. "Are all your boats this leaky?" Stone asked the man.

"None of them, until now. They've all been recently refurbished."

Stone inspected the little hole in the stern, then the sun glinted on copper. He reached into the boat and came back with a jacketed slug.

"What's that?" the dockmaster asked.

"Something that fell out of my pocket," Stone replied, looking carefully around for opposition but seeing none.

"Shall we get another boat?" Marisa asked.

"Let's go home and get some dry shoes," he said.

19

S tone and Marisa went upstairs to change, and he dumped his trousers, damp to the calf, into a hamper, along with his sweaty shirt and underwear, and put trees into his wet shoes. At least they had grown up wet, being alligator.

The phone rang, and he sat on the bedside and answered it. "Hello?"

"It's Ed Rawls. How you doing?"

"I'm not sure," Stone replied.

"That sounds ominous."

"I was on the boat lake in Central Park after lunch, and somebody put a round through the stern of my rowboat. I found a .23 slug in the bottom of the boat after we hauled it in."

"Just sitting there, not in your leg?"

"I figure it must have been fired into the water at the

stern, and that took a lot of muzzle velocity off it, otherwise it might have hit one of us."

"So you were rowing a lady around the Central Park boat lake? That doesn't sound like you."

"It doesn't feel like me, either," Stone said, "but I was cajoled into it with the promise of better things."

Rawls chuckled. "Better collect before she forgets."

"In the meantime, I've had a shot across my bows, even if it was into the stern."

"They're not going to go on warning you forever," Ed said. "Maybe it's time you made a move."

"Maybe so. You got any suggestions?"

"Well, my source tells me that Macher is spending a few days on St. Clair's yacht up here," Rawls said. "I've seen the chopper going back and forth from Rockland."

"You don't have a rocket-propelled grenade launcher handy, do you?"

"Well, no, but I could probably find you one pretty quick. But that might be more of a statement than you want to make at this point in the game."

"I guess so."

"I wouldn't rule it out for later, though," Rawls said, "if they hurt somebody. In the meantime there might be another alternative."

"Tell me."

Rawls told him.

"I like it," Stone said. "It's better than tit for tat, but it doesn't escalate things to the point where he'll have to respond with something life-threatening."

"I'll take care of it, then," Rawls said, and the two men hung up.

Marisa had sat down next to him, equally naked. "I

seem to recall promising you better things in return for the boat ride."

She pushed him back onto the bed.

"Do with me as you will," Stone said.

And she did.

ERIK MACHER AND his guests were just finishing their second bottle of wine with their lunch, when the captain came and motioned for Macher to leave the table.

"What is it?" Macher asked. "We're having lunch."

"I'm sorry, sir, but the Coast Guard has just hailed us, and they're coming aboard for an inspection."

"What kind of inspection?" Macher demanded. He didn't know anything about boats or the Coast Guard.

"It will be a routine equipment inspection," the captain said. "They'll want to see everything on the required emergency equipment list—life rafts, vests, flares, that sort of thing."

"Is there any reason why that should disturb our lunch?"

"I just wanted you to be aware of their presence," the captain said. "They're coming aboard now from a rigid inflatable. Please excuse me." He went to receive the boarding party.

A moment later, a young woman in uniform appeared in the dining room. "Good afternoon," she said. "I'm Lieutenant Graves of the United States Coast Guard. We've come aboard to conduct an investigation."

"An investigation?" Macher said. "I thought this was an equipment check."

"That, too," she replied. "Now, I'll need the names, addresses, dates of birth, and Social Security numbers of everyone aboard, crew and guests, and I'll need photo IDs for everyone. Please fill out these forms individually." She distributed documents and pens.

"We're in the middle of lunch," Macher said, outraged.

"Not anymore," she replied. "Please bring the completed forms, one at a time, to the afterdeck. In the meantime, members of my crew will be conducting a search belowdecks for contraband."

"Contraband? What sort of contraband."

"We'll know it when we see it," she said. "Now please fill out the forms, then come to the afterdeck, one at a time."

"I'm terribly sorry about this," Macher said to his guests, "but I suppose we'll have to permit it." Everyone began filling out the forms.

MACHER BROUGHT UP the rear of the procession to the afterdeck and handed the lieutenant his completed form. The yacht's captain was there, watching as she inspected the yacht's paperwork.

"Mr. Macher, you're the owner here?"

"The owner, as you will have seen in our registration documents, is a Delaware corporation," he replied stiffly.

"Do you represent the owner?"

"I am the president and chief executive officer of St. Clair Enterprises, which owns all of the stock in the corporation."

"Then you are the owner, for the purposes of our investigation."

"I suppose so."

"Who, may I ask, occupies the large cabin and sitting room forward in the yacht?"

"That is the owner's cabin, and I and my companion occupy it."

"Then," she said, holding up a zippered plastic bag half-filled with a white powder, "this belongs to you?"

"It does not," Macher said. "What is it?"

"I suspect it of being cocaine. I would think that there was more in the bag recently."

"I have never seen that before."

"Who occupied the cabin before you?"

"That would be Mr. Christian St. Clair, who is deceased. This is the first time I have been aboard the yacht, and I did *not* bring that powder, whatever it is, aboard."

"Were you personally acquainted with Mr. St. Clair?"

"I was. I was his principal colleague in the company."

"And did you know him well enough to suspect that he was an abuser of illegal substances?"

"We were not close personally," Macher replied.

"Very well, Mr. Macher. We will confiscate the powder and have it analyzed." She consulted his form. "This is your correct business and personal address?"

"It is."

"Then we will be in touch following the completion of the lab work. In the meantime, you may wish to consult an attorney with maritime experience."

"I shall certainly do so," Macher replied.

The coastguardsmen and their captain returned to their vessel and departed the yacht, and Macher was left to explain to his guests why they had been disturbed.

He was so furious he forgot about his planned afternoon tryst.

20

Jake Herman stood at a loose parade rest before Erik Macher's desk in Christian St. Clair's old library. He noticed that Macher seemed to have acquired a slight facial tic, the sudden lifting of his left eyebrow for no apparent reason.

"Good morning, sir," Jake said.

"Not so," Macher replied. "I have just had a long weekend of cruising aboard my yacht interrupted by a visit from the Coast Guard."

"Ah, yes, that happens, sir. They like to check to see if a boat has all the required emergency equipment."

"This was something more than that," Macher replied. "They did an investigatory search of the yacht, going through the guest cabins and the owner's cabin."

"Did they find anything of consequence?"

"They came up with a plastic bag containing a white powder."

"Uh-oh."

"It wasn't *my* white powder!" Macher yelled, losing it for a moment, then regaining control of himself.

"Of course not, sir."

"St. Clair must have left it there."

"Most probably, sir. Were there any consequences of this discovery?"

"A stern lecture from the captain of the Coast Guard vessel—a *woman*, for God's sake! She's having it tested in their laboratory, said she'd get back to me."

"I don't believe the Coast Guard has a laboratory, sir, so it probably went to the FBI lab for analysis. Have you taken any defensive steps?"

"The woman advised me to hire an attorney with maritime experience."

"That's probably good advice."

"I have a call in to Tommy Berenson, our corporate counsel."

"A good move."

"What happens if the powder is cocaine?" Macher demanded.

"Well, conceivably, charges for possession could be brought, or if there is a substantial quantity, a charge for intent to sell might be added."

"It was the first time I'd ever set foot on the yacht! I hadn't even unpacked my bags!"

"In that case, a good attorney might be able to persuade them not to bring charges, since it was clearly left there by a previous occupant—one now deceased, I might add, and that should stand in your stead."

"Jake, I smell a rat here, one named Stone Barrington. Do you think he might have been able to instigate these events?"

"Well, sir, anyone could call the Coast Guard and report that a yacht carrying drugs is sailing in Penobscot Bay, and the Coast Guard would be obliged to investigate such a report."

"Even if the report were anonymous? I can't imagine Barrington giving them his name."

"Yes, sir, even an anonymous report. Of course, any person making such a report that was false and malicious would be subject to arrest for making a false report."

"Aha!"

"However, if the substance found aboard turns out to be cocaine or heroin or some other illegal drug, the report would not have been false. In some circumstances he might even be financially rewarded, if the drugs were of sufficient value."

Macher made a groaning noise.

"Sir, I would suggest that this incident is unlikely to result in a prosecution because of insufficient evidence. I think the best thing would be to consult your attorney to see if any legal moves were indicated, then to just be patient and wait for the lab to issue its report."

"I am a little short of patience," Macher said.

"Sir, I originally came in to report on yesterday's incident in Central Park."

"Oh, yes, I had forgotten. What happened?"

"We found Barrington and the Carlsson woman in a rowboat on the Central Park lake. One of my men very carefully fired a silenced round into the boat, causing it to spring a serious leak."

"Heh, heh," Macher said.

"Barrington managed to get the boat to the dock before it could sink, but he was seen to recover the spent round from it, so he knows that he has received a warning."

"Now *that's* what I like to hear!" Macher said, brightening visibly. "Now he knows where we stand."

"Sir, this event took place early Saturday afternoon. When did your brush with the Coast Guard happen?"

"Late Saturday afternoon."

"So that event could have been in response to the earlier one."

Macher pondered that. "I see what you mean," he said. "So the ball could be back in our court?"

"Possibly, sir."

"Then we need to respond more forcibly."

"If I may suggest, sir, it might be prudent to wait to hear from the Coast Guard before proceeding."

"Oh, yes," Macher said, sounding disappointed.

"I could do some preplanning for a response and get back to you," Jake said.

"Yes, good, Jake, you do that."

"Please let me know about the lab report from the Coast Guard," Jake said. "It could affect our planning."

"Yes, of course, I'll do that."

Jake left Macher as he had found him, including the eyebrow twitch, which was still there.

Macher got Tommy Berenson on the phone.

"Good day, Erik," the attorney said.

"Good day. I may require some legal advice from an attorney with a knowledge of maritime law."

"Shoot."

Macher gave him an account of the stopping of the yacht and the subsequent search and powder found.

"First of all, Erik, I must ask you—and your reply is

covered under attorney-client confidentiality—was this powder yours, and is it cocaine?"

"Tommy, I have just explained to you the exact circumstances."

"Yes, but in this case, I need to know if we are up against an actual violation of the law, or just some awful coincidence."

"Do not make me recount the events. What I have told you is the truth."

"Then it is not cocaine?"

"I have no idea—it wasn't mine."

"Then it is not your cocaine?"

"Tommy," Macher said, and his voice was a little shaky, "if I have to explain this to you again, I am going to do so with my hands around your throat."

"I think it's best to wait for the lab report, then discuss how to proceed from there."

Macher slammed down the phone with a whimper.

21

Charles Fox listened to the recording from the tiny bug he had placed in Macher's office and smiled. The man sounded as if he were coming unglued, and that was exactly what Fox wished to happen. He knew that a board meeting had been called for later that morning, and he would record that, as well.

MACHER ROSE AS the board members filed into his office and took their seats at the conference table. He sat down opposite them. "Good morning, gentlemen. What is the purpose of this meeting?"

"The purpose," the chairman said drily, "is to discuss the failure of the takeover bid for the Carlsson Clinic."

"Are you implying that this is *my* failure?" Macher asked.

"Erik, you are the CEO—the buck stops with you."

"May I remind you that Christian St. Clair initiated the takeover bid, presumably with the agreement of this board? And that Christian made a bid that could only be described as 'lowball,' thus starting a bidding war?"

"While both of those things are nominally true," the chairman said, "they are irrelevant. We are discussing your actions."

"I took no actions," Erik said.

"Exactly. And there are times when no action is an affirmative action."

"Because of the lowball nature of Christian's bid, my only option was to offer a price higher than I deemed the clinic to be worth," Macher said through gritted teeth. "I am not in the business of paying more than a thing is worth. Had we offered the one hundred and fifty percent to begin with, we would now control the Carlsson Clinic. You may complain to the ghost of Christian St. Clair about that."

"Also," the chairman said, "it has come to the attention of the board that you are now a suspect in the smuggling of a large quantity of cocaine aboard the company yacht."

Macher shot a glance at Tommy Berenson, whose gaze was now directed at a point at the approximate height of the room's crown molding. "I want you all to listen to me very carefully," Macher said, and he gave them an account of the incident aboard the yacht. "I hope that is perfectly clear, because I am not going to explain it to you again."

"So," said the chairman, "as I understand it, we will not know for some time whether these charges are true."

"There are no charges extant," Macher said.

"I must tell you frankly, Erik, that if these charges are substantiated, we will be required to demand your resignation with immediate effect."

"What charges?"

"Surely you have heard everything I have said," the chairman said.

"Of course, but apparently you have heard nothing I have said. Let me put it this way—there are two possible outcomes to this investigation. First, that the substance found is not cocaine, in which case no charges will be filed. Second, that the substance is cocaine, in which case the culprit will be seen to be Christian St. Clair, who will not appear to speak in his defense."

"So you say."

"So I say. Is there anything else to discuss?"

"Not at this moment."

"Good. This meeting is adjourned. Tommy, you remain."

The men filed out, and Berenson remained. A thin film of perspiration had appeared on his upper lip.

"Erik, I have not violated your confidence," Berenson said.

"Then how did news of the incident aboard the yacht come to the board's attention?"

"I don't know. I didn't know it would be brought up."

"Tommy, if you are lying to me you will pay dearly."

"I swear to you, I had no knowledge of this, and I have spoken to no one about our conversation."

"Very well, I will take your word for it. You may go."

Berenson went, and quickly.

*   *   *

IN HIS OFFICE, Charles Fox listened with considerable amusement. When the recording had finished, he took out a cell phone and called Ed Rawls.

"Hey, Charley, what's going on around there?"

"In a word, Ed, pandemonium."

"I'm happy to hear it. Is this the result of our collaboration on the Coast Guard event?"

"It is, certainly. Macher, if he wasn't paranoid before, is now climbing the walls, and it would not surprise me if that has the effect of a more serious attempt on the Carlssons or Barrington, or all of them."

"Well, we knew that would have to happen before we achieve a resolution of this sorry affair, didn't we?"

"I suppose we did."

"And we will achieve a satisfactory resolution," Rawls said.

"I hope so."

"I think the time has come for you to meet Stone Barrington."

"I'd like that very much," Fox replied.

"Call him at this number in half an hour," Rawls said, dictating it.

22

Joan buzzed Stone. "Ed Rawls on one."

Stone picked up. "Yes, Ed?"

"Stone, I think it's time for you to meet my source at St. Clair."

"I'm up for that."

"His name is Charles Fox, Charley to his friends. He's going to call you in half an hour, and I suggest that you invite him to your home for dinner, rather than meet at a restaurant, and warn him not to be followed."

"All right. Tell me something about him."

"He's in his mid-thirties, a Southerner, scholarship to Yale, Rhodes Scholar, recruited to the Agency by a Yale professor. I've read his personnel file, and he got high marks from everyone during his training. When I was station chief in Stockholm, he was sent to me for an operation requiring an officer who was not connected to the embassy. He performed beautifully. He'll tell you the rest, including what he wants."

"All right, I'll look forward to hearing from him."

"By the way, I didn't thank you properly for dinner and the guest room. We had a wonderful time. See ya." Rawls hung up.

HALF AN HOUR LATER, Joan buzzed. "A man who won't give his name but says you're expecting his call."

"Right." Stone pressed the button. "Hello?"

"This is Ed's friend. May we meet?"

"Are you free for dinner this evening?"

"Yes."

Stone gave him the address. "Come here at seven, and we'll dine in. Ed says you should be careful of a tail."

"Right. See you then." He hung up.

AT SEVEN ON the dot, Stone picked up the phone to answer the front door. "Yes?"

"It's Fox."

Stone pressed the button to unlock. "Come in." He got up and walked from his study into the living room to greet his guest.

Charles Fox was about five-ten and thickly built— maybe two hundred pounds, sandy hair, pleasant mien. He moved like a man who knew how to take care of himself.

Stone offered his hand. "I'm Stone."

Fox shook it. "I'm Charley."

"Come into the study," Stone said, leading him in. "What will you drink?"

"I'm a Southerner, a bourbon man."

Stone poured two Knob Creeks and showed him to one of a pair of chairs before the fireplace, where a small fire blazed.

"Ed speaks highly of you," Stone said.

"I think highly of him. I thought he got a raw deal at the Agency, and I'm glad it got straightened out."

"Tell me a little about yourself—the sixty-second bio will do."

"Born Delano, Georgia, thirty-four years ago. Father and mother mill hands. Public schools, scholarship to Yale to study English lit, a Rhodes, spent at Oxford, then back at Yale, recruited for the Agency."

Stone nodded. "Did you like it there?"

"I did. I actually enjoyed the training, especially the physical stuff, which a lot of my classmates shied from. I got a couple of interesting assignments right away, including one in Stockholm, under Rawls. I spent two years in the London station."

"Who'd you work for in London?"

"Dick Stone. Ed says you were related."

"First cousins."

"A good man. He would have been director by now."

"Why'd you leave the Agency?"

"I was always a poor boy, and I wanted to make some money. A friend of a friend introduced me to somebody at Goldman Sachs, and they hired me as a trainee. I spent six years there, made partner after five."

"How'd you get to St. Clair?"

"He called me out of the blue, said a friend had suggested he talk to me. I'd heard of the man, of course, so I met him. He invited me up for a few days on his new yacht, and we got along. He gave me to understand that he needed somebody to work acquisitions, and that he wanted somebody who could rise to CEO quickly. He was backing a guy named Knott to run against Katharine Lee for President, and he told me that when his man was elected—when, not if, mind you—he'd be spending a lot of time in D.C., and if I worked out, I'd be minding the store in New York. I liked the idea. I found Goldman too regimented for me, too many committees, layers. He offered me two million a year, with a million-dollar signing bonus, and I jumped at it."

"I should think you would have," Stone said.

"I got there about a month before he blew himself up by opening what sounded like an Agency strong case the wrong way."

"What did you think of St. Clair?"

"He was a charmer, but I quickly learned that he liked cutting a corner or two, and I was uncomfortable with that. There was no management tree to speak of, so when he died, the place was adrift. Erik Macher stepped into the breach."

"And what did you think of that?"

"I stayed out of his way, until I could figure out what was going to happen. Macher didn't even know who I was. He was based in a security company in D.C. that was St. Clair's personal police force. He's no businessman, and I figured that, if I could edge him aside, I might still end up running the place. I checked up on his time at the Agency, and it was clear that the man was a thug. I figured that if I stuck around St. Clair and had to work for Macher, I'd end up in jail. I started collecting information that might stand me in good stead if the FBI or the New York Attorney General's Office came calling. There was a lot of gossip around the office, and I made notes, then I got into the company's most secure computer network. I've copied a huge lot of documents, more than enough to cover me."

"What do you plan to do with it?"

"I don't have a plan yet. I just want to get out of there before the place blows. Macher is a deeply paranoid character who reacts badly when he's crossed. He's in league with a lawyer named Thomas Berenson, who's corporate counsel, and during my computer searches I came up with a will for Christian St. Clair that Berenson had drawn, that pretty much handed the company to Macher. I also came up with the original will. Berenson had just substituted the new stuff for a couple of pages of the original, which had already been executed and which didn't mention Macher at all."

"That was pretty slick of Macher."

"He's a dangerous guy, in more ways than one. He had a reputation at the Agency for unnecessary violence. He's got a guy named Jake Herman, ex-FBI, who left the Bureau under unfavorable circumstances, and he's doing for Macher what Macher used to do for St. Clair, except out of the New York office, instead of D.C. The two of them make quite a pair."

Stone set down his drink. "Will you excuse me for a moment? I want to make a phone call."

"Sure."

Stone got up and called Mike Freeman. "I'm dining

with an interesting young man that you should meet. Can you join us at my house?"

"What time?"

"Now is good. We're still on drinks."

"I'll be there in fifteen minutes."

Stone hung up and rang Fred, letting him know they'd be three for dinner.

23

Mike Freeman arrived and was given a drink while Stone and Charley started a new one. Stone introduced Mike to Charley and filled him in on his background with Charley's help. Dinner was served, and Fred poured the wine.

"So, Charley," Stone said, "what do you want to do as soon as you can extricate yourself from Macher and St. Clair?"

"Well, if I can't run St. Clair, I'd like to go into the mergers and acquisitions business for myself, or with partners."

Stone and Mike exchanged a glance. "What sort of acquisitions interest you?" Stone asked.

"Start-ups, or interesting small companies with the potential for rapid growth, if they get the financing they need."

"What are you prepared to invest in such a business?" Mike asked.

"Five million to start. I made a couple of really good deals at Goldman, and I've still got my starting bonus from St. Clair."

"Is that everything you've got?" Mike asked.

"Not quite, and I'd need a salary to live on, of course."

"Where do you live?" Stone asked.

"I have a suite at the Lombardy Hotel, on East Fifty-sixth Street. It's expensive, but I get hotel services like room service, laundry, and maid, so I don't have to spend any time keeping house."

"How much time were you putting in on a weekly basis at Goldman?" Mike asked.

"Sixty to eighty hours a week," Charley replied. "It was what was expected of the younger guys, and it was too much. I want a life, too."

"That seems reasonable."

They chatted on through dinner and Stone got the strong impression that Mike wanted to go into business with Charley Fox. After dessert, he pulled Mike aside. "What do you think?"

"I think we need this guy," Mike said. "We've been acquiring slowly, catch as catch can, and we need somebody who can put together deals and do the due diligence."

"I think you're right, and I think he's the guy."

"I've got some free office space in our building. We can install him in there with a secretary and a small staff."

"Good," Stone replied. "What should we pay him?"

"A million a year, then bump him up to two as soon as he starts doing deals that will support it. I reckon we're going to be pumping in operating expenses for at least a year, but that's what we're for in the deal, the daddies."

"Are you going to kick in free rent?"

"Sure, until he generates the revenue to pay for it."

They went back to the dinner table. "I guess you've got a contract with St. Clair," Stone said.

Charley produced it from an inside pocket. "Christian drew it up, and I signed it."

Stone read it quickly. "Nothing to keep you from taking a hike whenever you feel like it."

"Or to keep him from firing me out of hand."

"Can you just walk out tomorrow?"

"I need a little more time with document collection," Charley said, "then I'm out." He paused. "If I've got someplace to go."

"Mike and I want to give you that place," Stone said. He outlined the deal he and Mike had discussed. "What do you think?"

"Do I get a piece of each deal?"

"You can invest up to a third of each one, if you can find the money."

Charley shook his head. "I want a fee for each deal, and that gets plowed in as an investment."

"What sort of a fee?"

"A third of a third of the investment. Sometimes I'll be able to ante up, sometimes not."

Stone and Mike exchanged a nod. "That's a very sweet deal, Charley," Stone said, offering his hand. "You'd better hold up your end."

"Agreed," Charley said, and he shook Mike's hand, too. "When I said I was interested in small deals, that won't always be so."

"When you've got the right deal, we can find the cash," Stone said. "From more than one source."

"Great."

"Okay, I'll draw up a contract and get it to you in a couple of days. Do you have a lawyer?"

"I'd like for you to be my lawyer."

"Not ethical. There's a guy at Woodman & Weld named Herb Fisher that you'll like. In fact, you talk to him, and he can draw up the contract."

"Charley," Mike said, "does anybody at St. Clair know where you live?"

"My address is in my employee records," he replied.

"You'd better get out of there before you make the move. It may piss off Macher, and we don't want you to be too easy to find."

"Tell you what, Charley," Stone said. "I own the house next door where my staff live. There's a furnished ground-floor rear apartment empty there, opens onto the common garden. You can move in there rent-free, until you decide where you want to live."

"Thanks, Stone."

"Call my secretary, Joan Robertson, when you want to start sending stuff over."

"It's just clothes—won't take long."

"You figure out when it's the right moment to bail out of St. Clair, and tell me how you want to do it."

"I'll want to vanish in a puff of smoke," Charley said.

"When you do, give Macher a proper letter of resignation. Do you still have family in Georgia?"

"Nope, they're all gone."

"Then tell him you have to go back there to deal with family matters. If he looks for you there, he'll find a dead end."

"Good idea," Charley said. "And there's something I should tell you."

"Okay," Stone said.

"I've got Macher's office wired for sound, and I have recordings of a couple of his meetings, including one with his board, which is exercised over something to do with the Coast Guard finding cocaine aboard the company yacht."

"I believe I'm acquainted with that incident," Stone said drily.

"Do you want me to keep the wire in there?"

"Yes, but for informational purposes only, since it's illegal. Make sure you shut it down without a trace when you go. You don't want them finding it later."

"Right," Charley said. "I'll be out of there in a week."

"Good. Be careful. Don't roil the waters there. We don't want our new partner to get hurt."

"Charley," Mike said, "I'm in the security business, you know. If you feel in danger at any time, call me on my cell, twenty-four/seven." He handed Charley a card. "I can put people on you or snatch you off the street, if necessary. And when you check out of the hotel, give them a forwarding address in Georgia, and after you leave, don't return to the hotel."

"Not even for a haircut?" Charley asked. "My barber's there."

"Find a new barber for the moment," Mike said.

"I get my hair cut there, too," Stone said. "I'll make excuses for you next time I'm in."

They walked Charley to the front door.

"Let me have a look outside," Mike said, "then I'll

give you a lift to the hotel." He did so, while Stone and
Charley waited.

"I think this is going to work well," Stone said. "Just
remember to stay safe. You've been trained on how to do
that, haven't you?"

"I certainly have," Charley said.

Mike returned. "Okay, into my car," he said, and the
two of them left.

24

Charley Fox turned up early the next morning and started going through his desk, cleaning out drawers and putting what he wanted to take away in his briefcase. He downloaded the cache of documents he had been saving onto a pair of thumb drives, numbered one and two, and tossed them into his briefcase. He deleted all his computer files and reformatted the hard drive. Finally, he disconnected the little amplifier hooked to the bug in Macher's office and tossed them into his briefcase, as well, along with the two burner cell phones in his drawer. That done, he typed up a letter of resignation, put it into his briefcase and locked it.

"Charles," a woman's voice said.

He turned to find Agnes, the group secretary, standing in his doorway. "Yes, Agnes?"

"Mr. Macher would like to see you in his office."

"I'll be there shortly, thanks."

"He said, *now*."

"All right." He got into his jacket, grabbed his brief-case, removed the resignation letter, put it into his jacket pocket, and walked upstairs. In the outer office, he set his briefcase down next to Macher's secretary's desk. "I'll pick this up in a few minutes," he said to her.

"Fine," she replied.

He knocked on the door and heard Macher shout, "Come!" He found Macher sitting at his desk and Jake Herman standing behind him, leaning against a book-case. This did not look good.

"Sit down, Charles," Macher said.

Charley did. "Good morning, Mr. Macher, Jake."

"Charles, have you heard anything about the company yacht being stopped by the Coast Guard last weekend?"

"Nope, not a thing," he replied. "They do equipment checks on yachts all the time, though. I wouldn't worry about it."

"Why not?"

"Because the checks are routine. They probably didn't single you out."

Herman spoke up. "You ever had any telephone con-versations with the Coast Guard, Fox?"

Charley shook his head. "Nope. I've never needed their help at sea."

"You sail?"

"Doesn't everybody?"

"Not everybody," Herman replied.

"Come on, Jake, what is this about?"

"Somebody tipped the Coast Guard to search the company yacht," Herman replied.

"What for?"

"Drugs."

"Did they find any?"

"Unlikely."

"Then what's the problem, and what do I have to do with it?"

Jake left the room and came back a moment later with Charley's briefcase. "Let's have a look in here," Herman said.

Charley leaned over as he passed and snatched the case out of Herman's hand. "Let's not." One of his burner phones would have the Coast Guard number in it.

"Charles, let Jake open the case," Macher said.

"For what purpose?"

"For whatever purpose I wish."

The secretary knocked, came into the room, and set some things on Macher's desk. "Your mail, sir," she said. "And there's one from the Coast Guard. You asked me to watch for it."

Macher picked up the envelope, ripped it open, and removed a letter. "Well, let's see what they have to say," he said, unfolding the letterhead and reading aloud. "'Dear Mr. Macher. Further to the search of your company's yacht on Saturday last, I wish to inform you that our laboratory has analyzed the white powder found in the owner's suite. The powder turned out to be an over-the-counter laxative called SuperLax. I wish to apologize for any inconvenience caused by our search and to thank you for your cooperation.'"

"Anything else?" Charley asked.

"That doesn't mean that you didn't call the Coast Guard," Herman said. He moved toward where Charley sat, reaching for the briefcase.

Charley stood up and kicked him hard in the knee, and Herman cried out and collapsed, clutching his knee. Charley turned to Macher. "Mr. Macher," he said, "I don't like working here anymore, so I'm resigning as of this moment. I got paid yesterday, so you don't owe me anything." He picked up his briefcase and started for the door.

"Now, Charles," Macher said placatingly, "let's talk about this."

"I've nothing to talk about," Charley replied, opening the door. "Good day." He closed the door behind him and started for the outer door, then he stopped, reached into his pocket for the resignation letter, and tossed it onto the secretary's desk. "I forgot to give this to Mr. Macher," he said. "Please give it to him for me."

"Of course, Charley," she replied.

A moment later, Charley was on the street, hailing a cab.

"The Lombardy Hotel," he said to the driver. "Fifty-sixth Street, east of Park."

At the hotel he got out, went upstairs to his room, packed his things, and called down for a bellman. When the man came, he said, "Put these into a cab for me, going to JFK Airport, while I check out."

"Yes, sir."

Charley took the elevator down and asked the woman at the desk for his final bill.

"Leaving us, Mr. Fox?"

"Yes, I have to head down to Georgia to tend to a family matter."

"Will you be returning to us soon?"

"Probably not for several months. I'll give you a forwarding address." He gave her his credit card, and she handed him a form. He filled it out, giving the address of the law firm that his family had dealt with, and signed the credit card slip. "Thanks for everything," he said.

"Come back to see us."

He gave the bellman a fifty, got into a cab, and as the driver pulled away, said, "Never mind the airport, I've another stop to make." He gave the man the address, then got out his cell phone.

"Stone Barrington."

"Stone, it's Charley Fox."

"Good morning, Charley."

"Things came to a head with Macher this morning, and I'm out of that place and the hotel. May I come there now?"

"Of course. Come in through my office entrance."

STONE BUZZED FOR FRED, then got up when Charley came in. Bob got up from near Stone's feet and greeted him.

"This is Bob," Stone said. "He's frisking you for food."

"Hi, Bob," Charley said, scratching his ears.

"Everything okay?"

"It is now." Charley gave him an account of his morning.

"It's just as well," Stone said. "Fred will take you next door and get you settled and show you how to work the security system. I'll call Mike Freeman and tell him you'll need your office space this afternoon."

"Thanks, Stone, I appreciate that."

*　　*　　*

JAKE HERMAN LIMPED into Macher's office. "I called his hotel," he said. "He's checked out, gave a forwarding address in Georgia, and took a cab to JFK."

Macher waved a letter. "Turns out he was resigning anyway. He'd already written this."

Herman looked at it. "Good riddance."

"I never knew what he did here, anyway," Macher said. "Still, I want you to keep tabs on where he is and what he's doing."

"Even in Georgia?"

"Anywhere he goes."

25

The following morning Jake Herman went to the Lombardy Hotel.

"May I help you, sir?" the desk clerk asked.

"Yes, I've been trying to reach a friend of mine, Charles Fox, who lives here, but the operator said he had checked out."

"Yes, sir, Mr. Fox checked out yesterday."

"Do you have a forwarding address? I want to repay some money I owe him."

She went to a file drawer and came back with a form, and he copied the address. A law firm. He found a seat in the lobby, called the number in Delano, Georgia. He was told that they had not seen or heard of Mr. Fox for more than two years and weren't expecting to.

Herman found the bell captain and inquired about Fox's departure the day before. The man called in the bellman who covered Fox's floor. "Did you put Mr. Fox into a cab yesterday?"

"Yep. He was going to JFK."

"Do you remember what cab company the car was from?" Herman asked.

"Yeah, it was the Ace Cab Company. We get a lot of their cabs waiting outside."

"Did you know the driver?"

"Name is Casey. I don't know if that's a first or a last name."

"What time did Mr. Fox leave?"

"About nine-thirty, nine forty-five."

Jake gave him a twenty and thanked him. He resumed his seat in the lobby, called the Ace Cab Company and asked for the dispatcher.

"Dispatch."

"This is Special Agent Jacobs with the Federal Bureau of Investigation."

"What can I do you for?"

"Yesterday around nine-thirty, nine forty-five, a driver of yours named Casey picked up a fare at the Lombardy Hotel on East Fifty-sixth Street. Can you tell me his final destination?"

"Hang on, let me pull up his trip sheet. Here we go, went to JFK—no, he changed his destination." The man gave it to him.

"That's in Turtle Bay Gardens, isn't it?"

"If you say so. Gotta run." The man hung up.

Jake Herman knew who lived at that address. He went back to St. Clair and downstairs to Fox's office, then searched it thoroughly. "As clean as a hound's tooth," he said aloud to himself, then he switched on Fox's computer.

That done, he went upstairs and knocked on Macher's door.

"Come!"

Jake went in and sat down. "Charles Fox didn't go to Georgia yesterday," he said. "He went to Stone Barrington's house."

"That little shit!"

"His office is empty, the cleaners have already emptied his wastebasket, and his computer's hard drive has been reformatted, so there's nothing on it."

"How the hell does he know Stone Barrington?"

"I don't know."

"Do you think he's been spying for Barrington ever since he came to work for St. Clair?"

"It's possible," Jake said. "There's no way of knowing, unless I get a chance to beat it out of him, and I'd welcome that opportunity." His knee still hurt.

"All right, stake out Barrington's house and snatch Fox at the first opportunity. Take him to that place you have where you do that sort of thing, and don't stop until you're satisfied you have every answer to your every question."

"Perhaps he should disappear permanently? He's already left the forwarding address of a law firm in Georgia."

"I think that might be the most convenient thing to do, but not until you know you've got everything."

"This will be my pleasure," Herman said.

STONE BARRINGTON SAT and read both of the wills that Charley had found on St. Clair's computer, then he buzzed Joan.

She came in. "Yessir?"

Stone handed her a thumb drive and gave her the two file names. "I want you to find a Kinko's or something like it, maybe on the West Side, not in this neighborhood, and print out half a dozen copies of these two wills. It's important that we don't print or copy it on any of our machines."

"Righto," Joan said, and left.

"Those could come in handy," Charley said from across his desk. Charley's cell phone rang. "Excuse me," he said to Stone, then went and sat on the sofa. "Hello?"

"Mr. Fox?"

"Yes?"

"This is Laura at the Lombardy. You checked out with me yesterday."

"Hi, Laura, what's up?"

"I thought you should know that a man came in this morning and inquired about your forwarding address, said he owed you some money and wanted to send it to you. And then he went and talked to the bellman who brought your bags down. He also sat down in our lobby for a few minutes and made some phone calls on his cell."

"What did the guy look like?"

"Maybe fifty, over six feet, heavy, looked like an ex–football player."

"Laura, thank you so much for letting me know. I want to send you a bottle of something. What do you drink?"

"Champagne," Laura replied.

"It's on its way." He hung up and called the liquor store he dealt with in the Lombardy's neighborhood and had a bottle of Dom Pérignon sent to her, then he went back and sat down across from Stone. "Looks like I've underestimated Macher," he said.

"How so?" Stone asked.

"His personal thug, Jake Herman, turned up at the Lombardy this morning and got my forwarding address, a law firm in my hometown. They would have told him they hadn't heard from me in years, and his next move would have been to find out where the cab took me, which was here. Clearly I wasn't careful enough."

"What do you think he'll do?"

"I think I'd give you three to one that he's got people outside right now, watching the house."

Stone picked up the phone and called Mike Freeman.

"Yes, Stone?"

"Charley Fox has been made by Macher's henchman, Jake Herman, when he came to my house, and Charley thinks he might have people outside right now."

"You want me to remove them?"

"For the moment, just photograph them and e-mail me the shots. Later, we might want them removed. You're going to need to put a couple of men on Charley, too, for the present. We don't want them following him to your building."

"Consider it done," Mike said, and they both hung up.

"Mike's on it," Stone said to Charley. "If you want to leave the house, go out of your apartment into the garden, and there's a wrought-iron gate that opens onto Second Avenue. Come back the same way, call Joan, and she will buzz you in until we can get you a key."

"I'm sorry to be all this trouble," Charley said. "I guess my tradecraft is a little rusty."

"Don't worry about it, just keep safe," Stone said.

26

Jake Herman went online to the New York City Department of Buildings website and searched for building permits at Stone Barrington's house. He was astonished at what he found.

Under the banner of the General Services Administration, a federal agency, he found detailed plans for improvements several years before, and the authorizing agency was the Central Intelligence Agency. For some reason they had seen fit to make Barrington's house extremely secure. The brick veneer at the front and rear of the house had been removed and half-inch steel sheathing had been applied, then the bricks replaced, and the same with the roof; the windows had been replaced with replicas conforming to the New-York Historical Society's rules with steel frames and inch-thick armored glass, and the electrical and utility wiring to the house had been reinforced and encased in stainless-steel pipes.

The goddamned place was a fortress. Clearly the Agency had some sort of relationship with Barrington. That made him wonder if Charles Fox had a connection with the Agency, but he didn't have the skills to crack their computers. He searched his mind for past acquaintances who had served there and came up with a woman about Fox's age, Kaley Weiss, whom he had interviewed for a job at Macher's security company a couple of years ago. He called the number he had for her.

"Hello?"

"Kaley Weiss?"

"Who's calling?"

"This is Jake Herman at St. Clair Enterprises. We met a couple of years ago."

"Oh, yes, the interview."

"We have an opening. Would you like to come by and talk about it?"

"Thank you, Mr. Herman, but I'm very well situated in a new job, and I'm not interested in moving."

"Oh? Where are you? I'll notate your record for the future."

"I'm afraid they insist on confidentiality from their employees."

"Of course. Oh, by the way, when you were at the Agency, did you know a guy named Charles Fox?"

"Yes, but not well. We were in a class together during training."

"Have you heard from him since? There's something here that might interest him, and I don't have a number for him."

"I'm afraid not," she said. "Thanks for thinking of me." She hung up and made a call of her own.

*   *   *

CHARLEY FOX'S CELL rang and he checked the number before answering. "Kaley?"

"Yes, Charley, how are you?"

"I'm very well, thanks, and you?"

"I'm doing great, thanks."

"Are you still with our former employer?"

"No, I left a couple of years ago. Now I'm with a security company called Strategic Services."

"I know them," Charley said. "What are you doing there?"

"Working for a woman named Vivian Bacchetti, who's chief of operations here. Listen, when I left our previous employer I had an interview with a guy at St. Clair Enterprises named Jake Herman, ex-FBI, thoroughly unsavory character."

"Oh?"

"Yes, and I just got a call from him asking about you."

"Aha. What did you tell him?"

"He asked if I knew you at the Agency, and I said we'd had a class together."

That was less than a full answer, Charley thought, since they had been sleeping together most of the time they were at the Farm. "Did you tell him anything else?"

"He wanted your number, but I got uncomfortable and didn't give it to him, just brushed him off."

"That's good," Charley said. "I worked at St. Clair for less than a month, then Christian St. Clair bought the farm, and I just got out of there."

"Well, Herman doesn't know anything he didn't know before. Where are you living?"

"I'm staying with a friend between residences. You want to have dinner one night soon?"

"Love to," she said. "This is my cell number. Call me when you like."

"Are you free this evening?"

"I am."

"There's a good cook where I'm staying. Why don't you come over, and we'll dine here?"

"Great."

He gave her the address of Stone's staff house. "I'm in apartment 1A. Seven o'clock?"

"You're on. See you then." They both hung up.

Charley, who had taken the call in the office next to Joan's, went into Stone's office.

"Stone, have you got an extra piece I could borrow while I'm here?"

"Sure. Any favorites?"

"Something light would do."

Stone went to his safe and removed a Colt Government .380 and a spare magazine. "How's this?" he asked, handing it over.

"Perfect."

"Do you have a New York City concealed carry permit?"

"No."

"Then don't take it out of the house."

"All right."

"I think it might be a good idea if you applied for a permit," Stone said. "You never know."

"All right, as soon as I can get out of the house."

"You can apply online, then they'll schedule you for an interview and fingerprinting. I might be able to grease the wheels a bit."

"Great. Listen, Stone, I probably should have asked, but do you mind if I have a woman for dinner in my apartment tonight?"

"Not in the least. Speak to Fred and he'll make your wishes known to Helene in the kitchen, and he'll find you some wine and booze, too."

"She's somebody I knew at the Agency. Her name is Kaley Weiss, and she works now at Strategic Services, for somebody named Vivian Bacchetti. You have a connection to that name, don't you?"

"I do. Her husband, Dino, and I were partners on the NYPD."

"And he's the police commissioner now?"

"That's right. You'll meet him in due course."

"Okay." Charley turned to go. "Oh, the way I got in touch was that Kaley got a call from Jake Herman."

"Uh-oh."

"She'd had a job interview at St. Clair a couple of years ago. He asked if she knew me, and she told him we'd been in a class together at the Farm. That was it, she hung up."

"So Herman now knows you were at the Agency."

"I guess so, though I can't think how that could matter."

"Probably not. Enjoy your evening."

Charley thanked him and went back to his borrowed office.

27

Charley Fox opened his door and found Kaley Weiss standing there in a cashmere dress draped over her tall, slim frame and high breasts. She looked much the same as the last time he had seen her, except there was a dent the size of a Ping-Pong ball in the right side of her forehead. She seemed to be missing a chunk of her skull.

They embraced lightly, and he showed her in.

"This is very nice," she said, looking around. "You said it belongs to a friend?"

"Yes, he lives in the house next door, but he owns this house, too, and he had an empty apartment. Let me get you a drink."

"Scotch," she said.

He poured her a Talisker and himself a Knob Creek. "Why don't we sit out in the garden for a while, before it gets too chilly?" He led her outside, where they found a comfortable outdoor sofa.

"This is lovely," she said. "I've heard of Turtle Bay, but I've never been here."

"You'll always be welcome."

"How long are you going to live here?"

"Stone has said I can stay as long as I like, but eventually I'll want to buy something."

"Wait a minute, Stone Barrington?"

"Yes. Do you know him?"

"No, but my boss and her husband are very tight with him."

"Right."

"Listen, I'd better explain about my face."

"You don't have to."

"Let's get it out of the way. After our training at the Farm I was stationed in various parts of the Middle East, the last in Israel. I was sitting in an outdoor café in Jerusalem with one of my local sources, and the place got hit in a drive-by, sprayed with automatic weapons fire. I woke up in a hospital two days later. A couple of days after that the Agency airlifted me home and put me in Walter Reed Hospital, where I had a number of surgeries over four months, then spent another seven months in rehabilitation. The Agency kept me on the payroll through all that, but afterward, I didn't want another foreign assignment, so I resigned and came to New York."

"You seem to be fine now," he said.

"I am fine—an occasional headache, but that's it. I still have one more surgery to go, but I'm glad to be out of the line of fire."

"I don't blame you," Charley said.

"What did you do after the Farm?"

"I did hitches in Stockholm and London."

"Did you learn Swedish?"

"No, I was playing the part of an American business-man, and nobody expected me to speak the language."

"I assume you didn't have that problem in London."

He laughed. "No, not once I got the hang of speaking Britslang."

"You said you had left St. Clair. What are you going to do now?"

"I'm going to work with Stone and your boss, Mike Freeman, doing mergers and acquisitions in a partnership we're forming. I'll be working in your office building."

"So you'll be conveniently located."

He smiled. "You, too."

THEY DINED AT a table in the living room as rain began to fall outside.

"I don't know any restaurants with food this good," Kaley said during the main course, "or with a better cellar."

"Stone lives well," Charley said. "Tell me, do you know anything else about Jake Herman, other than what you've already told me?"

"Not really, but I formed the impression that he was a pretty tough guy, and that he was doing dirty work for St. Clair, and I didn't want to be involved in that. He was inordinately impressed that I had served with the Agency, and he pressed me to tell him about the skills I'd learned at the Farm. I just told him I couldn't talk about it."

"Did you meet St. Clair?"

"Just in passing. He stopped by Herman's office, and I was introduced. He seemed much nicer than Jake Herman."

"He seemed that way to me, too, but then I wondered why he was employing people like Jake Herman."

"A very good point."

"Since St. Clair died, the place is being run by a guy named Erik Macher, who struck me as not much better than Jake. I viewed the place as a snake pit, and I got out after less than a month. Herman actually tracked me to Stone's house, although I made a minor effort to cover my tracks. Our instructors at the Farm would be ashamed. Macher's got a couple of guys in the block, now, keeping an eye out for me."

"What do they want from you?"

"I think they're worried about what I might know more than they think about how they do business. A pall of paranoia hangs over St. Clair."

"What did you find out while you were there?"

"Well, for a start, Macher and the company's lawyer falsified St. Clair's will in a manner that gave Macher control of the whole shebang. They also made an effort, though not an illegal one, to take over the Carlsson Clinic, but Stone got involved and put an end to their bid."

"I know a little about that. The clinic is our client now, and my boss, Viv, oversaw their security. It's still going on."

Fred Flicker came in to take their dishes, and Charley introduced him to Kaley.

"When you're ready to leave, miss," Fred said, "I'll drive you home. We have unwelcome visitors outside that you don't want to meet while looking for a cab."

"Thank you, Fred," Charley said. When he had gone, Charley told her about the butler. "Fred's an ex–Royal Marine commando, and tough as nails. You'll be safe with him, and you'll depart from the garage without being seen on the street."

"It's like being back at the Agency," Kaley said.

AFTER DINNER, it didn't take long for them to be back in bed together.

"Just like the old days," Kaley said, when they had both climaxed.

"Better," Charley replied. "We're older and wiser. And I have the feeling that the next few years are going to be the best I've known. Of course, I'll need your company to enjoy them fully."

"That's nice to know," she said.

"What sort of work has Strategic Services had you doing?"

"Personal protection stuff, at first, Secret Service–like. Viv and I have become close, though, and I'm working more with her on security evaluation and planning, and I like that. Occasionally, I still go out with a team, as I did at the Carlsson Clinic. I and another woman were assigned to Marisa, the daughter, and the old man became enamored of my partner. They've been seeing each other since. There's an age difference, but it doesn't seem to bother either of them."

AROUND MIDNIGHT, AFTER they had showered and dressed, Charley buzzed Fred, then he walked Kaley to the garage and put her into the Bentley. He made a point of getting back inside before the garage door opened, but he could hear the rain coming down hard.

"I hope you didn't bring an umbrella!" he yelled into the night.

28

The following morning Fred drove Charley Fox to the Strategic Services building on East Fifty-seventh Street, with his briefcase and a couple of boxes of office stuff. It was still raining.

"Mr. Fox, you'll be happy to hear your two tails got properly doused last night," Fred said.

"That does make me happy."

"There are two new ones there this morning, in raincoats, hats, and carrying umbrellas like weapons. They look like proper spies."

"They don't have wheels, do they?"

"No, don't worry, they're not following us. Still, I'll take further precautions." Fred made a couple of unnecessary course alterations, then pulled up under the portico of the building and carried Charley's boxes inside for him.

Charley presented himself at the front desk, showed them two picture IDs, then was photographed and presented with a newly minted security badge to clip to his breast pocket. A man in a black suit led him to an elevator and up to the fourth floor.

"My name is Chaney, Mr. Fox. You'll be pretty much alone on this floor," the man said, "as it's kept for expansion and for lone wolves like you. Two temporaries—a receptionist and a secretary—have been assigned to you, until you find your own."

"Thank you, Mr. Chaney," Charley replied.

They came to a double glass door on which had been affixed the words THE TRIANGLE PARTNERSHIP in large gold letters. An attractive young woman sat behind the front desk.

"Mr. Fox, this is Stella, your receptionist."

They shook hands.

"Welcome to Strategic Services," she said. "I'm sorry—to The Triangle Partnership."

"I'll have to get used to that myself," Charley said.

They continued to an office suite, where a middle-aged woman was occupying the secretary's desk.

"This is Maggie Everson," Chaney said. "She'll be running you."

Charley laughed and shook her hand. "I'll look forward to that, Maggie."

"He's all yours," Chaney said, and exited.

Maggie led him into a roomy corner office with a desk, a small conference table and other matching pieces of furniture, plus a seating area with a leather sofa and matching chairs. "We've got a warehouse full of stuff downtown, if there's anything you want to shop for," Maggie said. She opened the wide curtains, revealing a rain-swept garden below. "There's a lot of sun when it comes out."

"This looks very well equipped," Charley replied. It was much handsomer than his offices at either Goldman Sachs or St. Clair.

Maggie opened a desk drawer and handed him a box of business cards. "There's engraved stationery in the other drawers, and here's your new cell phone." She handed him the latest iPhone. "If you want to keep your old phone, as well, I can have your calls transferred to this one. It has some Strategic Services apps and security features that I'll take you through later. You should memorize the new number as soon as possible." She helped him open his boxes and distribute his belongings.

"Your computer is an Apple mini Mac, and our usual software has been customized for the purposes of Triangle." She took him through the operation of the computer, then showed him how the phone system worked. "You have a direct line for personal calls, three office lines, and three fax lines. Line one is the one on your business cards, and your new e-mail address is there, too—charlesfox-at-triangleparnership-dot-com. Stella is the phone operator, as well as the receptionist, and she answers all incoming calls, except your direct, private line. There are four other offices attached to this suite for future hirees. They have their own phone and fax lines. Your fax machine is outside, next to my desk." She opened a cabinet across the room to reveal a clever kitchenette, a well-stocked bar, with an ice maker and a coffee and espresso maker. "What else can I tell you?"

"Where's the men's room?" Charley asked.

She laughed and pointed at a door across the room. "That's your private one, and it has a shower, too. There's a bed, too, should you need to pull an all-nighter. Strategic Services frowns on sex in the office, but then this isn't their office, it's yours, and their rules don't apply."

Charley laughed. "Good to know."

"Visitors must check in first downstairs, as you did, and they'll be issued with visitors' passes. If some of your visitors are regular, they can be issued with permanent passes."

"That's fine."

"Two floors up there are two restaurants—a cafeteria for all employees and a more luxurious one called Safe House, with its own chef, for senior officers. You may use either. They'll swipe the bar code from your security ID and bill Triangle for all charges. Anything else?"

"Not right now. Thanks, Maggie."

She left, and a moment later there was a knock on the door, and Stone Barrington and Mike Freeman entered, one carrying a champagne bucket and the other a bottle of Veuve Clicquot Grande Dame.

"Welcome," Stone said, opening the bottle and grabbing three glasses from the bar. They raised them and drank.

"So," Mike said, "how much money have you made for us so far?"

"Zip," Charley replied, "but I have some ideas. I also have a list of companies that Christian St. Clair was interested in, glommed from his computer system. I think I'll start with those."

"You can hire anybody you want for receptionist and secretary," Mike said, "but if you're happy with these two, I'll transfer them."

"I'll let you know. There are also two people at Goldman that I'd like to steal from them."

"Go right ahead," Stone said. "You're going to need help."

"Make up your own office budget and send it to me," Mike said. "We'll also take care of background checks on the people you want to hire. Anybody who works in this building has to submit to that, and they're thorough. Don't commit to a hiring until that has been done. It rarely takes more than a few hours."

"Of course. What about polygraphs?"

"Only for senior Strategic Services staff, and those others we may have questions about."

"I'd like to have full workups on Erik Macher, Jake Herman, and Thomas Berenson, the St. Clair lawyer."

"Good idea," Mike said, "always good to know about the opposition. I understand you're acquainted with Kaley Weiss."

"You're very well informed."

"I try to be. What, may I ask, is your relationship?"

"Close," Charley replied. "We knew each other at the Farm, but our duties separated us after that. We had dinner last night and renewed our acquaintance."

"Well, we've already run our background check on you, Charley, and as far as Strategic Services is concerned, you are qualified to continue seeing her."

Charley laughed. "I'm relieved to hear it—it saves me from having to tell you to go fuck yourself."

Everybody laughed, but Charley had made his point.

29

Jake knocked on Macher's office door and was shouted in.

"What is it?" Macher asked sourly. He had been in a bad mood since Fox had so suddenly departed.

"Just an update," Jake said. "I'm getting no results on watching Barrington's house. His car has left the garage a couple of times, but the windows are tinted and my guys can't spot who's inside. Also, they weren't dressed for last night's unforecast big rain, and one of them has what sounds like walking pneumonia and is going to be in bed for a few days."

"Did you put new people on it? People with umbrellas, maybe?"

"Yes, sir, they're on station now, but they're getting nothing. Also, I think there may be a rear way out of the house, through the common garden, but we can't cover that. It's private, and somebody would immediately call the cops."

"Maybe it's time to hurt somebody."

"What would that accomplish, sir? We've lost the Carlsson takeover, and we can't get that back."

"All right, just annoy them, make them think we're thinking about them."

Jake sighed. "All right, sir. I'll have my men take out a couple of the Bentley's tires. That will take time and effort to correct. The car will have to be flat-bedded to a dealer."

"Call it a goodbye kiss," Macher said, managing what resembled a little smile.

"I'm on it."

"Oh, and I've made two new bids for small companies, ones that were on a list Christian was working from."

"What are they?"

"An electronic parts maker and a company that sends out mechanics to work on cars at people's homes or garages. They've already got twenty-five men working in the city, and they're ready to expand to other cities, if they can get fresh capital."

"Sounds great. I hope you didn't underbid, like Christian did."

"Get out of here," Macher growled. "And keep an eye on the computer file of those two companies."

"Yes, sir."

FRED WAS BACKING the Bentley out of the garage when he felt two small jolts to the car, one in back, one in front. He had a notion of what that was, but he waited until he had turned onto Third Avenue before getting out and inspecting the vehicle. There were two small marks, one on a rear tire, one on a front tire. He found a place at the curb and called his boss.

"Yes, Fred?" Stone asked.

"Mr. Barrington, our two watchers outside the house have taken a couple of potshots at two of our tires."

"With what effect?"

"No real effect, sir, since the tires are the special ones you ordered, constructed to absorb rounds and reseal. I just thought you'd like to know."

"Any reason to take it to the dealer?"

"I shouldn't think so, sir."

"Then carry on."

"Yes, sir." Fred got back into the car and continued on his mission.

STONE WAS THINKING this over when Dino called.

"Hey."

"You sound thoughtful," Dino said. "Something on your mind?"

"Yes. Macher has two people watching the house. We've been ignoring them, but this morning they tried to shoot out two of the Bentley's tires. No effect, since they're security equipment. Still, I don't think I should let it go unanswered."

"Are they still there?"

"They're always there. This morning they were both wearing trench coats, hats, and carrying umbrellas."

"Leave it to me," Dino said. "I'll get back to you."

"Okay."

"Dinner tonight?"

"Sure, just the two of us?"

"Yeah, Viv is traveling."

"You mind if I bring my new investment partner, Charley Fox? He's an interesting guy—CIA, followed by Goldman Sachs and St. Clair."

"Sure. P. J. Clarke's at seven?"

"See you then."

Joan came into his office. "I thought you'd like to know that I just saw the cops pick up our two watchers outside."

"I'm glad to hear it. Any trouble?"

"An argument, quickly resolved by the uniforms. They're gone."

JAKE HERMAN WAS at his desk when a call came in. "This is Jake."

"Jake, it's Martini. Gimlet and I got busted outside Barrington's house an hour ago. We need bail money."

"What's the charge?"

"Well, you told us to take out two tires on Barrington's Bentley, and we did, but it drove away. Fifteen minutes later we were busted, and Gimlet doesn't have his carry permit yet, and we're both charged with vandalism."

"Where are you?"

"At the Nineteenth Precinct. They're taking us downtown to be arraigned in a few minutes."

"I'll have a lawyer meet you there." He hung up and phoned an attorney St. Clair kept on retainer for such things. He didn't feel like telling Macher about this just yet; he'd let it ride until tomorrow.

*   *   *

STONE, DINO, AND CHARLEY met at Clarke's and had a drink at the bar before going into the back room for dinner. Dino and Charley got on immediately. Stone was impressed, because Dino usually reserved immediate camaraderie for cops and ex-cops.

"Thanks for clearing the street in front of the house," Stone said to Dino, when he got a chance to interrupt.

"No problem," Dino said.

"The security tires were a good move, I think."

"I don't use anything else on my official vehicles."

"I bridled at the cost, but not anymore."

"Somebody tried to shoot your tires out?" Charley asked.

"Your pal Jake Herman's people. Dino had them scooped up, and they got a few hours in the lockup."

Charley chuckled. "I wish I could see Macher's face when he finds out."

Dino chimed in, "Oh, that reminds me—you remember that other thing we talked about, that late-night visit?"

"I do," Stone said.

"How about I schedule that for soon?"

"I like the idea."

"I'm going to need a basis for a search warrant."

"I think I've got just the thing," Stone said.

Then they were called to their table.

30

Dino looked up from his steak. "Okay, what's my probable cause for a search warrant?"

"Thanks to Charley, here, I have two versions of Christian St. Clair's will that Erik Macher and Tommy Berenson, his lawyer, colluded on, and the second version gives full operating power of the whole company to Macher. The first one didn't mention him."

"I like it," Dino said, taking a swig of his cabernet. "These two copies were stolen, right?"

"Well, yes," Stone said, "but the original computer files are still in St. Clair's system. You can make your warrant for a search for the wills, which a reliable source told you existed, both physical and digital."

"I think that will fly," Dino said. "Remind me to call somebody after I finish this steak."

"Certainly."

"Dino," Charley said, "there's a button somewhere in

Macher's office that, when pressed, will scrub all their computer files clean."

"Uh-oh. Where is it?"

"I don't know, somewhere in that room. Just keep Macher and anybody else there out of that office until you've had a chance to search the files."

"Have you got locations and file names for the files?"

"Yes, you can print out the will there, then download them onto a thumb drive. I'm assuming you'll take an IT guy along on your raid."

"Right."

"If he has any problems, he can reach me anytime on my cell." Charley gave him his business card. "Macher lives on the top floor, in Christian St. Clair's old apartment, very handsome. Something else you should know, his taste in women runs to call girls. I heard him say once that picking up and seducing the amateurs was too time-consuming, so he's likely not to be alone when you bust in."

"There's another charge you can add to your list," Stone said.

"Who else lives there?" Dino asked.

"His secretary. Word around the office is, Macher likes her to be available for blow jobs, as well as her regular work. By the way, you want to keep her away from her desk and computer while you're there. Cuff her to a doorknob or something."

"Are there any other bedrooms?"

"There are several that are occasionally occupied by visiting business associates and others. It's quite an elegant house, really."

"What about Jake Herman, Charley?" Stone asked. "Where does he live?"

"He has an apartment in the neighborhood, but I've known him to stay the night at the mansion."

"Is he likely to offer resistance?"

"Nah, Jake is ex-FBI. He knows the drill. Macher knows the drill, too, but he won't like it. He could very well give you a hard time."

"I hope so," Dino said, grinning.

"So do I," Charley said. "I wish I could be there to watch the raid."

"We'll be doing a video," Dino replied. "I'll shoot you a copy so you won't miss any of the action."

"Great!"

"Forgive the change of subject," Stone said, "but is anything happening on the investment front, Charley?"

"I've had conversations with two companies on St. Clair's list—both are good bets."

"What are they?"

"DigiFlood is one. They make digital components for manufacturers. They're particularly interesting right now because they're working on a new kind of storage device that will be revolutionary. They need thirty million dollars to finish the development. The other is called Automobile Butler Services. They work on your car in your own garage or even parking space, if the weather is good. The great thing about them is that they're authorized warranty agents for the more expensive cars. They've got a couple of dozen offices in the tristate area, but they need capital to expand nationwide."

"Sounds good."

"They're both well managed and already profitable."

"Then move in whenever you're ready."

"I've also got two new people, starting the first of the

month, who I knew at Goldman, and they'll bring their own ideas with them."

"Great."

"One thing I should mention, though. St. Clair has already made overtures to both DigiFlood and Automobile Butler Services, so we're likely to make Macher angry again."

"Well, if he gets angry enough, maybe he'll do something stupid that will allow us to neutralize him."

"As long as you know what's happening."

"I'll have a word with Mike about it."

Dino finished his steak.

"You were going to call somebody," Stone reminded him.

"Yeah, an assistant DA who will get us our warrant." Dino made the call and discussed his raid for a few minutes, then hung up. "Done," he said. "He'll see a judge in the morning, and we should be ready to go for tomorrow night."

ON THE RIDE HOME, Charley spoke up. "Stone, would it be inconvenient for you if I stayed on in the apartment for a few months?"

"Not at all—as long as you like."

"I'm going to look for something to buy, but right now I'd like to put my time into getting Triangle up and running."

"Of course."

"And I'd like to pay rent. I can afford it."

"And I can afford not to collect it," Stone said, "so forget it."

As they pulled into the garage, Fred said, "Mr. Barrington, the street seems to be clean of the trash we've had in the block the past few days."

"That's good," Stone said.

"I expect Macher found it unprofitable," Charley said.

They drove into the garage and said good night.

STONE WENT UPSTAIRS and found a surprise waiting for him in his bed.

"Good evening," Marisa said. "I used my new key. Did you enjoy your boys' night out?"

"Not as much as I'm going to enjoy your company," Stone said, getting out of his clothes and slipping into bed with her.

She threw a leg over his and snuggled close. "Anything new in the world of skullduggery?"

"I think the skullduggers are getting weary," Stone replied. "The two guys out front have been withdrawn."

"Oh, good. May we dispense with the armed guards now?"

"Let's not be hasty about that," Stone replied. "Maybe another week."

Then he did his duty.

31

Erik Macher gazed up at the girl on top of him. "How's that, baby?" he asked.

"Oooh, good!" she replied, as she was expected to. "Why don't you just move me into your apartment, and we can do this all the time? Looks like you've got plenty of room."

"Don't ruin the mood," Macher said, then the doorbell rang. He glanced at the bedside clock: three AM. "What the hell?" he said, sitting up and unseating the young woman.

"What's the matter?"

The doorbell rang again, and there was a hammering on it, followed by muffled shouting.

"Don't you move," Macher said. He reached into his bedside drawer and withdrew a Glock. He grabbed a robe, and as he departed his apartment, he slapped the panic button on his security system, and a siren began to wail. As he reached the first floor, there was a huge bang, a splintering sound, and the front door flew open, followed by a man with a steel ram, surrounded by uniformed police officers wearing body armor.

"Drop the gun!" a cop yelled at him.

Macher had forgotten the Glock in his excitement, and he opened his hand, allowing it to fall onto the stairs. "What the fuck is this?" he screamed.

A cop handcuffed his wrist and fastened the other end to the banister rail. "What's your security cancellation code?" the cop shouted.

Macher told him, and the cop entered it into a keypad at the bottom of the stairs. The siren abruptly stopped. "I asked you, what the fuck is this?" Macher demanded anew.

A detective in a suit stepped forward and handed him a paper. "This is a warrant, allowing us to search the premises."

"Search the premises for *what*?" Macher demanded, tossing the warrant aside.

"Whatever the fuck we like," the cop replied. "You've been served, now shut up and cooperate. Who else is in the house?"

"My secretary lives on the second floor." As if on cue, the woman appeared, one landing up, tying a robe around her. "And there's a Ms. . . . . oh, I don't know what the hell her name is. She's on the top floor in my bed . . . ah, apartment."

"Is that your office?" the detective asked, pointing at a set of double doors.

"Yes."

"All right," he shouted to his group, "execute the

plan." He pointed at a young man in civilian clothes. "You—on the computers, now."

"Gotcha," the youth replied, heading for the double doors.

Macher sat down on the stairs, the cold marble freezing his ass through the thin silk robe, picked up the warrant and began to read. "Shit!" he said to nobody in particular.

AS DAWN BROKE over the Upper East Side, the policemen began departing, carrying boxes of documents and other evidence. The IT man approached the detective in charge and held up a thumb drive. "Got everything worth having," he said.

"Go back to the precinct and print it all out," the detective said, "then get yourself some breakfast and some sleep."

The detective walked over to Macher, who was still sitting on the stairs, handcuffed to the rail. "You got a permit for the piece?"

"I have," Macher said, "full carry."

The detective took out an iPhone and opened a departmental app, then tapped in the name. "Okay, you're licensed," he said a moment later. He uncuffed Macher, cleared the weapon and returned it to its owner. "Have a nice day," he said.

From the third floor, a young woman was heard to call out, "Do you want to go again? Or am I out of here?"

Macher started up the stairs. "Out of here!" he shouted.

*   *   *

STONE WAS AT his desk when Dino called.

"Good morning. How'd it go last night?"

"We got the will," Dino said, "and it's been turned over to the DA, who will decide whether to prosecute. My guys are still slogging through the printout from St. Clair's computers."

"I'm delighted to hear it."

"Something occurred to me—you know this strong case thing that had the bomb in it that killed St. Clair?"

"Yep, I know it, it lived in my safe for a couple of days."

"Describe it to me."

"It was a kind of briefcase, but bigger and thicker than the standard and covered in black leather. It had unconventional locks and a key that was a slab of titanium with some pointy things on it."

"Right, and was there some sort of procedure to unlock it without the bomb going off?"

"That's what I was told."

"What was the procedure?"

"I don't know," Stone said, "I never tried to open it."

"And who had the strong case before St. Clair opened it and got his head handed to him?"

"It was in the possession of Ed Rawls, at his house in Virginia, then Macher or some of his cohorts in his security firm broke into the house, roughed up Ed, and stole the case. Macher then took it to St. Clair and sat there in his office and watched while he opened it, then blooey!"

"The strong case was a CIA thing, wasn't it?" Dino asked.

"Yes. Holly Barker, who was visiting me at the time, knew about it from her days with the Agency."

"And Rawls was CIA once, that's where he got the case?"

"Right."

"And," Dino said, "Macher was CIA once, wasn't he?"

"Yes."

"Then he would have known something about the strong case and how it worked."

"Presumably."

"And yet he sat there and watched St. Clair open it and kill himself."

"Well . . . yes."

"Doesn't that sound to you like an awful good case for premeditated murder?"

"Well," Stone said, "if you can prove that Macher knew how the case worked and withheld that piece of information from St. Clair, yes."

"Did Macher or his men ask Rawls anything about the case when they took it from Rawls?"

"Ed says no, and in their rush he, ah, forgot to mention it to them."

"I'm liking this," Dino said.

"Then why don't you have a chat with the DA and see what he thinks?"

"You know," Dino said, "I believe I'll do that."

"Dino," Stone said, "if you can get Macher locked up without bail, that would solve a number of problems for me and my clients the Carlssons."

"Well, Stone," Dino said, "this department is always ready to oblige you." He hung up.

32

Stone was having lunch in the Strategic Services restaurant, Safe House, with Charley Fox.

"How'd the raid go?" Charley asked.

"As expected," Stone said. "They got the will, and the DA has it now. I hear he has forwarded it to the Bar Association and to the chairman of the board of St. Clair. Now we just wait for the explosions. If we're lucky, you'll be able to hear them in your office with the doors and windows closed."

"I would enjoy that," Charley said. "Now, my turn. After a few conversations, we have an agreement in principle for the investments in DigiFlood and Automobile Butler. I've spoken to Herb Fisher, and he's at work on the contracts."

"That went well!"

"Yes, it did. I want to send out a press release that combines the news of the investments and the forming of

Triangle and my appointment as president. That okay with you and Mike?"

"Sure. A nice piece in the *Journal* and the *Times* will probably invite new opportunities for investment."

"That would be good. I'm going to need seventy million in cash to close these two deals."

"I'll get on that. It should be in the Triangle account in a few days."

"How much capital do we have access to? I need to know so that I can have intelligent conversations with prospects."

"I think we can manage half a billion from our various sources, so for the moment, use that as a ceiling."

"Will it all come from you and Mike Freeman?"

"These first two deals will. As we need more cash, I can call on Marcel duBois, in Paris, and a client of mine named Laurence Hayward."

"I know who duBois is—the Warren Buffett of Europe. Who's Hayward?"

"He won six hundred and twelve million in the lottery a few months ago."

"Ah, yes, I read about that in the papers."

"The good news is, he hasn't spent it all yet, and he's looking for investments."

"I'll be happy to help him."

A FEW DAYS LATER, Erik Macher sat down at his desk in rather good spirits. He had spent a couple of nice days on the yacht with a girl, and since the raid, nothing terrible had happened.

He found the *Wall Street Journal* and the *Times* on his

desk, and he was alarmed to see a photograph of Charles Fox staring up at him from the front page of the *Journal*. He grabbed the paper and began to read the article.

Jake Herman had the misfortune to rap on Macher's office door at that very moment. He made to withdraw, but Macher had spotted him. "Get in here!" he yelled.

Jake crossed the twenty feet to Macher's desk cautiously, then took a seat, largely because his knees were weak.

"Have you seen this?" Macher demanded, slapping the *Journal*.

"Seen what?" Jake asked weakly.

"That fucking Fox!"

"What about him?"

"He's stolen the two companies we were going to bid on!"

"How could he do that?"

"With money! It says here that he's formed a new investment partnership called Triangle Partnership, and that he's backed by Strategic Services, the big security company, and Stone Barrington, a partner at Woodman & Weld!"

"That's very bad news, Erik. How can I help?" Jake very much hoped that would be a rhetorical question, but he was disappointed.

Macher got up and closed his office door, then returned and sat down at his desk. He stared at the leather tooling before him for a long moment before he spoke. "Jake," he said, in a low, earnest voice, "I want Fox dead."

Oh, Jesus, Jake thought. He had been afraid it might come to this, but it turned out to be worse.

"Barrington, too," Macher said.

"Erik," Jake said in his calmest possible voice, "one hit is a difficult enough thing. Two hits is almost certainly a one-way ticket to Sing Sing." He paused before adding, "For both of us."

Macher began blinking rapidly, always a bad sign. "It's worth the risk for me," he said.

Jake drew himself up to his full, seated height. "In that case, Erik, *you* knock them off. I work for you, but I'm not going to prison for you."

Macher stopped blinking, giving Jake hope. "You're right, Jake, it's too much to ask."

Jake discovered that he had been holding his breath, and he exhaled in a rush. "I'm glad you see that, Erik."

"Jake, what I need now is a partner whose loyalty to me is unquestioned, and it's beginning to appear that you are not that partner."

"Erik, I think that all my obligations to you are outlined in my employment agreement, and there's nothing in it that covers murder." Now he was afraid to inhale.

"Perhaps I didn't make myself clear, Jake. I viewed my request as something above and beyond your employment agreement, something that would require a substantial under-the-table, and therefore tax-free, payment."

Jake breathed again. "And what did you have in mind, Erik?"

"I was thinking of a quarter of a million dollars, in cash."

"That's an attractive number, Erik, if it's a quarter of a million *each*."

Macher began blinking rapidly again, but then he relaxed. "All right," he said.

It's not as if it were your money, Jake thought. "And it's very unlikely that I'll be able to do them both at the same time." He paused for effect. "However, I'll give it some thought."

"Of course, Jake, this is a business that requires careful planning, both in the execution and the follow-up."

"Follow-up?"

"By that I mean, there must be no evidence connecting me or the company to the occurrence. We also have to consider where I would be when it happens."

"Out of town, I expect."

"Of course."

Macher's secretary knocked on the door and entered, an envelope in her hand. "This just came for you, hand-delivered," she said.

Macher gazed at the envelope as if trying to divine its contents. Finally, he opened it and read the enclosed letter.

LEGAL NOTICE OF AN EMERGENCY MEETING OF THE BOARD OF DIRECTORS OF ST. CLAIR ENTERPRISES.

"Is something wrong, Erik?"

"The chairman of the board has called an emergency meeting of the board for ten AM tomorrow, in this office," Macher said.

"What kind of emergency?"

"It doesn't say."

Macher picked up the phone. "Get me Tommy Berenson at his law office," he said.

She came back a moment later. "I'm sorry, Mr. Macher, but the woman who answered—she wasn't his secretary—said that Mr. Berenson is not in and not expected."

"Thank you," Macher said.

"Do you have any idea what this is about, Erik?" Jake asked.

"No, but you and I have to put together some names for board memberships. New names."

"Why?"

"Because I have to fire the board before ten AM tomorrow."

33

Charley Fox was in his office after lunch when Stella buzzed him.

"Yes?"

"Norm Keller from Goldman Sachs for you."

Keller was Charley's last boss at Goldman. Charley picked up the phone. "Hi, Norm," he said.

"How you doing, Charley?"

"I can't complain."

"I saw the announcement in the *Journal*. Sounds like you've landed on your feet."

"If you say so," Charley said.

"I admit, I was envious of you when you left us for St. Clair. I figured you'd double or triple your income over there. Then St. Clair got blown up, and I wondered what had happened to you."

"Well, now you know."

"Is that Macher character still running St. Clair?" Keller asked.

"As far as I know, but a guy like Macher could evaporate at any moment."

"Interesting," Norm said. "I just got a hand-delivered letter from him, offering me a seat on the board at St. Clair. The money's good, and the use of the yacht is thrown in."

"Interesting."

"What's your take on this, Charley? Should I accept?"

"Just between you and me, Norm, I'd shred the letter and say nothing to anybody about it."

"Why?"

"I can't go into the details at the moment, but it's my opinion that Macher's position at St. Clair is precarious, to say the least, and dealing with him is an even more precarious state."

"One other guy here got the same letter," Keller said, "and he told me that a guy at Chase Private Bank got one, too."

"Sounds like Macher is looking for a whole new board, doesn't it?" Charley said. "Makes you wonder why, doesn't it?"

"Does he have the authority to fire and replace the St. Clair board at the drop of a hat?"

"If he does, it won't be for long, Norm. My advice to you and the others is to decline. Wait and see what happens."

"I expect that's good advice, Charley, and I thank you for it." He hung up.

Charley got Stone Barrington and Mike Freeman on a conference call.

"What's up, Charley?" Stone asked.

Charley related the content of the call from Keller. "What do you guys think is going on over there?"

"My guess," Stone said, "is that the St. Clair board has heard about the two wills, maybe from the DA, and I heard this morning that Tommy Berenson's license to practice law has been suspended by the Bar Association, pending a hearing. Remember, the bogus will gave Macher the authority to fire and replace the board, and that must be what he's trying to do."

"My guess," Mike Freeman said, "is that by this time tomorrow, Macher will be on the street, and the board will remain as constituted."

"Well," said Charley, "if that happens there might be some opportunities where the St. Clair assets are concerned. From what I gleaned from their computer files, the company has more than half a billion dollars in assets, all of it in just the kind of companies we're interested in acquiring, and St. Clair has no debt. Christian was always a very conservative businessman, and it's been a long time since he borrowed any money."

"Very, very interesting," Mike said. "Let's see what tomorrow brings."

"Call again," Stone said, "if you hear anything new." They all hung up.

Charley worked through the afternoon, and he was contemplating a drink when another call came in.

"Yes?"

"A Mr. Something-or-other Barnes on line one. I didn't get the first name."

Charley pressed the button. "This is Charles Fox."

"Mr. Fox," an elderly voice said, "this is Elihu Barnes. Does my name mean anything to you?"

"Yes, sir, it does. I believe you're a banker and chairman of the board of St. Clair Enterprises. We met when Mr. St. Clair hired me."

"You are correct, Mr. Fox, and I'm glad we don't have to waste any time establishing my bona fides."

"Certainly not."

"Mr. Fox, there is about to be a major upheaval at St. Clair, and I and the other two members of our board, Mr. Maximus Quinn and Mr. George Fineman, would like to meet with you, if we may."

"Of course, Mr. Barnes. I'm at your disposal."

"Our usual meeting place at St. Clair is not available to us at this moment. I wonder if we might meet at your offices?"

"Certainly." Charley gave him the address and explained the entry requirements for the building. "When would you like to meet?"

"Would six o'clock this evening be convenient for you?"

"Yes, sir, it would."

"Then we will look forward to seeing you at that time, in your offices." The two men hung up.

Charley reestablished his conference call.

"What's up, Charley?" Stone asked.

"Gentlemen, the board of directors of St. Clair Enterprises is going to be meeting at six o'clock—in my office."

Nobody said anything for a moment. Finally Stone spoke up. "Do you have any idea why?"

"Nothing that would make any sense," Charley said. "I was struck, though, at how solicitous Mr. Barnes sounded on the phone. His more usual style might be thought of as imperious."

"Charley," Mike said, "it sounds like these gentlemen want something from you. What might that be?"

"Perhaps investment advice?" Charley hazarded. "Christian St. Clair introduced me to them at the time he hired me, and he spoke to them of his hopes for me at St. Clair."

"Sounds like you impressed them," Mike said.

"Well," Stone said, "let's talk about what Charley might want from the board."

"How about their company?" Charley said. "I'd like for Triangle to own that."

"I doubt if that's up for grabs, but let's take a look at their assets. Do you have a list?"

"I do."

"Then why don't you run over that list before your meeting and see what plums you'd like to pick from their tree, and what each of them is worth to us."

"I can think, right off the bat, of two of their assets I'd like to own."

"And what are those?" Mike asked.

"Their building," Charley said, "and their yacht."

"I've been aboard the yacht," Stone said, "and it is gorgeous—made me salivate just to be on her. And she's brand-new, built in a small yard in Maine that Christian bought just to build the vessel. He told me the yard is already turning a profit, working on antique and traditional yachts."

"And what about the building?" Mike asked.

Charley spoke up. "It's a very large town house, maybe seventy-five feet wide, in the East Sixties. Beautifully renovated and decorated. It has an apartment upstairs, which was Christian's, another, smaller one for his secretary, maybe a dozen bedrooms, most of which have been converted to offices, and a garage on the lower level that will hold a dozen cars. It has a living room ideal for large cocktail parties, a dining room that will seat at least twenty, a beautifully designed garden out back, and a gorgeous library, which Christian used as his office."

"Both of those assets sound very desirable," Mike said.

"Listen, I'd like for both of you guys to be in the building while I'm talking to the board. I might need you on short notice."

"I'll come over," Stone said, "and have a drink with Mike while you have your meeting."

"We'll be available," Mike said.

"Be prepared to improvise," Charley replied, and ended the call.

34

The three-man board of directors of St. Clair Enterprises arrived, as one man, precisely at six PM. Charley figured they had all come in the same limo. Hands were shaken and acquaintances renewed. Charley seated them all in his collection of leather furniture.

"Mr. Fox," Elihu Barnes said, "I will come directly to the point, if I may."

"Certainly you may, sir," Charley replied, with appropriate deference.

"After a long and substantive discussion," Barnes said, "we would like to offer you the position of chief executive officer of St. Clair Enterprises." He held up a hand to deter protestations. "In our years of serving Christian St. Clair, we found him to be an excellent judge of both competence and character, and we were all impressed when he introduced us to you."

Charley allowed himself to breathe again. "Thank you, sir."

"Before Christian met his untimely death, he had not expressed to us any sort of idea of succession, and then Erik Macher came to us with a will appointing him CEO with extraordinary powers over the board. We have since learned that the will was fraudulent, concocted with the collusion of Thomas Berenson, our former corporate counsel."

Charley had noticed that Berenson was not present.

Barnes took a sheet of paper from his briefcase and handed it to Charley. "This is our proposal for authority, compensation, and perquisites. Please take as long as you like to peruse it."

It took Charley about six seconds to take it in, but he pretended to take longer. "Gentlemen," he said, "this is generous. As you may know, I have entered into a partnership with Mr. Michael Freeman of Strategic Services and Mr. Stone Barrington, a partner in the law firm of Woodman & Weld."

"We all read that in the *Wall Street Journal*," Barnes replied.

"If I may, I would like them to join us in discussing this matter."

"Of course, if you wish."

"If you will excuse me for a moment."

"Certainly."

Charley left the room and called upstairs from his secretary's desk. Mike Freeman answered, and Charley requested to be put on speakerphone.

"Go," Mike said.

"They've offered me the CEO job at St. Clair," he said.

"And what do you intend to do?" Stone asked.

"I think we should make them an offer for the company," Charley said.

"What sort of an offer?" Mike asked.

"I've been through the assets and the profit-and-loss statements, and I value them at about seven hundred million, including the building and yacht. I propose that we offer them half a billion for the lot. We can then dispose of the companies at our leisure and make a lot of money."

"Mike?" Stone asked.

"Good idea," Mike replied.

"Charley, you have our agreement," Stone said, "but we shouldn't buy the company, since we're not aware of what sort of liabilities it may have. Make the offer for the assets only."

"Right, now get your asses down here pronto!" Charley said. He hung up and waited another minute before returning to his office. "Mr. Freeman and Mr. Barrington will be here shortly," he said, dragging a couple of chairs over from his desk to the seating area.

As he resumed his seat there was a knock at the door, and Mike and Stone entered. Charley made the introductions.

"Gentlemen, may I continue?"

"Yes, please," Barnes replied.

"Regretfully, I must decline your generous offer." He gave them a moment to rearrange their faces. "However," he said, "the Triangle Partnership, that is, the three of us, would like to acquire all the assets of St. Clair Enterprises."

Barnes exchanged glances with his fellow board members and received an almost imperceptible nod from each, which indicated to Charley that they had previously discussed this move.

"What is your offer, Mr. Fox?"

"We offer half a billion dollars for all the company's assets, including the building and the yacht."

After a brief pause, Barnes said, "We have discussed this possibility, and we concur in our belief that a more acceptable offer would be six hundred million, the value of the assets being what it is."

"I can understand your feelings in the matter, gentlemen. You could certainly hire a firm like my previous home, Goldman Sachs, to come in, value each property separately, and dispose of them piecemeal. Alternatively, they could seek a buyer for the entire company, but I'm sure you realize that either process would consume many months of your time and many millions in fees and costs. We offer an immediate purchase, to close in, say, thirty days, and we will assume the responsibility of the preparation of the documentation for the sale, to be approved, of course, by your new counsel. Have you chosen one yet?"

"Frankly," Barnes replied, "we were considering offering Mr. Barrington that position."

"Thank you, gentlemen, but our offer would make that a conflict of interest. I could recommend someone, if you like."

"Mr. Fox, may we withdraw to your waiting room for a moment to discuss the matter?" Barnes asked.

Charley stood, and so did Mike and Stone. "Certainly," he said, and they waited until the board had closed the door behind them before sitting again.

"They're not going to take the offer," Mike said.

"I don't think so, either," Stone replied. "Suppose we offer them another fifty million?"

"Agreed," Mike replied, and Charley nodded.

"It was a smart move to offer the legal work," Stone said. "I can get that done wholesale."

"I figured you could," Charley replied. "I wanted to make it as easy for them as possible."

The door opened, and the three men returned. They didn't sit down, which worried Charley. "Gentlemen," Barnes said, "the board has voted to accept your offer."

Everyone broke out in smiles, and handshakes were exchanged all around. Charley produced a bottle of champagne from his bar, and toasts were drunk.

"I must say, Mr. Fox," Barnes said, "your offer took us somewhat by surprise, but I must admit that in making it, you confirmed our judgment of you. We are all sorry that we will miss the opportunity of working with you in years to come."

"Gentlemen," Charley said, "I believe that is the highest praise I have ever had."

When their glasses were empty, the group adjourned, and the board departed.

Mike grabbed Charley and hugged him. "This must be the most spectacular first week of any investment firm ever," he said.

Stone patted Charley on the back and said, "At the risk of being too late, why don't we run over that list of St. Clair's assets? I'd like to know exactly what Charley has gotten us into."

35

Stone tossed the documents onto the coffee table. "Charley," he said, "I think you've done a great job of placing values on these companies. In fact, I think you've been a little conservative. I believe they might be worth fifty or a hundred million more."

"I've been looking at these values since I joined St. Clair," Charley said, "so I've had plenty of time to come to my conclusions. However, I hope you are right. Now, how are we going to come up with half a billion dollars?"

"Mike and I have been talking about that," Stone said, "and I think we have a way forward. Mike and I can come up with seventy-five million each from our own resources."

"And go to Marcel duBois and your lottery winner for the rest?"

"No. As you may know, my late wife, Arrington, had been previously married to the actor Vance Calder."

"I don't think I did know that," Charley replied. "I know about Calder, though—that in addition to being a top star, he was a terrific businessman."

"He was, and his estate ran to something over a billion dollars. He left everything to Arrington, and after our marriage I oversaw the liquidation of most of his estate, mostly real estate, with the result that when Arrington died, she mostly held stock in Centurion Studios and in cash. My law firm had prepared her will, without my participation, or even knowledge of its terms. She left me a third of her estate and two-thirds to our son, Peter, in a trust of which I am the sole trustee. Peter doesn't come into it until he's thirty, but I have consulted him about the investments I've made for the trust. I think it would be a good use of the cash in the trust to invest three hundred million of it in Triangle, and use those funds to close the sale. I'll talk with Peter about it right away and confirm that."

"Great, but we're still missing fifty million."

"Mike and I are going to loan you that, secured by your share of the partnership, and you can repay the loan as profits come in from the sale of the St. Clair companies."

"That's extraordinarily generous of you both," Charley replied, moved.

"This transaction was your idea, and you brought the knowledge and skills to bear to make it happen. You deserve to be rewarded for that."

"There's something else I haven't mentioned," Charley said. "I think that three of the companies have come to the point where they can go public in the next year or so, and with our majority ownership, we will reap a huge profit from the initial public offering, and so will the original stockholders who sold to St. Clair. I think everybody will be very, very happy."

"Are there others on the list that can have IPOs later?" Mike asked.

"Most of them. Those that aren't ready we can sell separately."

"That's wonderful, Charley," Stone said. "Something else that Mike and I think you deserve is occupancy of St. Clair's apartment in the building."

Charley broke into a grin. "I can't say that that hadn't crossed my mind."

"Also, the yacht is owned by a Delaware corporation. We can sell that to ourselves, and Mike and I will loan you the money to buy your third. It shouldn't take you long to reap enough from the IPOs to repay it."

"Also," Mike said, "there are two airplanes and a helicopter owned by St. Clair. Strategic Services will buy one, and we can sell the helicopter, since none of us has much use for it. We can keep the other airplane as a Triangle company aircraft."

"What are the two airplanes?" Stone asked.

"One is a Gulfstream 450, which we will buy, if you agree. The other is a very new airplane from Cessna, a Citation Latitude, which has a big cabin and a range of twenty-seven hundred miles. It can live in our hangar complex at Teterboro."

"Suddenly, it seems," Charley said, "that all my personal needs have been taken care of." The three of them shook hands and parted company for the evening.

Stone headed home to call Peter, and then to have dinner and meet the personal needs of Marisa Carlsson.

*   *   *

ERIK MACHER WAS sitting at his desk the following morning when the board of directors of St. Clair Enterprises arrived, in the company of someone he didn't know, who was introduced as St. Clair's new corporate counsel. They all seated themselves at Macher's conference table.

"Good morning, gentlemen," Macher said. "To what do I owe the pleasure?"

"Believe me, Mr. Macher," Elihu Barnes said, "the pleasure is all ours. By a unanimous vote of the board, you are discharged from your position as CEO of St. Clair Enterprises, with immediate effect."

"Gentlemen," Macher replied, unperturbed, "I refer you to the will of Christian St. Clair, which denies you the authority for such an act."

"The will has been found to be fraudulent," Barnes said, with obvious satisfaction, "which is why Thomas Berenson is no longer our corporate counsel. Therefore, none of its provisions apply to our action. The matter rests with the district attorney, and I expect you will be hearing from him shortly. We welcome a civil action on your part, should you be unwise enough to bring it."

"This is outrageous!" Macher spat.

"No, the will was outrageous," Barnes replied. "Outside this room are two security guards who will escort you to the apartment upstairs and oversee the packing of such of your belongings there. There is a moving company present with a van to haul them away. You have one hour to clear the premises or be forcibly removed."

Macher's jaw dropped.

"Oh, also, you may inform Jake Herman and your secretary that they have been discharged as well. Herman will depart the premises immediately, and your secretary may have an hour to pack her things and have them removed. The van, upon departing, will deliver both your belongings to any address in Manhattan."

"I can't believe this," Macher said.

"Good day and goodbye, Mr. Macher," Barnes said. "Now get out, or we'll have you thrown out."

Macher stood up, went to his desk, and put a few things into his briefcase. He rang for his secretary, and she entered. He walked her into the vestibule outside. "You and I have been fired out of hand," he said to her. "Go and pack your things, and they will be moved for you. We have an hour. Oh, and go see Jake Herman and tell him he has been fired, too, and to clear his office."

She went pale. "Yes, sir," she said.

Two burly, uniformed security guards stepped forward and marched Macher upstairs to the apartment, followed by a team of moving men.

A volcanic anger began to build in Macher's breast.

36

Erik Macher and Jake Herman sat in Macher's new suite, a small one, at the Lombardy Hotel, surrounded by boxes. Macher's secretary had been dropped with her boxes at her sister's apartment building a few blocks away.

Macher poured Herman another drink. "You understand, Jake, you're still employed by my security company, which I owned before I met Christian St. Clair. The money isn't quite as good, but it will keep us afloat until we can feather our nests once again."

"And how are we going to do that?" Jake asked.

"Opportunities will present themselves, and we will capitalize on them."

"What kind of opportunities?"

"That remains to be seen, but believe me, they will materialize. Christian St. Clair was such an opportunity. There will be others."

"Okay, whatever you say."

"But before we make the move back to D.C. we have business to take care of here, with regard to Barrington and Fox."

"Uh-oh."

"Don't worry, there'll be the two of us working on it. You won't bear the entire responsibility. I would, however, be grateful for suggestions."

"A bullet to the brain has always worked for me," Jake said.

"Not in this case. There are three people to deal with."

"*Three?* Whatever happened to just the two?"

"Elihu Barnes will join Charles Fox and Stone Barrington on our list."

"Who the fuck is Elihu Barnes?"

"He's the chairman of the St. Clair board, the imperious prick who fired us."

"Oh. Well, in the circumstances I can hardly blame him," Jake said.

"*I* can blame him," Macher replied.

"Okay, then you kill him. I'll help with the other two."

"What I'd like your help on is to think of a way to get them in the same room. I'm well trained and experienced with explosives."

"Well, they must have further business together. Where would that take place?"

"I would think in the St. Clair mansion," Macher said.

"Why there?"

"Because I suspect that Barnes and the board are going to offer Charles Fox my job, and probably today."

"Why Charley?"

"Because St. Clair hired him, and I expect with the

promise of one day replacing Christian in the CEO's job. Barnes and Company would know that. They'd naturally turn to him, and Fox would take it in the blink of an eye."

"Well, if you can make a bomb, I guess I can get it into the library, where the board meets."

"You know that girl in accounting, the one you've been diddling since you came to New York?"

"Velma Ottley?"

"That's the one."

"She's not going to plant any bomb," Jake said.

"No, but she hears things around the office. She'll know what's going on."

"I guess."

"I think you should ask her to dinner tonight and prepare the ground for the sowing of seeds, so to speak."

"I guess I could do that."

"I got you a room down the hall. You can take her there after you dine. Make a reservation in the hotel dining room."

Jake picked up the phone.

"No, take your things down to your room," Macher said, handing him the key card. "Use your cell phone to call her."

"They took my cell phone when they threw us out."

Macher handed him a burner phone. "This will work."

Jake picked up his bags and left the suite.

Macher lay down on the bed, his head throbbing. He'd feel better when they were all dead.

CHARLEY FOX WALKED into Herb Fisher's office at Woodman & Weld and introduced himself.

"I hear you're Stone and Mike's new partner," Herbie said.

"That's right. And I hear you're the ace attorney Stone turns to when there's work to be done."

"I'm his man."

Charley set his briefcase on Herbie's desk. "These were delivered to me this morning," he said. "It's all the papers you'll need to prepare the sales contract and the closing statement."

Herbie took the papers from the case and ran through them, making notes on a printed form.

"What's the form?" Charley asked.

"It's a checklist of everything we need for closings— helps bring order to the process."

"When do you think we can close?"

"When do you think you can come up with a cashier's check for half a billion dollars?"

"Pretty quick. It's already in the works."

Herbie completed his list. "Whaddya know, Mr. Barnes is very well organized. We have every piece of paper we need to move this forward. I just have to write the sales contract. My secretary can put together the closing statement. If I work this weekend, I can be ready to close on Monday morning."

"Well, Herb, that's really moving. Stone and Mike will be delighted, and I'll be in my new apartment on Monday afternoon."

"Where's your new apartment?"

"On the top floor of the St. Clair mansion, about three thousand square feet of it, according to the plans."

"Very nice."

"And my office will be in the library on the first floor. Can I schedule the closing for noon on Monday?"

"Sure, as long as there's no hitch. It helps that the banks are not involved. There's no mortgage on the building, for instance. I'll call you if any impediment arises, but I think we're in good shape."

"Thank you, Herb. Listen, I'm going to need a personal attorney to handle my affairs. Would you like the job?"

"I'd be delighted, Charley." He reached into a drawer and pulled out another printed form. "Here's a Woodman & Weld client agreement. It sets out our terms. Read and sign it at your leisure."

Charley took out his pen, signed the document, and handed it to Herbie.

"Welcome aboard," Herbie said. The two shook hands, then Charley left him to get on with his work.

JAKE HERMAN GOT out of a shower and into a freshly pressed suit. Tonight, he would begin a charm offensive on Velma Ottley, one designed to bend her to his will.

37

Jake was awakened early on Saturday morning by an insistent Velma. They had dined well the evening before, and had adjourned to Jake's room, where they had done things to each other twice, before rendering each other unconscious.

"It's Saturday," Velma said. "No work."

"You mean there's nobody at the office?"

"Nobody works Saturdays since St. Clair died."

"That's good news," Jake muttered.

"Why?" Velma asked.

Jake thought about that for a moment. "Because you don't have to be there, and you can fuck me again."

"How nice you put it, Jake," Velma replied, rolling him over and climbing on. "And I'm going to want eggs Benedict after you're helpless again."

"Deal," Jake said, then did his duty.

*   *   *

JAKE RANG MACHER'S bell at mid-morning, and his boss was awake and dressed. "Come in here and see this," he said to Jake.

On the dressing table in Macher's bedroom was a chunk of plastic explosive the size of a brick, with a burner cell phone taped to it. "No telltale wires," Macher said. "Entirely self-contained."

"Very pretty," Jake said, "but are you going to need that much of the plastic stuff? That could bring the building down, couldn't it?"

"Not likely," Macher replied, "but who gives a shit?"

"Velma says the coast is clear on Saturdays—nobody works weekends since St. Clair went away. Oh, she says the board is meeting to sell the company at noon on Monday."

"And I've still got my keys to the building," Macher said. "Nobody relieved me of them, and I'll bet money they haven't changed the alarm code, either."

"When do you want to do it?" Jake asked.

"As soon as we've had a nice brunch," Macher said.

STONE, MARISA, CHARLEY, and Kaley were having a Saturday brunch in the Carlyle Hotel dining room, eggs Benedict and mimosas for everybody.

"You two are looking very self-satisfied," Kaley said.

"I think the word describes us very well," Stone replied.

"Why so happy?" Marisa asked.

"Charley has done good work," Stone said.

"So have we all," Charley replied.

"What have you done?"

"We have pulled off a coup that wouldn't have been possible without Charley," Stone said. "We've bought all the assets of a company called St. Clair Enterprises."

"That guy who tried to buy us out of our clinic?" Marisa asked.

"One and the same."

"And a yacht," Charley said, "and a gorgeous house."

"Yacht, where?" Marisa asked.

"The yacht is in Rockland, Maine," Stone said, "a stone's throw from your own fine vessel. And this one doesn't need sails to sail."

"A stinkpot?"

"It's very beautiful, don't call it names."

"And when do we get to sail aboard her?"

"How about next weekend? Everybody up for that?"

Affirmative noises were made by all.

"And where's the house?" Kaley asked.

"Not a dozen blocks from where we sit," Charley said. "Would you like to see it?"

"How do we get in?" Stone asked.

"I still have my keys, and I'll bet they haven't changed the alarm code, and nobody will be there on a Saturday, because both St. Clair and Macher have gone."

"Check!" Stone called to their waiter.

JAKE CHECKED OUT the block while Macher found a parking spot. No security guards, and no one stirring in the building. Macher appeared from around a corner, and Jake waved him on.

They were inside in a moment, and Macher let them into the library.

"Where are you going to put it?" Jake asked.

Macher looked around the room. "The wood box, next to the fireplace," he said. It was an antique box of rusting iron. "It will make wonderful shrapnel."

Jake opened the box and found it full of firewood.

"Stack it neatly next to the fireplace, and don't make a mess, somebody might notice," Macher commanded.

Jake did as he was instructed.

Macher removed the device from a shopping bag and checked its connections. He read the number from a label taped to the back of the phone and entered the number into his own burner, setting it to speed dial when the number nine was pressed. "There," he said, "we're all set. I can call this phone from anywhere in the world by just pushing a button."

"Swell," Jake said. "Now can we get out of here?"

"I need to run upstairs to my apartment for a moment," Macher said. "I left my razor in the bathroom."

"Your razor? You can get one at any drugstore."

"Not like this one. It's a straight razor, with a blade of Damascus steel and an ivory handle. I had it made in Istanbul, eight hundred bucks. I hope to God one of those security guys didn't cop it." Macher handed Jake his car keys. "The car is around the block, in the next street. You bring it around while I get my razor."

"Okay," Jake said, then left.

Macher took the elevator to the top floor and let himself into the apartment and looked around. The heat was running, and it was hot in the room. The bed had been stripped and the place cleaned by the maids. He wished that he had had the chance to take the pictures with him. Christian had had superb taste in art, and Macher knew nothing about it. He made his way to the bathroom and opened the medicine cabinet. There it was, where he'd left it. He put the razor into his jacket pocket and started to leave. As he opened the door, he heard voices downstairs. Who the hell could that be on a Saturday? He pulled a handkerchief from his pocket.

CHARLEY LET THEM into the house amid oohs and aahs in the marble entryway. "You folks go and see the library, up there," Charley said, pointing to the double doors. "I want to show Kaley my apartment." They started up the stairs.

Stone opened the double doors.

"Oh, this is magnificent," Marisa said, looking around. "When was this house built?"

"My guess would be in the twenties," Stone said. "Lots of money around then and not much in taxes. Some robber baron must have built it to show the world how rich he was." They browsed among the books.

AT THE TOP of the stairs Charley saw the open door. "I'm glad the maids have been in," he said. "I don't have a key for this door yet." He led Kaley into the apartment and they stood, admiring the finely carved fireplace and the pictures on the walls.

"That's a Picasso," Kaley said, pointing, "and that's a Matisse."

"Wow," Charley said, taking off his jacket and tossing

it onto the sofa. "Hot in here. Will you open a window? I need to use the john."

Kaley opened one of the French doors leading to an outside balcony, and fresh autumn air poured in. Then she followed him into the bedroom. Charley was walking into the bathroom.

Charley had just stepped onto the marble floor when a figure in dark clothes and a cloth cap appeared before him, wearing a handkerchief tied over his face. His first thought was a Western movie he had seen as a child. Then the figure swung an arm, and he felt a searing pain across his abdomen. His hand went to the wound automatically, and it was warm and wet. The figure brushed past him, and he heard Kaley scream before he collapsed onto the bathroom floor, blood pooling around him.

He heard heels on marble and Kaley shouting his name.

38

Stone heard Kaley screaming and started for the stairs, then he saw the elevator, its door standing open. He pulled Marisa in and pressed the button for the top floor. As the car rose, he saw through the stained glass of the doors a figure running down the stairs and out the front door. At the top, they got out and ran into the apartment, looking for Kaley and Charley.

They found them in the bathroom, Charley lying on his back, glassy-eyed, while Kaley tried to stanch the flow of blood from his belly with a towel.

"Let me in here," Marisa said, pushing Kaley aside. She examined the wound, then applied a fresh towel to it.

"I'll call nine-one-one," Stone said, whipping out his cell phone.

"No," Marisa barked, "dial this number." She recited it for him. "Now give me the phone." She listened for a moment. "This is Marisa, give me Nihls, *now*." She waited.

"Nihls, I'm bringing in a man with a major abdominal knife wound. Send an ambulance to this address." She recited it. "Prep OR 1 and start scrubbing. Wait."

Charley was trying to say something. Marisa bent over him and listened.

"A positive," Charley murmured, then closed his eyes.

Marisa went back to the phone. "Order four units of type A positive for the ambulance and eight for the OR, stat!" She hung up. "Nihls is the best trauma surgeon in the city," she said. "He did his surgical residency at Bellevue, and he's seen more knife wounds than anybody."

Somewhere out in the street, an ambulance siren could already be heard. "I'll get them up here," Stone said, and ran down the stairs.

NEARLY FOUR HOURS LATER, Stone was shaken awake by Kaley. He had fallen asleep in a chair in a waiting room. Nihls Carlsson stood before him, his surgical scrubs mottled with blood. He looked exhausted. "He's stable and in recovery," he said. "There wasn't too much organ damage, just an awful, twelve-inch wound. He's young and strong, and he'll make it."

Stone shook his hand. "Thank you, Nihls. When can we see him?"

"Give him until tomorrow morning," Nihls said. "He needs to rest."

"Will you ask someone to tell him Kaley and Stone were here, and we'll be back tomorrow morning?"

"Of course." Nihls went looking for a nurse.

*   *   *

STONE AND MARISA dropped Kaley off at her apartment. "Are you going to be all right?" he asked her.

"Sure, now that I know he will be."

"We'll pick you up at nine tomorrow morning."

"Make it ten," Marisa said.

"All right, ten."

She closed the door to the cab, and they continued downtown to Turtle Bay.

"I'm really glad you were there," Stone said.

"So am I," Marisa replied. "If it had taken five minutes longer to get him a transfusion, he wouldn't have made it."

"It's a good thing you requested blood in the ambulance."

"A nine-one-one ambulance might not have had it aboard."

OVER DINNER, Stone didn't have much to say. Now that Charley's recovery seemed assured, he started to think about how to proceed without him. "How long will his recovery be?" he asked Marisa.

"Assuming no infection or other complications, he'll be out of the hospital in four days or so, and he'll need to recover at home, with a daily visit from a nurse to change his dressings, for another week. Then he'll be ambulatory. They'll remove the stitches about two weeks out—the nurse will know when it's time—and then he'll need some rehab to get his abdominal muscles in shape again. He can work during that time, if he feels like it. In a month to six weeks he should have a full recovery."

"Send his medical bills to me," Stone said. "We haven't had time to arrange for company insurance."

"I've already spoken to Dad. The costs are on us, in gratitude for all you did for us during the takeover bid."

"That's very kind of all of you. I know Charley will be grateful, too."

He was already thinking about how to handle the closing, with Charley out of commission. He and Herbie could get it done, and he had already moved the money and asked the bank for a cashier's check.

THE FOLLOWING MORNING, Charley looked better than Stone had expected. He had been moved to a lovely private room, which, magically, had been filled with flowers. His bed had been raised a little, to make it easier for him to talk. "How're you feeling?" Stone asked.

"Exhausted."

"You were on the table for three and a half hours," Stone said. "That's hard work." He told Charley what Marisa had said about his recovery schedule. "Charley, was it Macher or Herman?"

"It wasn't Herman," Charley said. "Not big enough. It could have been Macher, but there was a handkerchief tied over his face, so I couldn't make him."

"Never mind."

"Can you and Herb close the deal without me?" Charley asked.

"Sure, did you think you were indispensable?"

Charley smiled. "Well, yeah, sort of. Stone, will you give Kaley and me a few minutes?"

"Sure, I'll see you tomorrow."

"No, you'll be closing. Just call and let me know how it went."

"Okay. Talk to you then." Stone left.

CHARLEY PRESSED THE button that raised his bed a little more. "Listen," he said, "I was going to say this yesterday, but I got interrupted."

"Yes, you did, and you scared me to death."

"I'm sorry about that. What I was going to say to you was, why don't you move into the new apartment with me? Let's live together for a year or so, and if we can still stand each other, let's get married."

Kaley smiled. "What a good idea! Yes, on all points!"

"Quit your job, if you like. You're not going to need the money."

"I like my job, so I'll keep it. Maybe I'll take some time off to get us moved in, so it will be ready when you are. In the meantime, I'll stay with you in Stone's apartment, to see that you're taken care of."

"That would be great," Charley said. "Now I need to get some sleep, right after you kiss me."

Kaley kissed him, and he closed his eyes. She tiptoed out of the room.

39

Stone got to his desk on time the next morning and rang for Joan.

She picked up the phone. "Yes, boss?"

"Will you please run over to the bank, see Mr. Baird, and pick up a cashier's check for me?"

"Sure thing. Be right back." She hung up.

Stone reviewed his copy of the sales contract and closing statement, and by the time he had finished, Joan was back with the check.

"That's a very nice round number," she said, handing him the check.

"It's going to buy a dozen or more companies," he replied, "for Triangle."

"How's Charley doing?"

"He was fine when I saw him yesterday. He ran me out and told me to call him today when we've closed."

"Good luck," she said, and went back to her desk.

Stone gathered his papers together, put the check in his inside pocket, and got into the Bentley for the trip to the St. Clair mansion.

AS HE WALKED up the front steps, he was joined by a young man with an elderly yellow Labrador retriever leashed to his wrist.

"Yes?"

"I'm Eliot Crenshaw, the new corporate counsel for St. Clair. We're here for the closing."

Stone scratched the Lab behind an ear. "Who's your colleague?"

"This is Bessie," he said. "Sometimes I take her to work. Do you mind?"

"Not in the least. I've one at home a lot like her, named Bob."

"Then you must be a very happy man."

They went into the building and into the library, finding themselves the first there. Crenshaw unleashed Bessie and told her to go lie down. Instead, she began circling the room, sniffing.

The three members of the board of directors and Herb Fisher arrived, and Stone shook all their hands. "I'm sorry that Charley Fox couldn't be with us this morning. He had an accident over the weekend and is spending a few days in the hospital."

"Nothing serious, I hope," Elihu Barnes said.

"It was, but he received quick attention, and he's recovering normally."

"I'm glad to hear it." They all took seats at the table.

"I'll turn this over to Herb Fisher, of Woodman & Weld," Stone said.

Bessie began to growl at the fireplace.

"Does she detect an intruder?" Stone asked Crenshaw, interrupting Herbie.

"Bessie doesn't do intruders," he replied. "She spent eight years at JFK as a sniffer dog."

"Drugs?"

"No, her specialty was bombs."

Stone froze. "Excuse me, gentlemen," he said, "but would you all grab your papers and get out of the building as quickly as possible?"

"What?" Barnes asked.

"*Get out of the building now!*" Stone commanded.

"Let's go, gentlemen," Herbie said, and began herding them toward the door. Only Crenshaw stayed.

Stone walked toward the fireplace, surveying the area. Bessie seemed to be concentrating on the wood box. The logs, Stone noted, were stacked neatly beside it, instead of *inside* it. He reached out for the latch and opened the lid a quarter of an inch, then he looked around the gap for any sign of wires. Nothing. He opened the lid.

There was no ticking clock, but there was a cell phone taped to a large brick of what looked like modeling clay. "Eliot," Stone said, "take Bessie and go, right now." Crenshaw hurried for the door, but Bessie had to be dragged.

Stone looked at his watch: two minutes before twelve; people had arrived a little early. He would normally have called Dino and asked for the bomb squad, but he had the very strong feeling that this phone was going to ring at noon. He ran over to the desk and found a large pair of scissors, then returned to the wood box. He snipped the tape that clamped the phone to the brick, and it came away attached to a single wire, running from the earbud receptacle on the bottom of the phone to a cylinder he believed was a detonator, pushed into the soft material. He unplugged the wire from the phone, and as he did the instrument lit up and rang.

Stone jumped back and dropped the phone, expecting the explosive to detonate. Then the phone rang a second time, and a third. He picked it up and pressed the send button. "Hello?"

"What number is this?" a male voice asked.

"What number did you call?" Stone asked.

There was a dead silence at the other end of the phone, then the man spoke in a half-whisper. "*Barrington?*"

"Yes, Mr. Macher. Who or what were you expecting, Mr. Boom?" The connection was broken.

Stone got out his own phone and pressed the favorites button, then another.

"Bacchetti," Dino said.

"It's Stone."

"Is it important? I'm with some people."

"Is one of them a bomb expert?" Stone asked.

"Funny you should mention that," Dino said.

STONE LEFT THE phone and the bomb in the wood box and joined the others on the street.

"Mr. Barrington," Elihu Barnes said, "would you mind explaining what's going on here?"

Stone went over and hugged Bessie against his leg.

"This young lady, Eliot's Bessie, who is a retired sniffer of bombs at the airport, has just saved all our lives, and probably those of half the neighborhood."

Approaching sirens could be heard.

TWO HOURS LATER, sitting at a lunch table with the others around the corner from the house, Stone answered his phone. "Stone Barrington."

"Mr. Barrington, this is Lieutenant Marconi. Nice job on deactivating your bomb. We've secured it and searched the building for any other explosives. We didn't find anything else, so you can return to the building whenever you wish."

"Thank you, Lieutenant," Stone said, "and please thank your squad for arriving so quickly and making us feel safe again." He put the phone away. "Gentlemen, I am informed that the house is now safe, and we may resume our business there."

Everybody got up, Stone paid the bill, and they walked back to the mansion together. Forty minutes later, all *i*'s had been dotted and *t*'s crossed, and a check for half a billion dollars had changed hands.

"Congratulations, Mr. Barrington," Barnes said, "you and your partners have just become the owners of a fine business."

"Thank you," Stone replied, and began escorting everyone out.

Along the way, Barnes leaned over and whispered into Stone's ear, "Was it Macher?"

"Yes," Stone replied, "but it's going to be hard to prove."

40

Stone went straight to the hospital to see Charley Fox.

"When you didn't call I began to think something had gone wrong," Charley said.

"You could say that," Stone replied. He related the events of midday.

"Macher!" Charley said.

"Of course, who else?"

"Can we nail him for it?"

"I've already talked to Dino, who has talked to the DA. There were no prints on the bomb, and the phone was bought at a convenience store in New Jersey. And I can't swear it was Macher on the phone. It's called 'insufficient evidence to indict.'"

"I'm glad there's a guard on my room," Charley said.

"There are a dozen Strategic Services people in the building. You're quite safe."

"When I'm out of here," Charley said, "Macher and I are going to have a reckoning."

"Don't let that weigh on your mind," Stone replied. "You'll internalize your anger, and it will affect your recovery."

"I feel an intense need to deal with it on a personal level."

"I can understand that, but it's not the way to go about it. The DA is still considering whether to charge Macher with the murder of Christian St. Clair, so he's far from out of the woods."

"Something else," Charley said.

"What?"

"He's not going to stop."

"Charley . . ."

"No, I'm happy about that—it will give us other opportunities to kill him legally."

"Not while I'm your attorney," Stone said.

"Then at some point I'll just have to fire you."

"You know who we should talk to about this?"

"Who?"

"Ed Rawls."

Charley managed to sit up a little straighter in his bed. "You're damned right," he said. "Ed is smarter than any of us, and he knows more ways to skin a cat than anybody alive."

"What can I get you to make your stay more pleasant?" Stone asked. "Magazines? Books?"

"They have a very good library here. A lady comes around every day with a cartful of reading material."

"Anything else?"

"A bottle of single-malt scotch and a straw."

"All in good time."

"I must be getting better—I'm horny."

"Maybe you should discuss that with Kaley," Stone said.

"Don't you worry, I will. Oh, I didn't tell you—Kaley's going to move into the mansion with me."

"Now that's good news."

"She's out shopping now for enough new furniture and stuff so that we can forget Macher ever lived there. She's going to keep her job at Strategic Services."

"By the way, there's a locksmith at the mansion as we speak, rekeying the locks, and Mike's people will change the alarm code. I'll send everything over to Kaley as soon as the locksmith drops off the new keys."

"I think you'd better call the old employees—the accounting people and the cleaning and cooking staffs—and tell them to come back to work tomorrow."

"All that's in hand. There'll be somebody there to let them in. There's enough cash in the company accounts to pay their salaries and other operating expenses, for the moment. I've already sent the bank new signature cards with my and Mike's signatures. We'll add yours later."

"Right. Stone," Charley said, "there's something else you can do for me."

"Anything at all."

"Your pistol and my knife are in my desk drawer in the apartment. Could you get them over to me? I'd be more comfortable with them on hand."

"Did you get your application in for the carry permit?"

"Yes."

"I'll ask Dino if he can rush it, and I'll get the knife to you. That'll have to do until you're licensed."

"Oh, all right. I was always better with the knife than the gun when I was in training."

"By the way, Marisa's father has said that your medical bills and your stay here are on him, so don't worry about that."

"That's very good of him."

"You can thank him when you see him. In the meantime, I'll have a word with Arthur Steele at the Steele Insurance Group and get a full corporate package put together for Triangle, you, and the new employees."

"You think of everything."

"I'll have to, until you're well enough to think." Stone said goodbye and went home.

"GET YOUR closing done?" Joan asked.

"By the skin of my teeth." He told her of the day's events.

"Sheesh! That Macher is a bastard, isn't he?"

"If that's the worst name you can think of."

"Oh, the locksmith dropped off the new keys to the mansion," she said, handing him a set.

"Please messenger a set and the new alarm code to Kaley Weiss at Strategic Services. Oh, and Charley has a knife in his desk drawer in the apartment—include that in the package, but not the gun."

She went to get it done, and Stone called Dino.

"Bacchetti."

"Thanks for the help of the NYPD today," Stone said. "They did a great job."

"Don't mention it."

"Charley Fox has applied for a carry permit, and since

he's already been attacked, I can't see any impediment, can you?"

"Nope. I'll oil the machinery and get it done. Shall I send it to him at the clinic?"

"That will make him feel much better."

"As long as he doesn't hunt Macher down and shoot him."

"Don't worry, I've already had that conversation with him."

"Bad news," Dino said. "The DA called and says he can't move against Macher on the murder charge."

"Don't tell me, not enough evidence."

"You took the words right out of my mouth."

"I'd certainly feel better if he were behind bars, no bail, awaiting trial."

"I'm sorry, I can't provide that service without some paperwork from the DA, and these days I can't send somebody out to hunt him down and kill him."

"You never could do that," Stone said.

"Wouldn't it be wonderful if I could?"

"I always knew you had fascist tendencies."

"Don't tell anybody."

"Dinner later?"

"Sure. Patroon?"

"Done."

41

Stone called Ed Rawls, who answered immediately.

"Ed, I need your advice," Stone said. He told him of Macher's effort to blow up the St. Clair building. "We don't have enough evidence to prosecute him. Have you any advice as to how to proceed?"

"Shoot the son of a bitch and don't get caught," Rawls said.

"That's excellent advice, Ed, but I need a way ahead that doesn't involve life in prison without parole."

"I said don't get caught, didn't I?"

"Ed, I was a homicide detective for a long time, and I never encountered a perfect murder. These days, there are too many kinds of evidence that didn't exist all those years ago."

"Yeah, DNA, and all that crap."

"Right. How do we defend ourselves from somebody

with no scruples at all? Somebody who's willing to do anything?"

"Stone," Ed said, "if I knew that, Macher would already be dead."

LIEUTENANT GEORGE MARCONI, who commanded one of the NYPD's bomb squads, sat at his desk and stared at the burner cell phone that had been attached to the bomb found in the St. Clair mansion. He pressed the recent button and found a single phone number. Could this possibly work? He retrieved a small recorder from a desk drawer and plugged it into the cell phone, then pressed send. It was answered on the third ring.

"Hello?"

"Mr. Macher, this is George Marconi, how are you?"

"Okay, I guess, *who* are you?"

"I want to be sure that I've got the right person," Marconi said. "Is this the Erik Macher who, until recently, ran the St. Clair company?" He heard Macher suck in a breath, then stop.

"I don't know what the hell you're talking about," Macher said, and hung up.

Marconi sighed. Nearly had him. Macher wouldn't be answering that phone again. He went to his computer and found a secure directory of all cell phone numbers in the Northeast, entered his password, then did a search for Erik Macher. There! He called the number.

"Erik Macher," a gruff voice said. The same voice he'd just heard on the burner.

"Mr. Macher, it's George Marconi again. Why did you hang up on me?"

"How'd you get this number?" Macher demanded.

"Oh, I can get anybody's cell number," Marconi said, "even a burner number."

A long silence, then, "What's a burner number?"

"That's a number on a throwaway cell phone, like the one you attached to your bomb at the St. Clair mansion."

"Who are you?"

"I told you, I'm George Marconi."

"That doesn't tell me who you are."

"I'm curious, Mr. Macher, where did you get the design for your bomb?"

Another silence, then, "Bomb? What bomb?"

"Come on, Erik, you're not going to play dumb, are you? Would you like me to go to the police and tell them you're the guy who planted the bomb at the St. Clair mansion, and I can prove it?"

"Prove what?"

"That you're the man who planted the bomb."

"You're insane."

"I'm a reasonable man," Marconi said, trying to get him talking, "I can be bought off, and for less than you might imagine."

"Bought off?"

"Do I have to spell it out for you? Okay, you pay me twenty-five thousand or I'll tip off the police and give them your whereabouts. Is that clear enough for you?"

"What's clear to me is that you're a crazy person. I don't know anything about any bomb." He hung up.

Marconi's phone rang almost immediately. "Lieutenant Marconi."

"Marconi, this is Bacchetti."

"Afternoon, Commissioner."

"What are you turning up on the bomb at the St. Clair
mansion?"

"Funny you should mention that, sir. I was just on the
phone with Erik Macher. I called the phone number that
the burner phone attached to the bomb heard from—the
one that Mr. Barrington answered?"

"And who did you get?"

"Erik Macher. And I recorded the two conversations I
had with him."

"Play the recordings for me."

Marconi did so.

"That was a really good idea," Dino said, "except for
the part about it not working."

"It nearly worked, Commissioner."

"So, it was a really good idea that didn't work."

"I guess you could put it that way."

"How about coming up with an idea that works?"

"I'm working on that, Commissioner."

"You do that, Lieutenant." He hung up.

Marconi hung up and called his lab.

"Yes, Lieutenant?"

"Have you come up with anything on that explosive I
sent you?"

"Funny you should mention that, Lieutenant. I just did."

"Tell me."

"You know, a few years back, there was an experimental program started that was supposed to help us trace
explosives?"

"No, I didn't know that. What kind of program?"

"The idea was that the manufacturer would place a marker in the explosive that would allow it to be traced back to the manufacturer, who would keep a record of who the explosive was sold to."

"Did it work?"

"Sure, it worked, but Congress wouldn't pass a law allowing that to be done. There was another suggestion that ammunition could be marked the same way, and they were apparently afraid the NRA would shout that they were infringing on gun owners' rights, so they wouldn't approve it for either ammunition or explosives."

"So why are you telling me all this?"

"Because, Lieutenant, the explosive you sent me was apparently part of the experimental program. It contained a tracer element."

"So, did you trace it?"

"Yes, sir. I called the manufacturer, and they were able to look it up and tell me who they sold it to."

"Don't keep me in suspense, man, who did they sell it to?"

"The CIA."

Marconi's jaw dropped. "You're telling me that the explosive I sent you came from the CIA?"

"That's what I'm telling you, Lieutenant. So I called the CIA, and eventually I got connected to somebody in the technical services division, who would have issued the explosive to somebody at the Agency."

"And who did they issue it to?"

"They wouldn't tell me."

"What? Did you explain that the explosive was part of a criminal investigation?"

"I did, sir, but they denied all knowledge of it. So I guess it was kind of a dead end."

Marconi groaned. He thanked the man and hung up. He called the commissioner back but got his voice mail, so he left a message describing his conversation with the lab.

42

S tone got to Patroon first and ordered drinks for
both himself and Dino. They arrived just as Dino
did.

"I'm impressed with your timing," Dino said.

"You're easily impressed—I just wanted a drink, and I
didn't want to wait for you."

"I figured. I just thought I'd make you feel better after
what must have been a depressing day."

"Why would you think it was a depressing day? I got
the deal closed, and I'm going to make zillions of dollars
from it, eventually."

"Gee, I don't know, I thought it might have been depressing for you to come within a second of getting your
ass scattered all over the Upper East Side."

"On the other hand, it was exhilarating for that to *not*
happen. You have to look on the bright side, Dino. Otherwise, who would have had a drink waiting for you?"

Dino took a swig. "You're right, I feel better already."

"I'm so glad."

"Listen, I got some interesting news from my people this afternoon."

"I'm always interested in the interesting."

"Turns out the explosive in Macher's bomb was an experimental batch that contained a trace marker that allowed the manufacturer to have a record of who it was delivered to."

"You're right, that is certainly interesting. To whom was it delivered?"

"The CIA."

"Aha!"

"Don't aha so fast, my friend, they won't tell us who—rather, to whom—they issued it."

"Well, that's annoying of them, isn't it?"

"It certainly is, but we have an in with the Agency, don't we?"

"And who is that?"

"That is you."

"You think they'd tell me?"

"You're Lance Cabot's fair-haired boy—he'd tell you."

"I question your assessment of the fairness of my hair in Lance's eyes, so let me rephrase the question. You think Lance would tell me who checked out the explosive, then testify to that in open court? I think he might well express a certain reluctance to participate in that scenario."

"You have a point, but you're making it without reference to your gift of persuasion, especially where Lance is concerned."

"Oh? Kindly quote me an example of when I persuaded Lance to do something for me. It's always the other way around, and Lance's persuasion is always tainted with a veiled threat about what might befall me if I should not be persuaded."

"Okay, you persuaded him to sell you that house in Paris that the Agency owned, and at a minimal price, if memory serves."

"That was only because Lance desperately wanted something from me."

"And what was that something?"

"I don't recall offhand, but it must have been something really important to make him that desperate. Also, it was very expensive for the Agency to maintain the place as a safe house, and they hardly ever used it. I'm sure the General Services Administration was pleased to have it off their books."

"I forget what point I was trying to prove."

"You were trying to persuade me that I could persuade Lance to give me the name of the person who signed out the explosive, and then to testify to that in open court."

"Oh, yes, I remember now."

"I'm so relieved. I had thought you were exhibiting signs of early-onset dementia."

"Not in the least. Will you call Lance?"

"Only if we can think of something to give Lance in return, something that he really wants."

There followed three minutes of silent contemplation.

"I can't think of a thing," Dino said finally.

"Neither can I." Stone got out his cell phone. "I'll call Lance."

"Good idea. Put it on speaker."

Stone did so.

"This is Cabot. Why are you calling me at this time of night?"

"Because I know you work at all hours, Lance."

"Ah, Stone, to what do I owe this dubious pleasure?"

"I thought, Lance, that you might derive some satisfaction from helping to imprison a former CIA agent, a thoroughgoing rogue who is a contemptible and murderous swine."

"As inviting as imprisoning a contemptible and murderous swine sounds, I cannot imagine how I could help."

"Then I'll clear it up for you. The former agent checked out a quantity of plastic explosive from your technical services division some time back, and after performing whatever task he had in mind, he retained a considerable portion of that explosive until this very morning, when he deployed it in an attempt to murder everyone at a meeting at which I was in attendance, not to mention a few dozen innocents in adjacent buildings on the Upper East Side of this city. We were saved only by a passing Labrador retriever who was skilled in the arts of explosive sniffing."

"A passing Labrador retriever? One on the sidewalk, sniffing for a place to do his business, who just happened to zero in on some plastic explosive at your meeting?"

"It was a she, name of Bessie, but all right, she was actually attending the meeting, in the company of her owner, when she began barking at the fireplace. The bomb was contained in a wood box next to same, which, at Bessie's suggestion, I opened just in time to disconnect a cell phone attached to said explosive. A moment later, it rang."

"I hope you answered it."

"I did, and on the other end was the aforesaid contemptible, murderous swine, name of Erik Macher."

"Ah!" Lance said. "I believe I do recall that person, and you have described him accurately."

"Thank you."

"And what is it you want me to do to him?"

"Just instruct your director of Technical Services to testify that the explosive was checked out to Mr. Macher, and that he did not return any of it."

"Forgive my asking, but how would my man determine that the same explosive he issued to Macher was contained in the bomb of your acquaintance?"

"Because the manufacturer of said explosive took part in an experimental program to add trace markers to their product, and they have a record of having delivered explosive containing that marker to your own estimable agency, and the NYPD has identified the marker. All we need is the Agency's confirmation that it was issued to Macher and none was returned."

"Stone," Lance said, "I believe you are well acquainted with the level of secrecy under which we operate, are you not?"

"I am, but I don't see how getting a contemptible, murderous swine off the streets would compromise that secrecy."

"Because the world at large is not aware that our technical services division even exists, let alone the name of its director, nor does it know for certain that we sometimes find uses for explosives. We do not wish to implant that information in the consciousness of unsuspecting citizens, which might later emerge to bite us on the ass in a congressional hearing, or other such venue, which it surely, as night follows day, would. Please give my warm regards to Bessie, and I bid you a pleasant good evening." Lance hung up.

"You see?" Stone asked Dino.

"You weren't persuasive enough," Dino replied.

43

Stone arrived at the Carlsson Clinic just before noon and opened the door to Charley's room to find Charley and Kaley close together, both a little breathless and flushed.

"I hope I'm not interrupting anything," Stone said, dragging a chair up to Charley's bedside.

"Of course not," Charley panted.

"I was just leaving," Kaley said, checking her appearance in her compact mirror and refreshing her lipstick. She kissed Charley and left.

"You got here just in time," Charley said. "I might have expired."

"Lovely way to go," Stone observed.

"I'd just as soon hang around for more," Charley replied.

"I thought I'd bring you up to date."

"Shoot."

"First of all, I checked with Ed Rawls and asked his advice on how best to quietly remove Macher from the scene."

"And what did Ed suggest?"

"He suggested shooting him in the head and not getting caught."

"You know," Charley said, "that's not a bad idea."

"I gave Ed the benefit of my experience as a homicide detective in a past life and explained that I had never encountered a perfect murder."

"But wait," Charley said, "in a couple of days I'm going to be ambulatory. I could creep out of here, off Macher, and creep back in. I'm an invalid—no one would ever suspect me. How perfect is that?"

"Imperfect," Stone said. "You forget that we have no idea where Macher is, or whether he is predisposed to getting shot in the head by an invalid, who would probably pop his sutures and bleed to death in the street before he could creep back into the Carlsson Clinic."

"There is that," Charley said, looking sad. Then he brightened. "I could get Kaley to shoot him. She'd like that, and God knows, she's been trained for it."

"Right," Stone said, brightening, too, "and she could take the rap for it, as well. You and I would go scot-free. I like it."

"All right, that was a little unchivalrous of me."

"It was."

"Still . . ."

"Put it out of your mind, Charley."

"You know the three most important things about a successful murder, Stone?"

"Like real estate—location, location, location."

"Well, yes, but . . ."

"What were your three things?"

"I've forgotten."

"That may be the best idea of all," Stone said, "just forget it."

There was a knock at the door, and a nurse entered with an envelope. "This was just hand-delivered to you by a policeman," she said, handing it to Charley.

Charley opened the envelope and examined the contents. "It's my carry license," he said, beaming.

"I spoke to Dino about it." Stone pulled the little Colt Government .380 he had loaned Charley from his pocket and handed it to him. "There you are, and all legal."

"I feel much better," Charley said.

"And that greatly simplifies our problem," Stone said. "All we have to do now is to pull all your guards off, wait for Macher to come in here to kill you, then you can shoot him."

"Great!"

"If you don't fall asleep while you're waiting for him to show up, in which case he will kill you."

"You're such a killjoy," Charley said.

"Remember, that thing is loaded, and there's one in the chamber. Is six rounds enough to dispatch Macher when he shows up?"

"I should think so."

"It's a light caliber—go for a head shot. We don't want him lumbering about the clinic like a wounded bear, knocking over things."

"I'll keep that in mind," Charley said.

"Okay, I'll get out of here, then. I'm having lunch with Marisa at her apartment upstairs."

"Don't do anything I wouldn't do."

"Or haven't just done." Stone left and took the elevator upstairs to Marisa.

She gave him a big kiss. "I haven't seen Charley today," she said, "how is he?"

"Well enough to accept a little fellatio from Kaley," Stone replied. "I nearly caught them at it."

"What a nice idea," Marisa said. "Are you up for a little fellatio? Or cunnilingus? It's a smorgasbord—take your pick."

Stone grabbed her. "A little of everything, please."

She fended him off. "It will have to wait until after work. I have an appointment with a patient in twenty minutes."

"I'll make it fast."

"You're forgetting lunch."

"You're lunch."

"Think of me as a canapé at the cocktail hour."

"I can't wait around here all day, waiting for the cocktail hour."

"Let's have lunch, then you go home, and I'll join you at the cocktail hour for a smorgasbord. I'll undress in the cab on the way, so there'll be no waiting."

"I like that. I'll try to contain myself until then."

They had lunch, and he went home, atingle with anticipation.

ERIK MACHER AND Jake Herman were having a room-service lunch at the Lombardy Hotel.

"What went wrong?" Jake asked.

"I don't know. I rang the cell number, and Stone Barrington answered."

"He found the bomb? How'd he do that?"

"How the hell should I know? Why would he be expecting a bomb?"

"The guy is supernatural."

"No, he's just very lucky," Macher said.

"Same thing. What about Charley Fox?"

"He's still in the Carlsson Clinic, and there's a heavy Strategic Services presence there."

"What will you do about him?"

"Wait until he gets out, for a start," Macher replied.

"And then what?"

"I don't know. Do you have any ideas?"

Jake thought about it for a minute. "No."

"You're being unhelpful, Jake."

"Don't put this off on me. I don't have any reason to kill either Charley or Barrington."

"Have you become uninterested in money?"

Jake sighed. "I'll think of something."

44

t the end of Charley's first week as an invalid, he was examined by his surgeon, Nihls Carlsson, and discharged as a patient. "Just be careful," Nihls said, "no abdominal exertion, no running or exercise program. Move about gingerly for another week, then we can start rehab."

Charley readily agreed, and he was met by Fred in the Bentley outside. "Where's Kaley?" Charley asked.

"Waiting for you at home," Fred replied, and drove away.

Charley closed his eyes and relaxed, and when Fred opened the door for him, he found himself in front of the St. Clair mansion, and Kaley was waiting for him on the doorstep.

Fred offered his arm, and Charley climbed the steps, one at a time, embraced Kaley, and then was whisked upstairs in the elevator.

The apartment had been transformed from St. Clair's to Kaley and Charley's. Several pieces of comfortable, but less flamboyant pieces of furniture replaced some of those St. Clair had chosen, and there were flowers everywhere. The beautiful pictures remained where St. Clair had hung them.

Kaley began unbuttoning his shirt. "Now you should get into bed," she said, "doctor's orders."

"What else did the doctor order?" Charley asked, and Kaley showed him. When he was completely re-laxed and she had helped him into a pair of new silk pajamas, she picked up a remote control and made the bed sit up.

"Wow," Charley said. "Does your side do the same?"

"Yes, it does." She pressed another button and a huge TV set rose from the floor before the fireplace. "Now you can watch the game while we wait for lunch to be served by the staff."

"What game?"

"Whatever game." She handed him the remote control. "You choose. It's satellite, there are a zillion channels."

Charley found a game.

AFTER LUNCH, Stone called. "How are you feeling?"

"Never better," Charley replied honestly.

"Do you think you'd be up for a few days of cruising in autumnal Maine, starting Friday?"

"You bet your ass I would."

"Fred will collect you at nine AM. We'll be aboard for lunch."

"I'll be ready." Kaley came into the room. "We're cruising aboard our new yacht this weekend," he said.

"I know, I've already packed."

"You're not going to need much in the way of clothes," he said.

"The Stones, the Mikes, and the Dinos will be aboard."

"I'm sure they're all broad-minded."

"Maybe, but I'm not. My flesh is for your eyes only—well, *that* part of my flesh, anyway."

MACHER PUT DOWN the phone and turned to Jake. "They're going to be aboard my yacht for a long weekend in Maine," he said.

"How do you know that?" Jake asked.

"Intelligence operative aboard."

"Do we know where?"

"They won't be hard to find," Macher said. He went to a bottom drawer in his bedroom and removed a cardboard box.

"What's in there?" Jake asked.

Macher opened the box to reveal a block of plastique.

"How much more of that stuff have you got?" Jake asked.

"Enough to do the job," Macher replied.

"Tell me how you're going to do it."

"I seem to recall, Jake, that you own a wet suit and have considerable experience as a diver."

"True on both counts."

"That is how," Macher said.

*   *   *

THE MORNING DAWNED brightly with the hint of a nip in the air. They breakfasted on their terrace overlooking the garden, then Kaley put their luggage into the elevator and sent it down.

Fred awaited them, and fifteen minutes later he pulled the Bentley up to the pad at the East Side Heliport, where Stone, Marisa, Mike, and his girlfriend awaited, then he put their luggage aboard. They made themselves comfortable inside the leathered passenger cabin, and the blades began to turn.

"How long to Rockland?" Charley asked.

"We're not going to Rockland," Stone replied.

AN HOUR AND a quarter later, the helicopter, now at low altitude, made a turn, and Charley saw the yacht, cruising slowly into the wind. A moment later the chopper set down gently on the upper deck, and half a dozen crew members rushed it, emptying the luggage compartment and escorting everyone down the stairs to the main deck. When the copter pad was clear, the machine revved its engines and lifted free of the yacht, turning to the south.

Charley was made comfortable in a soft reclining chair on the afterdeck, and Kaley tucked a cashmere blanket around him, while a steward stood by with two drinks on a silver tray. Charley gratefully sipped his first bourbon in almost a week while the yacht got under way.

THEY LUNCHED ON lobster salad, of course, that being the obligatory culinary introduction to Maine, then the captain came to their table. "Mr. Barrington, as you suggested, we have waited for the latest forecast before choosing our destination, and we may look forward to sunshine and light winds. Therefore, we have set a course for Martha's Vineyard, and we'll be at a mooring off the yacht club for dinner."

"Very good, Captain," Stone replied. He rose and called the man aside. "For this weekend, as I explained on the phone, we require an upgrade in our security."

"I have already personally inspected every corner of the yacht," the captain replied.

"Excellent," Stone replied. "And every night that we are aboard, I want a crew member on the top deck with binoculars, a spotlight, and a rifle. Every morning before sailing, I want a crew member in a wet suit to inspect the hull, right down to the keel, for any unwanted attachments."

"Yes, sir," the captain replied.

Stone returned to the table.

"What are you and the captain cooking up?" Marisa asked.

"Just a word about the menus and the wines for our cruise," Stone replied, resuming his seat.

"You were right," Marisa said, "this is a very beautiful yacht, and I'm sorry I called it a stinkpot."

"You are forgiven," Stone replied, "and I promise you that, when under way, you will be standing vertically, and not at an angle to the deck."

"I'm sure I will enjoy that," Marisa replied.

Stone raised his glass: "To the wonderful good taste in yacht building of Christian St. Clair," he toasted.

"Hear! Hear!" the others replied.

*   *   *

A MILE AWAY, Erik Macher, at the helm of a rented forty-foot cabin cruiser, fell in behind them. "They appear to have set a course for Provincetown, or perhaps the Cape Cod Canal," he said to Jake Herman. Jake opened another cold beer.

45

They cruised the whole of the afternoon and, as the sun was low in the sky, they picked up a mooring in Edgartown Harbor, near the yacht club. The harbor was not as crowded in the early autumn as in midsummer, but there were still many yachts about, and they received the admiring attention of those passing. Mike Freeman handed a triangular flag to a crewman and requested that it be flown at the bow of the yacht.

"What's the flag?" Charley asked.

"It's the burgee of the New York Yacht Club," Mike replied, "of which I am a member, so we are entitled to fly it. It occurs to me that you and Stone, since you are yachtsmen, should be members, as well, and I would be delighted to propose you both."

"I accept," Charley said, and Stone agreed.

*   *   *

THEY TOOK COCKTAILS on the afterdeck, then, as the evening grew cooler, moved inside for dinner. Before they entered the saloon, Stone took note that there was a crew member on the upper deck, with a pair of binoculars around his neck.

AFTER DINNER THEY adjourned to the saloon and watched a movie on the yacht's video system, then everyone sleepily headed for their cabins.

MARISA MARVELED AT the comforts of the owner's cabin, which Mike and Charley insisted should always be Stone's. "It is more comfortable than my bedroom at home," she said, "but not more comfortable than yours." She got into bed and snuggled with Stone. "I'm glad we could make this trip now, because I have to go to Sweden next week to attend to some family business. I'd ask you to come, but you seem to have your hands full here."

"You're right, I'm afraid," Stone said. "How long will you be gone?"

"A week, perhaps two."

"Send me postcards."

"I'll be back before they would be delivered," she said, fondling him. "We must make this weekend memorable, to last us until I'm home again."

Stone found the idea entirely agreeable, as he responded to her touch and returned the favor.

*   *   *

"HOW FAR CAN you swim underwater?" Macher asked. They were moored at the other end of Edgartown Harbor.

"Not that far," Jake replied. "Not at night, anyway. Besides there are too many yachts here, even for this time of year. Your object is not to attract attention, isn't it?"

"Hardly," Macher replied. "We will just enjoy our cruise, until the right opportunity presents itself."

THE FOLLOWING MORNING after breakfast, everyone went into town on foot for some shopping and sightseeing, then stayed ashore for lunch at an Edgartown restaurant.

"The foot traffic here in summer is so thick you can hardly walk down the street," Mike observed. "This time of year is so much better."

Everyone agreed.

MACHER WATCHED THROUGH binoculars as the party was taken ashore in the yacht's tender. "They're all ashore. I think now would be a good time for you to reconnoiter, Jake."

"Don't you want to come with me?"

"No, I might be recognized by one of the crew, and it is not in our interests for them to know I'm around."

"What do you want me to reconnoiter?" Jake asked.

Just circumnavigate the yacht and look for a likely spot to deposit our payload—the antenna has to be mounted above the waterline."

"If you don't mind my saying so," Jake said, "I think

it would be best to detonate the thing after they've left Edgartown and are not within easy reach of a port."

"My guess is they'll head to Nantucket from here, and that's thirty miles of Atlantic Ocean for them to cross," Macher said. "And deep water."

STONE HAD DIFFICULTY sleeping that night, which was unusual for him. Around three AM he disentangled himself from Marisa, put on a cashmere robe and some slippers, and went up to the saloon, where he poured himself a cognac. He strolled out onto the afterdeck and had a look at the lights of the village reflected in the water, and the anchor lights of the neighboring yachts. A large moon was rising.

He took a turn around the deck, and when he was coming aft again, noticed the shadow of the yacht cast by the moon. He looked for the shadow of a man on the upper deck but saw nothing.

He walked up the stairs, his slippers soft on the steps, and emerged onto the moon-flooded upper deck. On a sofa on the port side, a human figure was stretched out, snoring softly.

Stone walked over and kicked the bottom of the sofa, rousing the crewman.

"What's wrong?" the man asked.

"How can we tell, when you are asleep?" Stone asked.

"Well, there was nothing going on."

"And how would you know? Our lives are at risk here, and so is yours. Had that not occurred to you?"

The man got to his feet, and Stone picked up the rifle from the deck and handed it to him. "Tell you what," he said, "tomorrow after sunup, you can volunteer to survey the hull from below."

"Yes, sir," the man said, slinging the rifle onto his shoulder.

Stone went back down to the saloon and refreshed his drink, then sat on the afterdeck, a throw over his lap, watching the moon rise.

He didn't have many periods of contemplation in his life; he was too busy, so now he took the opportunity. He thought about what it might be like to be married to Marisa, and the thought was pleasing, though he felt no compulsion to propose such a thing. Maybe after a few months, when the new had worn off. She would probably want children, he mused, though the subject hadn't come up. He wondered how he would handle an infant in the house, and what sort of father he would be. He had missed that part of Peter's life; the boy had been a teenager when they first met.

He thought about business. Charley would be fully enough recovered to handle all that in a few weeks, but until then, matters rested on his shoulders. He had a feeling that Charley and Kaley would be married before too long.

He heard a noise, then a bottle being uncorked, then Dino sat down beside him.

"You couldn't sleep, either?"

"No. I don't know why."

"Because we're being stalked," Dino said. "I can feel it."

"I know, I feel it, too. I found the guy up top sound asleep."

"That's not very reassuring, is it?"

"No, it isn't. I hope I put the fear of God into him."

"I hope so, too."

They finished their drinks, then went back to their beds.

AT THREE AM, Jake Herman, wearing a wet suit, set off in the rubber dinghy, rowing instead of using the outboard. He tied up the dinghy to the mooring buoy of a yacht thirty yards from *Breeze*, the St. Clair yacht, removed his equipment from a duffel, and let himself slowly into the water. Using a long snorkel, he swam toward the big yacht breathing comfortably.

An hour later, he was back aboard the cabin cruiser.

46

The following morning after breakfast they weighed anchor and left Edgartown Harbor for the forty-mile run to Nantucket.

Stone visited the bridge, where the captain was alone, monitoring their progress under autopilot.

"Good morning, Mr. Barrington," the captain said.

"Good morning."

"Is everything all right?"

"I don't know," Stone said, "is it?"

"Is there some problem?"

"I took a stroll last night and came across your crewman on the top deck, sound asleep."

The captain winced. "That's Yancy Tubbs. I should have given someone else the first watch," he said.

"Has he not been otherwise satisfactory?"

"Lazy, mostly. Also, he was tight with Mr. Macher, and I don't know if that's a good thing."

"It is not a good thing," Stone said. "Perhaps he could fly home from Nantucket."

"He's already gone," the captain replied. "He volunteered to go under the yacht for a look at the hull, which surprised me, but I let him do it, then I broke the news to him and sent him ashore."

"That's a relief," Stone said. Then he thought about it for a moment and said, "Captain, please stop the ship."

"What?"

"I want her dead in the water right now, and I need a wet suit, a snorkel, and flippers. Also, some wire cutters."

"Mr. Barrington, what's wrong?"

"I have a feeling your ex-crewman might not have done a good enough job in looking at the hull."

The captain switched off the autopilot and pulled the throttles back to idle. The yacht slowed, then finally stopped.

STONE GOT INTO the wet suit and flippers, adjusted the snorkel, and snapped the wire cutters into a pocket, then he dropped off the stern into the water.

A MILE BEHIND the yacht, Erik Macher pulled his throttles to idle.

"What's wrong?" Jake Herman asked.

"They've stopped. Give me the portable radio."

Jake took the new unit out of its box and handed it to him.

Macher turned on the unit, but no lights came on. "I need batteries," he said.

"What kind?"

Macher removed the back of the radio. "Four double A's," he said.

"Do we have batteries on board?"

"The radio affixed to the bomb came with batteries."

"There are none in the box."

"Well, goddamnit, find some!"

STONE DOVE DOWN the centerline of the boat and worked his way forward, holding his breath. He had to stop halfway, surface to snorkel height and breathe for a moment, then he continued to the bows. From there, he worked his way aft on the port side, just below the waterline, looking and feeling.

"HERE WE GO!" Jake said. "They were in a galley drawer."

"Put them into the radio!" Macher ordered.

Jake fumbled with the batteries and dropped one, which rolled under a settee.

"Get another one from the drawer," Macher said.

"There were only four." Jake dropped to his knees and reached under the settee, feeling for the battery. "Got it," he said after a minute.

"Then load it."

Jake did so and handed Macher the radio. "You do it," he said. "I don't want to."

Macher snatched the radio from him and switched it on.

*   *   *

STONE FOUND AN antenna taped to the stern near an exhaust pipe. He followed the wire until it came to the explosive, which was held to the hull with waterproof tape. He scratched at the tape with his nails, but couldn't dislodge it. Finally, he got out his wire cutters and began scraping at the tape. As he pulled it free, the whole thing slipped from his grasp and went down.

Stone swam as fast as he could, then ran out of wind and surfaced.

MACHER TUNED IN the proper channel, took a last look at the yacht, and pushed the send button.

STONE WAS SUDDENLY lifted by a force beneath him, and he landed with one hip on the boarding platform.

"What the hell was that?" Dino yelled from above.

Stone tossed his flippers onto the deck and climbed up. "That," he said, "was a bomb. Fortunately, I lost my grip on it, or it would have been on deck."

"Are you all right?" the captain asked.

"I am," Stone said. "How much water are we in?"

"About sixty feet," the captain replied, then he pointed aft. "Look."

Stone and Dino looked aft and saw dead fish floating on the surface.

"Look back there," Dino said, pointing.

A smaller craft, perhaps a mile off, was turning and heading back toward Martha's Vineyard.

"I could call the local cops or the Coast Guard," Dino said, "and get him hauled in."

"On what evidence?" Stone asked.

"You have a point," Dino admitted.

The others had gathered on the afterdeck now, as Stone struggled out of the wet suit.

Dino explained to them what had happened.

"What do we do now?" Marisa asked.

"Continue to Nantucket, Captain," Stone said. "Macher ran for it, and even if he hadn't done so, I doubt if he had any explosive left."

The captain headed for the bridge, and they were shortly under way again.

MARISA STRIPPED OFF Stone's swimsuit and toweled him dry. Stone wrapped the towel around him and flopped into a chair. "Dino?" he said.

"Yeah?"

"Do you think you can find me a large brandy and soda, no ice?"

"It's one of the things I do best," Dino said, heading for the bar.

A minute later, Stone was letting the alcohol find its way to his toes and fingers.

"You know something?" Dino said. "I'm getting tired of these close calls."

"Not as tired as I," Stone replied, polishing off the rest of his drink.

47

They spent two nights in the Nantucket marina, enjoying good weather, then Stone summoned the helicopter to meet them at the airport. By midday they were back in New York, and Fred met Stone at the East Side Heliport, while the others took cabs home.

"Dinner tonight?" he asked Marisa.

"I'd love to, but I have to pack for Sweden. I have a morning flight."

He dropped her at the clinic and Fred drove him home. Stone dined alone at home that evening, already missing Marisa.

THE FOLLOWING MORNING, Ed Rawls called.

"How are you, Ed?" Stone asked.

"Uncomfortable," Rawls replied. "I've been uncomfortable since our last conversation. You hear any more from Macher?"

"Well, yes. He stuck a bomb to our hull in Edgartown a couple of days ago. I got lucky and jettisoned it before it went off."

"It went off?"

"Killed a lot of fish," Stone replied, "but none of us."

"I saw *Breeze* pass by late yesterday, on the way back to her berth, I guess. Are you going to lay her up for the winter?"

"Not until the weather turns," Stone replied. "We might want to use her again or we might send her south. The skipper will keep an eye out for signs of Macher."

"I would enjoy killing Macher for you," Ed said, "if I got the chance."

"You've already been to prison once, Ed. Did you enjoy it?"

"No, I guess I didn't."

"Then don't do anything that might send you back there."

"I might be the victim of an irresistible impulse, if I saw Macher again."

"Resist the irresistible," Stone said.

"I'll try."

"Do you know where Macher lives, Ed?"

"He has that security business—in Arlington, I think. He might live somewhere around there."

"I'll look into that," Stone said. They said goodbye and hung up.

Stone had a thought; he called Dino.

"Bacchetti."

"It's Stone."

"Thanks for a great weekend," Dino said.

"You're welcome. You've got a way to find cell phone records and trace them, haven't you?"

"Sure, I can do that. You looking for Macher?"

"Yes. It might have a 202 area code."

"Just the address?"

"I'd like to know where he is," Stone said.

"Let me get back to you."

Stone went back to handling his correspondence from his time away; an hour or so later, Dino rang back.

"I've got something for you," he said, reciting an address in Arlington.

Stone noted it. "Maybe I'll run down there and have a word with him," Stone said.

"No need to leave town," Dino replied.

"He's in New York?"

"We've got him on East Fifty-sixth Street, between Park and Lex, north side of the street."

"That's the Lombardy Hotel," Stone said. "Charley Fox used to live there."

"Macher is stationary at the moment, not on the move."

"Can you think of any defensible reason to haul him in for a chat?"

"I thought about that, and no. We can't put him in the Cape Cod area, and we had nothing left of his bomb for evidence."

"That's discouraging."

"I gotta go. You want to meet for dinner at Clarke's?"

"Sure, seven?"

"See you then."

*　　*　　*

MACHER AND JAKE were having a drink in Macher's suite.

"I'm getting discouraged," Macher said.

"Here's an idea," Jake said. "Why don't you go back to D.C. and run your business for a while? It could probably use your attention, and Barrington will still be around."

"It's a thought," Macher said. "I just hate to leave a thing undone."

"You can still do it, just at your leisure."

"Maybe you're right."

STONE AND DINO met in the bar at P. J. Clarke's and had a drink before dinner.

"You feeling any better?" Dino asked.

"I should be feeling great—I've just had a wonderful cruise to places I enjoy. I got some sun and spent time with friends. What have I got to be unhappy about?"

"You're missing Marisa, then."

"You've got me there. I had become accustomed to having a sex life again, after Holly."

"Have you heard from her?"

"Not since she went back to Washington. She's got to get Kate reelected, plus help run foreign policy at the Security Council, so she's got her hands full."

"And when is Marisa due back?"

"A week or two, she said."

"Maybe you should pop down to Washington and call on Holly?"

"I can't just drop in, she has to plan to get any time off."

They were called to their table and had hardly sat down when Stone's phone rang. He checked the calling number, but it was blocked. "Hello?"

"It's Holly," she said.

Stone mouthed her name for Dino. "Well, hi there."

"Where are you? It's noisy at your end."

"At Clarke's, having dinner with Dino."

"I won't interrupt you, then."

"Please interrupt me. Dino is boring me rigid."

She laughed. "All right, I have some news."

"Shoot."

"You remember we had a conversation about Kate moving me back to my old home after the election?"

"Yes, she was going to run with Lance on the ticket, but she didn't do that."

"Lance didn't want to leave the Agency, he loves his job."

"So what's in store for you?"

"I hesitate to even mention it. I'm superstitious, I guess."

"Then don't. Let's talk about something else."

"I don't want to talk about something else," she said.

"Then take a deep breath and tell me."

"All right, here goes. I'm going to be the next secretary of state."

"*What?*"

"You heard me."

"Adamson doesn't want to serve another term?"

"He's burned out, he says. He wants to leave immediately after the election, and since Kate is already in office, she doesn't have to wait until after the inauguration to appoint me."

"Well, that's fantastic, you'll be very good at it. After all, you've been practicing for the job for four years at the NSC. It's the logical next step."

"I guess that's the optimistic way to look at it," she said.

"It's the only way to look at it. Can you get away for a few days in New York?"

"No, it's crazy here. Maybe after the election, before I make the move to Foggy Bottom."

"Great, I'll look forward to it."

"I've gotta run, there's a meeting. I just wanted to tell somebody."

"I'm glad you told me." He hung up.

"Adamson doesn't want to serve another term?" Dino said. "Does that mean Holly is going to replace him?"

"It means exactly that—right after the election."

"I'll drink to that," Dino said, raising his glass.

They both did.

48

Stone was at his desk the following morning when Joan buzzed him. "Dr. Carlsson is on line one for you."

"Okay, I'll bite—which Dr. Carlsson?"

"Oh, sorry, the patriarch of the clan."

Stone picked up the phone. "Paul, good morning."

"Good morning, Stone. I've been talking with my sons, and we think it's time to return our security status to normal. They find the presence of guards uncomfortable, and some of our patients have commented on it as well."

"Well, Paul, the worst seems to be over for the clinic, so a return to normal might be all right, but there are still risks. What if we reduced the presence by half? That could still give you a margin of safety. Then, in a week or two, we could end it."

"All right, then," Carlsson said, "a fifty percent reduction immediately, and in another week, we end it."

"I think that's a good move. Have you heard from Marisa?"

"Ah, yes," Carlsson said, seeming to hesitate.

Stone had had two e-mails, and she sounded cheerful enough. "Is everything all right in Sweden?"

"Everything is always all right in Sweden," Carlsson said, laughing. "Stone, I'm not sure you understand how strong our bond is with that country and its language."

"Perhaps not," Stone replied.

"We all feel at least half Swedish, and we make a point of visiting our ancestral home as frequently as we can find the time. We even have a smaller version of our clinic in Stockholm."

"I didn't know that," Stone said. "Marisa never mentioned it."

"Perhaps she should have," Carlsson said. "Well, if you'll excuse me, I'd better get back to work. Will you speak to Mike Freeman on my behalf about reducing the security presence?"

"Of course, Paul. Thank you for calling." Stone hung up and called Mike Freeman.

"Good morning," Mike said. "I suppose you're calling about Erik Macher's continuing presence in New York."

"No, but Dino spoke to me about it. Macher is apparently living at the Lombardy."

"That's our information. You should keep that in mind when moving around the city."

"I'll do that. Mike, Paul Carlsson just called me, and he wants to reduce the security presence at the clinic."

"And what's your opinion on that?"

"I suggested a fifty percent reduction immediately, and if the week passes with no problems, then an end to it—unless a new threat develops."

"All right, I'll get that done right away."

"Paul would appreciate that."

"Anything else?"

"Keep me posted if there's anything new on Macher."

"I will, certainly." The two men hung up.

Stone checked his e-mail and found one from Marisa.

Stone, I'm sorry if I've seemed uncommunicative, but I've been very busy at our clinic here. Did I mention that we have a clinic in Stockholm? In any case, we're losing two of our best doctors, who are going into private practice, and I'm in the midst of interviewing candidates to replace them and, perhaps, reorganizing some of our services as a result. I'm afraid it's going to take me at least a month to get everything running smoothly enough for me to return to New York. I wanted to tell you now, so that if you're contemplating any social plans, to go ahead without me. Needless to say, I maintain my liberal Swedish attitude about sex!

Dad tells me that he's reducing, and eventually eliminating, the security presence at the New York clinic. I'm glad of that, as it will make the atmosphere less tense for our patients.

I hope you're well and that you understand why I must remain in Stockholm for a while. Take care of yourself.

Fondly,
Marisa

THAT NEWS WASN'T good and he was concerned by the lack of expressed affection in the letter. He found it businesslike, and not much more, except for the perceived invitation to have as much sex as he wanted.

Joan came in. "Are you having lunch at your desk? Shall I order you something from Helene?"

"Yes, thanks, a sandwich will do."

"What kind of sandwich?"

"Tell Helene to surprise me."

"Boss, is something wrong? You look a little unwell."

"No, I'm just fine, thanks." He was a bit surprised to find that he wasn't.

JAKE HERMAN RANG the bell to Erik Macher's suite and was admitted.

"What's up?" Macher asked.

"Not much, I'm afraid. I saw my girl from accounting at St. Clair last night, and she tells me that Charley Fox and his girlfriend have redecorated the upstairs suite and moved into it. She also says that all the locks have been changed and the security system revamped."

Macher had no response, just glared at him.

"I tell you this because it means that the mansion is not as good a target as it might have been in the past."

"I still can't figure out how they discovered my bomb in the library," Macher said.

"Oh, she told me about that. The new corporate counsel has a Labrador retriever, and he brought the dog to the board meeting. The animal is a retired sniffer dog at the airports, and she smelled something that led Barrington to open the wood box."

"Well, shit!" Macher yelled.

"I know it's a blow, but if the thing had gone off, we would now be up to our asses in investigators. Perhaps it's just as well it didn't."

"You have a point there," Macher said.

"And about the yacht. Our man on the crew volunteered to check the hull that morning, and shortly after that, he was fired and sent ashore in Edgartown. He says that the bomb was still in place when he left the yacht, and he doesn't know what went wrong."

"Barrington is the luckiest bastard I've ever known," Macher said.

"Maybe we should go back to D.C. and tend to business there. I'm hearing that not much work is getting done in our absence."

"Oh, all right," Macher said. "We're certainly not getting anything done here, and I'm running up a hell of a hotel bill."

"I'll go get my things together. What time do you want to depart?"

"Call for a bellman in half an hour, and ask him to bring the car around."

"Certainly," Jake said. He went to his room, relieved that there would be no more attacks on Macher's enemies, at least for a while.

Macher, if he had known what Jake was thinking, would not have agreed with him.

49

Kaley Weiss left the offices of Strategic Services at 11:30 to go and prepare lunch for Charley, something she did each day, even if there was a cook on duty at the mansion.

She started across Park Avenue, but the light caught her on the center island, and she had to wait there for it to change. As she did, she saw a stopped car on East Fifty-seventh, headed west, waiting for the light to change. She recognized the driver from photographs: it was Jake Herman. That must mean that the man sitting next to him in the front passenger seat was Erik Macher. As she watched, the light changed, and the car drove across Park Avenue. She noticed a hanging garment bag and a suitcase in the rear seat, as if the trunk must be full. She turned and watched the car proceed up East Fifty-seventh Street, and she watched it from a distance until it disappeared, going west.

Kaley called Stone Barrington.

"Yes, Kaley?"

"Good morning, Stone," she said. "I'm at the corner of East Fifty-seventh and Park Avenue, and two men in a Mercedes S550 just drove past me, heading west. The driver was Jake Herman, and I'm assuming the front-seat passenger was Erik Macher. The backseat had luggage in it, which I take to mean that the trunk was full, and that car has a pretty big trunk. I watched them drive all the way west, as if they were headed for the bridge or the tunnel."

"That's an astute observation, Kaley," Stone said. "I expect they're leaving the city to drive back to D.C., where Macher has a condo, across the river in Arlington."

"Then that's good news?"

"It is. How's Charley doing?"

"Better and better. I'm headed over to the mansion now to fix his lunch and to make sure he isn't doing too much yet."

"That's good of you, and thanks for the information." He hung up.

STONE CALLED DINO.

"Bacchetti."

"Someone I know thinks she saw Jake Herman and Erik Macher headed across town, west, probably headed for the tunnel, thence to D.C."

"Hang on, I'll bring up the app." He paused a moment. "I've got him on Eleventh Avenue, just north of the tunnel. He's waiting in traffic. Now he's moving, and he's turning into the tunnel."

"Let's get his direction when he gets to Jersey."

"What would you like to talk about in the meantime?" Dino asked. "This job leaves me with so much time on my hands."

"Hang up, if you're needed."

Dino hung up.

Stone waited patiently for another fifteen minutes, then his phone rang. "I'm here."

"He turned south on I-95, which means he's headed either to D.C. or Miami, or some point in between. Satisfied?"

"For the moment."

"See ya." Dino hung up.

Okay, Stone thought, Macher is headed for D.C. Now what?

KALEY CAME INTO the bedroom carrying a tray containing a sandwich, to find Charley sitting up in bed watching a soap opera. "Gotcha!" she said. "A soap opera, yet!"

"I was just channel surfing," Charley said, accepting the sandwich and taking a big bite. He switched to MSNBC.

"Guess who I just saw headed out of town?"

"Who?"

"Erik Macher and Jake Herman. At least they *seemed* to be heading out of town."

"You should tell Stone."

"I already have. He thinks they're headed for D.C."

"If that's true, it's good news." Charley's phone rang, and he picked it up. "Charles Fox."

"It's Stone. I just talked to Dino. He's tracking Macher, and he's headed south on I-95, we think to D.C."

"Great," Charley said. "Can we relax now?"

"A little," Stone said. "Let's not get overconfident."

"I'm going back to work tomorrow," Charley said.

"You are not!" Kaley shouted. "You're going to stay in bed for at least another week."

"Listen, I went yachting and nearly got blown up, and I didn't pop any stitches."

"That's not the same as working."

"Yeah, when I work I sit in a chair and talk on the phone and tap the computer keyboard a little. Does that sound too strenuous to you? I'll tell you something, watching a soap opera is more strenuous than that. The music alone makes me antsy."

"Charley," Stone said.

"You heard all that?"

"How could I miss it? Do as Kaley says—your life won't be worth living if you fight her on this."

"Then I'm going to need a lot of dirty magazines," Charley said.

"Dirty magazines?" Kaley asked. "What am I, chopped liver?"

"Charley," Stone said, "*you're* going to be chopped liver if you don't do as she says. Don't you know anything about women?"

"More than I want to," Charley said.

"Humor her."

"All right, Kaley, I'll stay in bed awhile longer, but as soon as the stitches are out, I'm back at work, clear?"

"We'll see," Kaley said.

"I'll leave you to your fate," Stone said, and hung up.

Kaley sat on the edge of the bed, pressed the down button on his bed's remote control, pulled back the covers, and began unbuttoning his pajamas. "Okay," she said, "think about dirty magazines, if you need to."

Charley didn't need to.

BOB CAME OVER to Stone, sat down at his side, and stared up at him. "It's not time, Bob," Stone said to the dog, glancing at his watch. "Now go lie down."

Bob retreated a couple of feet and lay down. Ten minutes later he was back, and this time he placed a paw on Stone's knee.

Stone looked at his watch; the stroke of noon. He buzzed Joan.

"Yes, boss?"

"Bob says it's lunchtime, and he's giving me the paw."

"Oh, no, not the dreaded paw! I'll be right in."

Joan came in, got a scoop of dog food from a cabinet and tipped it into Bob's dish, then she refilled his water bowl. Bob inhaled the food, then nudged Joan.

"He wants his cookie," Stone said, and she gave it to him.

Bob went to his bed near the door, climbed into it, curled up, and began his after-lunch nap.

LATE IN THE AFTERNOON, Joan buzzed Stone. "Dino for you on one."

Stone picked up the phone. "I'm here."

"Macher is in Arlington," Dino said, "parked at his office address."

"Great. What do we do now?"

"I haven't been able to think of anything," Dino said. "How about you?"

"Not a thing."

50

Erik Macher arrived at his office an hour earlier than his small staff, after a fitful night's sleep. Barrington was an itch he couldn't seem to scratch, and the thought of him, alive and well in New York, was too much to bear.

He went into his office, locked the door, and opened the walk-in safe in a corner of the room. His firm's weapons were kept there—handguns, holsters, assault rifles, and a couple of fully automatic machine guns. In a rear corner was a wooden case, and he opened that. It was half-full of plastic explosive bricks, each weighing one kilogram, or 2.2 pounds. Next to that box was another, containing detonators and timers.

He spread a plastic cloth on his desk, pulled on a pair of latex gloves, and retrieved two of the explosive bricks, setting them on the plastic sheet on his desk. This time he was taking no chances.

He pressed two detonators into the plastique and attached wires from them to an empty battery holder, then attached another two wires running from there to the terminals on a timer. He didn't set the timer yet. He pressed a fresh lithium-ion battery against his tongue and felt the tiny shock. Good battery. He clipped it into the holder, and he had himself one hell of a bomb.

He stepped outside into the alley, where a box held packaging materials, and selected a heavy, two-ply cardboard box and a bag of foam peanuts, then took them back into his office. He laid a layer of foam at the bottom of the box, then pressed the two bricks into the yielding material, then filled the box with peanuts, leaving only the timer exposed. For added impact, he took two boxes of double-ought shotgun shells from the safe and with a craft knife cut each of the two dozen shells open and poured the shot into the box. He also scattered the powder over the foam.

He found a shipping label in a storage cabinet and snipped off the return address and waybill number, then affixed it to the top of the box, then he sprayed the container with Windex to remove any fingerprints or DNA. All that remained was to set the timer, tape the box shut, and send it on its way. He heard the outside door to the building open and close, and someone tried his office door, then knocked.

"Erik," Jake said, "it's me."

Macher let him in. "Sit down, Jake," he said.

Jake sat. "What's in the box?"

"Think of it as a gift." He went back to the safe and found an explosive-suppressing woven steel blanket and set it on his desk. "What we've got here is two kilos of plastique, a lot of buckshot, and a timer," he said.

"You're going to try this again?" Jake asked doubtfully.

"Just once—once and for all," Macher replied.

"And you want me to deliver it?"

"No, I don't want that, you're going to need an iron-clad alibi."

Jake looked relieved.

"Name a man who can be trusted to deliver this and to do it right."

"Swenson," Jake said without hesitation. "He's young, but reliable. He did two tours in Iraq and Afghanistan, and he knows what it means to follow orders precisely."

"All right, Swenson," Macher said. "He's single, isn't he? Lives alone?"

"Yes. How do you want him to handle this?"

"I want the package placed outside the street entrance to Barrington's office, which is downstairs in his house."

"Right."

"I want it set in place at three tomorrow morning. That will give Swenson plenty of time to drive up there, place the package, and drive back, arriving at work at his usual time."

"Got it. What's the steel blanket for?"

"I want Swenson to wrap it around the box on the street side, like this." Macher demonstrated how to do it. "That will help direct the explosive force away from the street and into Barrington's office. There's enough explosive here to destroy the secretary's office near the street, then push into Barrington's office, destroying it and him, and I anticipate that the force of the explosion will cause his house to collapse on top of his office. That way, in the unlikely event that he survives the explosion, he'll die in the rubble while the fire department is trying to dig him out."

"That sounds thorough, Erik. I assume you've taken steps not to leave any prints or DNA on the box."

Macher held up his gloved hands.

"Got it," Jake said.

"When we had his house under surveillance before, our men determined that Barrington's secretary gets to her office around eight-thirty, and that Barrington comes downstairs between nine and nine-thirty, so I'm setting the timer for ten."

"Suppose someone tries to enter from the street and discovers the box?"

Macher grabbed a pencil and pad. "The front of the office entrance protrudes from the house, like this." He drew the outline. "There are concrete flower boxes under the windows on either side of the entrance. I want Swenson to pull one of them out far enough to place the package behind it, along with the steel blanket. The flower box will hide the package from the street and help the blanket do its job."

"I see." Jake sat immobile and silent.

"What is it, Jake?"

"I'm just running through it in my mind. When the secretary comes to work, she might notice the new position of the flower box."

"She lives next door, and she enters the Barrington house from there and goes into her office from inside the house. Should FedEx or some other person get buzzed in from inside, he won't notice the position of the concrete flower box."

"That's good," Jake said. "You appear to have thought of everything."

"I believe I have," Macher replied. He got up from his

seat, opened the box, and began to set the timer. "I'm setting the timer now, for ten AM, tomorrow's date." He did so, then closed the box and taped it securely shut.

"That's it?"

"That's it." Macher handed him a box of latex gloves. "Now put these on and take the box and the blanket down to your office. You can explain it to Swenson there, and make sure he has gloves for handling the material. All he has to do is stop at the curb, get the box out of his trunk, place it and the blanket, and he's out of there in a minute or so. Also, while he's at it, tell him to tape his license plate and leave the tape on until he's well clear of the house."

Jake picked up the box. "I'll keep thinking about it and see if there are any other possible hitches."

"You do that," Macher said. He sat down, feeling much better than he had an hour before.

51

Dan Swenson was sitting at his desk, reading a gun magazine, when his phone rang. "Swenson."

"Dan, it's Jake Herman. Come to my office, will you? I have an assignment for you."

"Be right there, Jake," Swenson said, excited. He had been sitting around for weeks with little or nothing to do, and he hoped for an assignment of some consequence.

Swenson knocked on Herman's door.

"Come!"

Swenson opened the door and walked in. "Good morning, Jake."

"Good morning, Dan. Take a seat."

Swenson did so.

"I expect you must be itching for something to do," Jake said.

"You bet I am."

"This involves driving to New York, setting a package

in place outside a town house, then driving back here in time for work tomorrow morning."

"I can do that."

"If you do this job exactly as instructed, some bad people are going to get hurt."

"I don't have a problem with that," Swenson said, meaning it.

Jake reached across the desk and handed him a pair of latex gloves. "Put these on."

Swenson did so.

"You are to wear those at any time when your hands come in contact with this package," Jake said, indicating the box on his desk. "It's entirely for your protection."

"I understand," Swenson said.

"You are to depart here at ten PM tonight and drive to this address." He pushed an index card across the desk. "At approximately three AM, you will park at the curb in front of the house, take the box and the accompanying steel blanket from the trunk of your car, and go to the downstairs, street door, which has a brass plate on it with the name of a law firm engraved, 'The Barrington Practice.'"

"I see."

"To the left of the door, under a window, is a concrete flower box. You are to slide the box out enough to admit the package, set it there, then wrap the street side of the box in the steel blanket, then push the flower box back in place to hold the package there."

"I understand," Swenson said.

"You are then to return to your car, close the trunk, and put masking tape over your license plate, then drive away. When you are several blocks away, you are to remove the masking tape, then drive back to your home in time to leave for work at your usual hour. Is there anything you do not understand about these instructions?"

"No, Jake."

"Repeat them to me," Jake said.

Swenson did so flawlessly.

"After you have successfully completed your mission, there will be a ten-thousand-dollar cash reward paid to you for service above and beyond the call."

"Thank you, Jake, that's very generous. I would have done it for nothing."

"Remember this—you are not to put the cash into any bank account. You may keep it in your safe at home or your office or in a safe-deposit box at your bank, and use it as you see fit, but it must not pass through any bank account. Is that clear?"

"Of course—a normal precaution."

"You should put the box in your car trunk now, before the rest of the staff get here."

Swenson put on the latex gloves, set the steel blanket on top of the package, picked it up, and walked it to the alley behind the building, where the company cars were parked. He set the box in place and put the blanket beside it, then went back inside, got a roll of masking tape from his desk, and returned to the car, where he set it beside the box and closed the trunk, locking it.

"You forgot this," a voice said from behind him, causing him to jump. Jake was standing there holding an index card. "It's the address. You might put it into your car's GPS, but don't forget to delete it after your mission is completed."

"Got it," Swenson said, pocketing the card.

*   *   *

THAT NIGHT STONE had dinner alone in his study, then went up to his bedroom, undressed, got into bed, and switched on the TV. He found an interesting movie among those he had TiVoed for later viewing and switched it on. As the credits were rolling, he picked up his iPhone and checked his appointments for the following morning. Only one: Eliot Crenshaw, the new corporate counsel for the St. Clair company, was coming to drop off the company's books and some other computer records at 9:30. He made a mental note to be at his desk by that time.

DAN SWENSON HAD a late dinner with Jake Herman, as part of his alibi for the evening, then returned to his apartment. He watched a little TV, put on some fresh clothes and a shoulder holster and his 9mm H&K semi-automatic, which he was licensed to carry in Virginia and D.C., and left his apartment at 10:30 for the drive to New York. He checked his fuel level—plenty for the drive up and back, no stopping for gas—then he started the car and entered the address of his target house into his on-board GPS. Shortly, he was on the interstate, driving toward New York.

He left the tunnel at half past two, then drove to the address in his GPS. He stopped, got out of the car, looked around, then drove around the block again. He pulled to a halt on the uptown side of the street, immediately in front of the target address, then he got out of the car and went to the door, finding the promised brass plate.

He went back to the car, opened the trunk, pulled on his latex gloves, then set the blanket on top of the package and carried it to the door. He had another look around, found the block deserted, then pulled the concrete flower box away from the wall, which was harder than he had thought it would be.

He picked up the box, set it down behind the flower box, then unfolded the steel blanket and wrapped it around the three sides of the box and pushed the flower box back into place. He examined his work and thought it looked good.

He went back to his car, opened the trunk, removed the masking tape, and knelt down to tape over his license plate. He had just finished when a set of headlights turned the corner and a car stopped behind his car, emitting a short blast on its whooper.

Swenson stood up to face the two policemen getting out of their patrol car. "Good evening," he said to them.

"Yeah," the driving cop said. "Tell me, how come you are obliterating your license plate with tape? Don't you know it's a serious misdemeanor to drive with an obliterated tag?"

"I'm sorry, Officer," Swenson said, but he didn't have a story ready for this, and he was stuck.

"Let me see your license, registration, and insurance card," the cop said.

"Of course, Officer," Swenson said. "I'll have to get it from the glove compartment."

"Go ahead, but keep your hands in sight."

Swenson felt a rising wave of panic. If the cops discovered the package, he would be in serious trouble, and it suddenly occurred to him that he was not licensed to carry in New York City. He turned to walk toward the driver's door.

"Hold it," the cop said.

Swenson stopped.

"The glove compartment is on the other side of the car."

Swenson turned slightly to hide his right hand, then he drew the 9mm from his shoulder holster, turned, and fired a round each at the two cops. Both went down immediately.

He turned to get into the driver's seat when he heard and felt two shots in the middle of his back, and he fell into the gutter.

52

Stone was sleeping soundly when he was awakened by a distant popping, sounding like gunshots. He listened for a moment more, then drifted off again.

THE PHONE RANG. Stone opened an eye and glanced at the bedside clock: 6:10 AM. He reached for the phone. "Barrington," he croaked.

"It's Dino. How come you're still asleep? Don't you know what happened?"

"No, because I'm still asleep."

"There was a police shooting in front of your house about three AM."

"Why?" Stone asked, still foggy.

"Why? Who the hell knows why? A patrol car rumbled some guy who was putting tape on his license plate. They asked for his paperwork, and he shot both of them, then both of them shot him."

Stone was awake now. "Anybody dead?"

"Not yet. The cops were wearing vests, and the shooter drilled them both dead center, so he was no amateur."

"What about the shooter?"

"He's in Bellevue, still unconscious. I've got detectives standing by to question him when he wakes up."

"I can't think of any reason why any of that might have happened in front of my house," Stone said.

"I figured."

"Then you could have called me in another hour, and I could have slept on."

Dino hung up.

It was too early for breakfast to come up in the dumb-waiter, so Stone switched on the TV and surfed the morning shows. He got half a report from a local station about the shooting, but no new information. He called Dino on his cell.

"Bacchetti."

"Anything new from the shooter in Bellevue?"

"He's still unconscious. I told you I'd call you when I know something. Oh, the shooter's car is registered to an Arlington, Virginia, company, EMServices. Guess who that is?" Dino hung up.

AT SEVEN THE dumbwaiter rang; breakfast arrived with the *Times*, and Stone began his day all over again. He remembered he had a 9:30 appointment, so he was sitting at his desk on time. He finished the crossword and buzzed Joan. "Any sign of Eliot Crenshaw?"

"He called to say he was running late."

"Thanks." Stone finished the crossword. He glanced at his watch: 9:52. Bob, who was sitting at his feet, suddenly sat up and barked once.

"What is it, Bob?"

Bob barked again, then, surprisingly, he got an answer from outside. That set off a cascade of barking both indoors and out.

Stone got up and went to Joan's office. "What's going on? Bob's going nuts."

"So is a dog outside."

Stone went to the door and opened it. Outside, Eliot Crenshaw stood, his briefcase in one hand and Bessie's leash in the other. "What's happening, Eliot?"

"Bessie is locked onto your flower box," the lawyer said.

"Inside, quick," Stone said.

Joan appeared in the doorway. "What's happening?"

"Joan," Stone said, "take Eliot and his dog, Bessie, and go sit in the garden."

"The garden?"

"Right now, please!" She finally obeyed him, and the barking moved inside. Stone went to the flower box and saw the object behind it. There was a steel blanket, like those at construction sites, hiding something. He tugged at it, exposing a cardboard box, taped shut. He took a penknife from his pocket and slit the tape, then opened the box and brushed away some foam peanuts.

Inside the box, a digital timer was counting down from fifty-nine seconds. Foolishly, he turned over the box and emptied the contents: two blocks of plastique. "Oh, shit," he said aloud. He followed the wires from the timer to the detonators and pulled them out of the explosive, then he threw the timer with the detonators still attached onto the sidewalk. Almost immediately, the detonators exploded, like two cherry bombs, knocking him backward. His cell phone started ringing.

"Hello?"

"It's Dino. The shooter at Bellevue is awake, and he told my detectives that he planted a bomb outside your house. The bomb squad is on their way."

"Tell them they're a little late, but to come ahead anyway."

"The bomb went off?"

"The two detonators did. Fortunately, I had separated them from the two blocks of plastic explosives."

"Two blocks?"

"About a kilo each, I'd estimate."

"Well, get the fuck away from it! It could still go off."

Stone went inside and walked through his office and the kitchen to the rear garden. The two dogs were dancing around each other, making dog noises.

"I heard shots," Eliot said.

"Not shots, detonators," Stone replied.

"Not again," Eliot said.

"Again," Stone replied.

LIEUTENANT MARCONI of the bomb squad came into Stone's office. "You're all clear," he said. "You're becoming our best customer, you know."

"I'm sorry about that," Stone said. "I'd prefer not to be."

"That was high-quality stuff," Marconi said. "Just like last time. It would have done serious damage to your house and both sides of the street, and that concrete flower box would have become very dangerous shrapnel."

Stone held up a hand. "Don't tell me any more, I won't sleep tonight."

"As you wish. Good morning." Marconi left, and a moment later Dino joined them. "How you feeling?" Dino asked.

"Still scared."

Bob and Bessie went to greet Dino.

"Dino, this is Eliot Crenshaw, a lawyer for St. Clair. This is his second bomb scare with me, and his dog, Bessie, saved our asses again, with a little help from Bob."

"Good dog," Dino said, patting her. "Our shooter at Bellevue is talking," he said.

"Did he implicate Macher?"

Dino shook his head. "Not Macher, but Jake Herman, his guy. He's the one who briefed the bomber, whose name is Daniel Swenson, ex-Army special forces. He's being charged with two counts of attempted murder of a police officer—and, of course, for the bomb. The Arlington cops are on their way to pick up Herman now."

"Jesus, Dino, offer this Swenson whatever you have to to get him to implicate Macher. Let's put them both away."

"I'd like nothing better," Dino said, "but Macher never spoke a word to Swenson about this. Herman did all the talking. Still, Arlington is getting a warrant to search Macher's offices."

"Thank God for small favors."

53

Erik Macher was on his way to the office, listening to satellite news, when he heard the report.

"Last night in New York City, in the wee hours, an NYPD patrol car came across a man in the East Forties putting tape over his license plate. When the two officers questioned him, the man drew a pistol and shot them both, then was shot in return by the two officers. A police spokesman said that both officers were wearing ballistic vests and are not seriously injured, and the shooter is at Bellevue Hospital and talking to officers. He is expected to recover."

Macher called Jake Herman on his cell.

"Yeah?"

"Have you heard the news?"

"Barrington is dead?"

"No, but Swenson is in Bellevue with two gunshot wounds, and he's talking."

"Oh, shit."

"You'd better not come to work, and don't go home, either."

"I'm at home now."

"Well, get out of there and call me at mid-morning. I'll deal with the police."

"Where am I supposed to go?"

"Go get some breakfast or something, just go!" Macher hung up. He drove to his office and parked out back, then let himself into the building and ran to his office. He opened his safe, pulled on some latex gloves, and put his timers and detonators into the box containing the remainder of his explosives, then took it out of the safe and into the alley. He walked fifty yards away and put the box carefully into a neighbor's dumpster, then returned to his office and had a good look around for any trace of the explosives. He went to Jake's office and did the same, then he went back to his desk and sat down.

THE POLICE ARRIVED around 8:30. They hammered on the front door, and he raced to open it before they crashed in.

"Good morning," he said to the four armed and suited men and two detectives. "Can I help you?"

"Mind if we come in?" a detective asked.

He led them to his office and sat down. "Now," he said, "what's this all about?"

"Have you listened to the news this morning?"

"I'm afraid not. Is there something I should know about?"

"Do you have two employees named Jacob Herman and Daniel Swenson?"

"Yes, but they aren't in yet. I usually get in before anyone else."

"Do you know their whereabouts?"

Macher glanced at his watch. "I suppose they're on their way to work. You're welcome to wait for them. Would you like some coffee?"

"No, thanks, but while we're waiting, let me serve you with this warrant to search the premises." He handed Macher the document.

Macher dropped it, unread, on his desk and spread his hands. "Please help yourself," he said. "You don't need a warrant, I'm happy to help."

"Where are your two employees' offices?"

"Mr. Herman's is to your left at the end of the hall. Mr. Swenson is to your right at the other end."

He turned to his men. "Okay, two of you in each office, we'll take this room." He turned back to Macher. "Stand up."

Macher stood up, backed away from his desk, and leaned against the wall. "Let me know if I can help."

The two detectives went methodically through his desk and filing cabinets and asked him to open the safe. "I'm happy to do so. When do I get to know what this is all about?" He worked the combination.

One detective started on the safe. "You have permits for all these weapons?"

"In the box on the right-side shelf, along with my business license," Macher replied.

"It's like this," the other detective said, "last night in

New York City a patrol car came across your employee Swenson putting tape over his license plate."

"Swenson isn't supposed to be in New York," Macher said. "He's due here for work, like always."

"Well, he's in Bellevue Hospital, instead, with two bullets in him."

"Why would they shoot him?"

"Because he shot them first. Luckily, they were wearing protective gear."

"This is crazy!" Macher said, giving his best performance. "Swenson is a good man, a decorated veteran of the wars in Iraq and Afghanistan."

"Well, now he's charged with two counts of attempted murder."

"This is insane. What does Swenson have to say?"

A uniform came back. "The offices are clean of anything that could be of use to us."

"Listen," Macher said, "it sounds like Swenson went off his rocker. He's had problems with post-traumatic stress disorder, going back to his army days. I can't think of any other reason he'd go to New York, shoot two policemen."

"We don't know. We were hoping to find some answers here. When did you last speak to Mr. Herman?"

"Yesterday when he left work. I called him on the way to work this morning but got his voice mail. He should have been at work an hour and a half ago."

The detective gave him a card. "When you hear from Herman, give us a call, and tell him not to go anywhere until we've talked to him."

Macher took the card. "I hope you'll ask your colleagues in New York to treat Dan Swenson like a wounded veteran, instead of a criminal suspect."

"We'll pass along the information." The detectives thanked him for his cooperation and left.

Another fifteen minutes passed before Jake Herman called.

"Where are you, Jake?"

"Down the street in a diner. You know the one."

"The cops have already been here and torn the place apart, but they didn't find anything."

"I don't want to talk on the phone," Jake said. "We need to meet."

"Where?"

"I don't know, someplace they'd never look for me."

"I can think of a place," Macher said. "It belongs to Ed Rawls, but he's at his house in Maine. It's an hour, hour and a half from here." He gave him directions. "If you get there before I do, break in, but disable the alarm first. I'll get there as fast as I can."

"Okay."

Macher's secretary walked in. "This place is a mess," she said.

"I have to go out," Macher said. "Please tidy up. Jake and Dan won't be in today."

"When will you be back?"

"Tomorrow, the next day, maybe. We've got a new client."

Macher went into the alley, removed the explosives from the neighbor's dumpster, and put them in the trunk of his car. He chose weapons from the safe, then got the car started and headed south.

54

Jake Herman got to the house first. He found the junction box for the alarm system and disconnected it, then he picked the lock on the back door, went in, unlocked the other doors, and made himself some coffee in the kitchen. The phone rang, but it soon stopped.

He liked the house, particularly the study, and he made himself at home in there with the *Washington Post* and the *New York Times*, which he had picked up at the diner.

MACHER, USING A burner phone, called Jake's cell from the road.

"Yeah?"

"Where are you?"

"At the house. Pretty nice."

"I thought you'd been there before. We had the place under surveillance for a few days a while back."

"Nope. I didn't get that duty."

"Did you disconnect the alarm?"

"I did."

"What are you doing now?"

"Reading the papers and having some of our host's coffee. There's no food in the house, so if you're planning to be here for a while, you'd better pick up some groceries."

"Okay, I'll do that. See you in an hour or so." Macher hung up and turned into a shopping center, where there was a supermarket. Half an hour later he was back on the road with a trunk full of food and drink.

STONE WAS AT his desk when Joan buzzed. "Ed Rawls for you on one."

"Hello, Ed."

"Morning, Stone. Anything unusual happening there?"

"Well, let's see. In the middle of the night there was a gun battle in front of my house, and the perpetrator is in Bellevue with a couple of slugs in him. Turns out, he had planted a bomb outside before he was arrested, but we got that taken care of before it could go off."

"Sounds like Macher."

"Sounds exactly like Macher. The perp's car was registered to his Virginia security company, and the Arlington police have searched his offices, looking for Jake Herman, his number one man, who was implicated by the shooter. Macher was in his office in Arlington, but he's probably on the run by now."

"Funny you should mention that," Rawls said. "I got a call from the alarm system monitor for my Virginia house. Someone has disconnected the alarm."

"I'll call Dino and see that the local police are notified."

"My house is in the country, and the local sheriff's office is understaffed. They don't think much of domestic alarm system calls, since nine out of ten are homeowners who have entered the wrong code or otherwise fucked it up."

"What do you want to do, then?"

"I'm headed to Virginia this morning, anyway. It's getting too cold for me in Maine. I was going to drive, but I think I'll charter a light airplane from the Rockland airport. If I start now, I can be down there in, say, three hours."

"You'd better go armed, if Jake Herman is in your house."

"Where do you think Macher is?" Ed asked.

"No idea. I'll see what Dino knows and get back to you."

Stone dialed the number.

"Bacchetti."

"It's Stone. Can you get another fix on Macher's cell phone?"

"Hang on." Dino put him on hold for a minute, then came back. "He's still in Virginia, but he's moved south to a spot not far from the workplace of your buddy Lance Cabot."

"That sounds like Ed Rawls's house."

"Is Ed down there?"

"No, but he's headed that way. Thanks." Stone hung up and called Rawls.

Rawls was packing when Stone called. "Hello?"

"Ed, Dino's got a fix on Macher, and he's at a location not far from Langley. That sound familiar?"

"You bet your sweet ass, it does. I gotta run." He called the airport and ordered up their Cessna 182, then finished packing. He called a local cab to take him to the airport.

STONE CALLED DINO.

"Bacchetti."

"I just got a call from Ed Rawls. Somebody has disconnected the alarm at his house in Virginia. I told him about your hit on Macher's phone, and he's on the way down there. I don't want him to walk in on them. Can you call the cop shop down there and get them to check the house?"

"Listen, I can't call out the local gendarmerie in some Podunk place in another state, just because Ed Rawls has a hair up his ass. Does he have a security system?"

"Yes, and it went off this morning."

"If they get an alarm anomaly, somebody'll check it out. I'm not going to get involved."

"Do the Arlington police know where Macher is now?"

"He was in his office an hour ago, when they left."

"Okay, thanks." Stone hung up and Googled Macher's company, then called.

"EMServices," a woman said.

"Erik Macher, please."

"He's out at the moment. Who's calling?"

"A friend. When do you expect him back?"

"It may be a day or two, he said."

"Thanks." Stone hung up and called Rawls back.

"Rawls."

"Macher's office says he's gone for a couple of days. Does he know about your house?"

"He certainly does. He had surveillance on it for several days."

"What's the nearest airport?"

"I'm flying into Manassas. They're picking me up in half an hour to go to Islesboro Airport."

"Tell you what, I'll fly into Manassas, too. Meet me there."

"Okay. Whoever lands first can just wait."

"Right. Are you armed?"

"You bet your ass."

"I'm not licensed down there."

"The rural law tends to look kindly on that sort of thing if you're licensed anywhere at all."

"Okay, Ed, I'll see you when I see you." They hung up. Stone buzzed Joan.

"Yes, boss?"

"I've got to go somewhere. Please call the airport and have the airplane brought up and refueled, pronto, and tell Fred I need a ride."

"Will do."

Stone hung up and went upstairs to pack a bag. Fred drove him to the airport, and he filed a flight plan for Manassas on the way. The airplane was on the ramp when he arrived; he did his usual preflight inspection, then ran through the cockpit checklist and got a clearance. That done, he started the engines, finished his checklist, and got permission to taxi. There were a few corporate jets ahead of him, and it took another half hour to get off the ground.

The flight time was a little over an hour, so he stayed fairly low, at 20,000 feet, instead of climbing to 41,000. It burned more fuel down there, but it saved time on ascent and descent. The weather was clear at both ends, so he anticipated no delays.

55

Jake read one of Rawls's books for a while but felt antsy. It was nice outside, so he went for a little walk. The first nip of autumn was in the air, and there was a hint of color in the trees around the house.

As he strolled around the ample backyard he noticed a pile of dirt behind the garage. Closer inspection revealed a brand-new propane tank set in the hole, and an old, rusty one on the ground beside it. The new tank appeared to be connected, and the heat was on in the house. A backhoe stood beside the hole. Apparently, the tank had been installed and the backhoe operator had left until the plumber arrived to make the connection.

He strolled on until he came to a barbed-wire fence that seemed to separate Rawls's property from the farm beyond. A few dairy cattle grazed beyond that. He felt a hunger pang and wished Macher would hurry up.

On his way back, he inspected the garage, found it

unlocked and an old Mercedes inside. He thought it would be a good idea to get his own car out of sight, so he moved it into the garage and closed the doors.

MACHER WAS NEARLY to the house when his cell rang.

"Yes?"

It was his secretary. "Someone called for you half an hour ago."

"Who?"

"He said he was a friend, wouldn't leave a name."

"If he calls again, give him my cell number."

"As you wish." He hung up. That wouldn't have been the police, since they had already visited, and a client would have given his name. He considered Barrington as a possibility, but dismissed it as being too far-fetched. He drove on toward his destination.

STONE GOT THE Manassas automated weather: the wind was from the south at ten knots, so he called the tower and requested runway 16 and set the airplane down there. He rolled out and taxied back to the FBO, expecting Rawls to come out to greet him, but he didn't show. Probably still in the air.

Inside he requested fuel and hangar space and rented a car. Half an hour later a Cessna 182 rolled up to the FBO, cut its engine, and Rawls got out. Stone met him on the ramp and put his bags into the car, along with his own. Rawls headed inside for the head, then came back and got into the car.

"I'll need directions," Stone said, and Rawls gave them.

"What's your plan when we get there, Ed?"

"Don't have one," Rawls replied. "I don't think we'll just walk in, though. Why don't we stop for a late lunch, then take our time. I'd rather approach the place after dark. If Herman is there, he'll have a light on."

"Makes sense."

Rawls guided Stone to a country restaurant, and they had a leisurely lunch.

"We could pay Lance Cabot a surprise call," Rawls said. "The Agency is ten minutes from here, and we go right past it."

"I don't think Lance and I have anything in particular to say to each other right now." He told Rawls about Lance's disinterest in connecting the CIA explosives to Erik Macher.

"That sounds like Lance," Rawls said. "There was nothing in it for him, so he said no."

MACHER PULLED UP to the house in the late afternoon. He didn't see Jake's car, so he approached the house with caution. Jake saw him through a window and opened a door to admit him.

"Where's your car?" Macher asked.

"I put it in the garage."

"Is there room for mine?"

"No, Rawls's car is taking up the other space."

Macher parked next to the house. "Have you had a look around?"

"Yeah," Jake said, "I took a walk."

"Anything unusual going on?"

"There's a backhoe parked behind the garage, waiting

to bury a new propane tank, apparently just installed, so tomorrow somebody might turn up to fill the hole. I don't think he'll need to speak to us. Did you bring food?"

"Yep, booze, too. I could use a drink."

"I could use one, too," Jake said, "and something to eat."

They went inside the house, collecting Macher's bag on the way. Jake saw the explosives in the box in the trunk. "Why did you bring the plastique?"

"I wanted to get it out of the office. The cops have searched it once, but I moved it to a dumpster. You never know when they'll come back."

"What did they say about Dan Swenson?"

"That he's expected to recover."

"Did they mention the bomb?"

"No."

"That must mean it didn't go off. What time were they at the office?"

"They left a little before ten."

"So the bomb might still have gone off?"

"I don't think so," Macher said. "I had the satellite radio news on the whole way down here and there was no mention of it."

They went into the kitchen, and Jake heated up a can of chili while they sipped a scotch.

STONE AND RAWLS cruised slowly past the house as the sun was going down and saw Macher's Mercedes.

"What does Macher drive?" Ed asked.

"A Mercedes S550, just like that one," Stone replied. They drove on past.

56

tone, directed by Ed Rawls, found a spot to park in some high weeds, within sight of the house. Stone left the satellite radio on a jazz station so they wouldn't have to talk, but Rawls wanted to talk anyway.

"This is like old times, in my younger days with the Agency," he said. "Except I would be on my belly in the grass, instead of sitting in a comfortable chair and listening to good jazz from the sky."

"Did you like those days?" Stone asked, just to keep him going.

"I did," Rawls replied. "In fact, I loved them. I was serving my country and at the same time, venting my hatred of the Soviets and the harm they were causing in the world. Every time we hurt them I felt genuine satisfaction."

"What about later, when you were running agents instead of being run?"

"Running others was harder than being run. The only safety I could give them was in the planning. Once they were out in the field, all I could do was worry, and I did."

"Did many of them not come back?"

"A few. I could name their names and tell you their records, which I memorized. We hardly ever got to bury them. They're just stars on a wall at Langley, not even their names."

"You said you'd heard of Macher while you were still in harness. What did you hear?"

"I told you some of it—a propensity for violence, whether called for or not. He'd shoot the opposition if he had the chance. It caused a backlash from the Soviets and the East Germans that did not react to our benefit. For that, I hate the son of a bitch, to this day."

"Do you mean to kill him tonight?" Stone asked.

"If he gives me an excuse that will work with the cops. I'm not willing to go to jail for it. Are you going to back me?"

"If I can," Stone replied.

"That's very reassuring," Rawls said sarcastically.

"After all, he's tried to kill me a couple of times—tried hard, too. I just got lucky."

"I should think that would be reason enough just to put two in his head," Rawls said. "What does it take to get you riled enough to do something about it?"

"I haven't figured that out yet," Stone replied.

"Well, you'd better think on it, because if we get within range of these two, I think we can count on rounds coming our way."

"That would certainly call for a response," Stone said.

They sat quietly for a while, waiting for dark.

Rawls finally spoke again, and his voice was without its hard edge. "You know, I've known a lot of people in my life—still know a lot of them—but I think you're the only friend I've got."

"Why do you think that is?" Stone asked, genuinely curious.

"Kate used to be my friend," Rawls said. "I was her mentor, and I was a good one, too. But when I had my trouble, she took great personal offense, and we weren't friends anymore."

Stone knew about that.

"Since that time, you are the only person who has laid it on the line for me, and I want you to know I'm grateful for that."

"You're welcome, but let's not overstate the case."

"I'm not overstating nothing. Who else would be with me here right now?"

Stone didn't have an answer for that.

They were silent for a while, and Stone began to doze a bit. Some time later, he wasn't sure how long, Rawls poked him in the ribs.

"What?" Stone asked.

"A light just went on in the house," Rawls said. "In my study, I think."

"Nothing else?"

"Nothing else."

"Then that would mean they're both in your study, wouldn't it?"

"No," Rawls said, "that would mean that at least one

of them is in my study. The other could be upstairs, asleep, or napping on the living room sofa. Let's drift down there and see."

As the car began to move an outdoor light came on behind the house.

MACHER GOT UP from the living room sofa, where he had been napping and making decisions. He went to the study door where Jake was reading. "Jake?"

"Yep?"

"Come show me this backhoe out back."

"What for?"

"I'm curious about something."

"What?"

"Show me, and I'll tell you, if it means something."

Jake put down his book and stood up. "All right, follow me." He took out a flashlight, led the way to the rear of the house and out the door.

As his foot touched the back steps, Macher turned on the outside light. "Easier to see," he said.

Jake led the way behind the garage, then switched on his light to illuminate the shadows.

"You know how to run a backhoe, Jake?" Macher asked.

"Yeah, I worked construction summers during college. I can handle most gear. We shouldn't cover it up, though—somebody will be back to do that."

"Right." They were standing on the edge of the pit, looking at the new tank. "Let me have your flashlight for a minute," Macher said.

"Sure," Jake said, handing it over.

Macher shot Jake in the back of the head; he crumpled, then fell into the pit, alongside the tank. He was still moving. Macher reached out and put one foot on the tank, his other still on the edge of the pit, straddling Jake. Being careful not to hit the tank, Macher put another round into Jake's head. He crumpled, relaxed, and fell deeper into the pit, below the tank. If you weren't looking for it, Macher thought, you wouldn't see it.

Still, he had to be sure.

COASTING DOWN A small hill with the windows down, Stone and Ed heard the first shot and saw the flash from the rear of the garage, then they heard the second shot.

"Somebody's in that pit with my new propane tank," Rawls said.

"Pit?"

"I ordered a new tank. The plumber has hooked it up, but they haven't finished the job yet. The hole still has to be filled."

"Which one do you think is in the pit?" Stone asked.

"It would be unlike Macher to be," Ed replied.

USING JAKE'S FLASHLIGHT, Macher found a shovel. He holstered his weapon, held the flashlight in his teeth, and began shoveling dirt into the crevice where Jake's body lay. It only took a few shovelfuls to make the body invisible. He returned the shovel to its original position and trudged back toward the house.

He needed a night's sleep before he returned to Arlington. He was relieved to have Jake out of the way; it left him in the clear, and the trail from the New York incident would stop with Jake. They might have their suspicions, but they wouldn't have the evidence. He would send someone in a day or two to pick up Jake's company car.

57

S tone had passed the house, now. He made a U-turn, and Ed told him to park in the weeds again.

"He's going to need sleep," Ed said. "Let's let him settle in awhile."

"And then what?" Stone asked.

"Then we can capture us a murderer," Ed replied. "Whichever one it is, then we call the cops."

"You're still making this up as you go along, aren't you?" Stone asked.

"Yep. Let's get a little sleep ourselves." He laid his head against the seat back and seemed instantly asleep.

Stone dozed, too, and when he awoke the moon had set, and it was pitch-dark: no lights in the house. As he shifted his weight, Rawls woke, too.

"Ah, good," Ed said, "I feel better rested now."

"What's your plan?" Stone asked.

"I want to get a look inside that Mercedes," Rawls said.

"What if it's locked?"

"Who would lock his car out here in the wilderness?" He got out of the car, closed the door softly, and, followed by Stone, crossed the road and walked toward the house. At the entrance to the driveway, which was paved, Rawls stopped and took off his shoes, and Stone followed suit.

"Don't use your flashlight unless you have to," Rawls said. He walked silently up the driveway, stopped, and signaled for Stone to wait, then he went to the driver's-side door of the Mercedes, shone his light inside briefly, and the trunk lid opened without a sound.

Rawls walked to the rear of the car, set his shoes inside the trunk, then played his light around the interior. He seemed to open a box, then he set down his light and worked for perhaps a minute at something, then he switched off the light, picked up his shoes, silently closed the trunk lid, and joined Stone.

"Let's go have a look behind the garage," Rawls said.

Stone followed him, keeping the garage between them and the house. Ed waited until they were standing on the edge of the dark pit before he switched on his flashlight. "Well," Ed said, holding the beam steady, "you wouldn't notice unless you were looking for him, would you?"

"No," Stone replied, "you wouldn't."

"Let's go back to our car," Rawls said.

Stone followed him back to the road, where they put their shoes back on and walked the few yards to the car. "Why aren't we rousting Macher?" he asked.

"Well," Rawls said, "I'd rather not tiptoe into the house and up the stairs to the bedroom, where he's likely sleeping with a gun next to him. It's an old house, and it's creaky in places. I'd rather wait until he comes downstairs in the morning and gets into his car. I'll give him the option of running."

"I'll take the backseat," Stone said, opening the door and crawling in. He was, shortly, fast asleep.

STONE WAS AWAKENED at sunrise by the starting of the car. He sat up as Rawls put it into gear and drove the fifty yards that separated them from the house. To Stone's surprise, Rawls parked on the opposite side of the road at the entrance to the driveway, leaving it clear.

Ed switched off the engine. "Now," he said.

Stone got out of the car, peed into a ditch, then got into the front passenger seat. There was no traffic any-where. "Now what?" he asked.

"Mr. Macher has stirred," Ed said. "I caught a whiff of coffee on the air. He'll be leaving soon."

"Why do you think that?"

"Because he won't want to be here when the backhoe operator arrives, in case the fellow should notice that there's a corpse in the hole with the tank. Macher will stop somewhere nearby where he has a view, and make sure the operator does his work and leaves without the cops arriving. That done, he'll drive home a free man, with no evidence of anything against him. Then, in due course, he'll find a way to murder you."

"I'm tired of people trying to murder me," Stone said.

"Well, he's screwed up three times. Fourth time lucky, I reckon. He'll take the greatest care next time."

"You're very encouraging," Stone said.

"Not to worry," Ed said, "he won't get far, then he'll have a terrible accident."

"I don't understand," Stone said.

"You will in a little while. By the way, I think you should keep your weapon in its holster."

"You won't need help?"

"I'll have all the help I need, and I and my weapon are legal in Virginia."

"Whatever you say," Stone said. He was hungry; he started thinking about eggs and bacon.

"HERE WE GO!" Rawls shouted. He began getting out of the car.

Stone looked up to see Macher, carrying a small suitcase, come out of the kitchen door and start for his car. He didn't seem to notice the car parked across the road with a man leaning against it.

Macher got into the Mercedes, made a U-turn, drove to the head of the driveway, and stopped. Now he was staring straight ahead at Ed Rawls.

"Does he know you?" Stone asked.

"Maybe, maybe not," Rawls replied. "Stop! Murder!" he whispered aloud.

Then Macher saw Stone.

"What's your plan, Ed?"

"I'm going to put a few rounds into the man's trunk, where he has stored two bricks of gelignite."

"I've got bad news for you, Ed."

"What's that?"

"You can fire all the bullets you like into gelignite, and they won't ignite it."

"We'll see," Ed said.

Macher decided it was time to move. He started a right turn into the road and accelerated. Ed began firing at the lower right of his trunk. The fourth round bore fruit.

Fortunately, the car was far enough away to protect the shooter and his friend, because the explosion was like what Stone thought would be produced by a missile from a passing fighter plane. Assisted by the fuel in the tank, the car erupted into an enormous fireball, and the noise pinned their ears back, and the shockwave knocked them down. Small bits of the car rained down around them, some of them flaming.

The two men got to their feet. "You're right, Stone," Ed said, "a bullet into the plastique wouldn't ignite it, but if there were half a dozen detonators plugged into it and the bullet struck one of those, then that, as you can see, would do the job."

"I can't bring myself to disagree," Stone said, brushing himself off.

Ed reached into the car and turned on the emergency blinkers. "Why don't we go into the house, have some breakfast, call the cops, and get our stories straight?"

58

Stone and Rawls sat across the kitchen table from a Captain Sawyer, chief of the Virginia State Police Bureau of Criminal Investigation, who looked tired and a little baffled.

"Mr. Rawls," Sawyer said, "I have to tell you, in thirty years of serving in law enforcement, that is the most complicated story I have ever heard."

"That's the way it happened," Rawls replied. "Sometimes life is complicated."

"Life is *usually* complicated," Sawyer replied, "but not *that* complicated." He looked at Stone, who had remained mostly mute. "Mr. Barrington, is that the way you saw it happen?"

"Captain, I'm Mr. Rawls's attorney. I wouldn't let him lie to a law enforcement officer."

"Well, I spoke to Commissioner Bacchetti, in New York, as you suggested, and he backs you up about the threat constituted by Jacob Herman and Erik Macher. After hearing about them, I'm not surprised there were explosives in the trunk of Macher's car."

"I was surprised," Rawls said. "I was aiming at his right rear tire, not his trunk."

Stone kicked him under the table.

"But that's all I've got to tell you," Rawls said.

Stone breathed a sigh of relief.

"Lieutenant," Sawyer said to the uniformed officer leaning against a kitchen counter, "I'm satisfied with Mr. Rawls's and Mr. Barrington's accounts of what happened here. You may remove Mr. Herman's body to the state crime lab. Have you found any of Mr. Macher?"

"A few charred pieces of bone," the lieutenant replied. "I guess everything else was just vaporized."

"I'm not surprised," Sawyer said. "That must have been some explosion. We got nine-one-one calls from miles around. Most folks thought there had been a plane crash."

"I'm not surprised," Rawls said.

Sawyer slapped his palms on the table. "Well, I'm outta here, Lieutenant. You got anything else?"

"That's it for us, Captain."

The officers shook hands with Stone and Ed and filed out of the house. A moment later, the last of their vehicles had left the property.

"I'm glad that's over," Stone said, then he jumped as there came a knock on the door.

Rawls answered it and found a man in work clothes standing there.

"Mornin', Mr. Rawls," he said. "Is it okay now if I fill up that hole and get my backhoe outta here?"

"Go right ahead," Rawls said, "and send me a bill." He came back and sat down at the table.

"I thought you were going to talk us right into prison," Stone said.

"I've always been a good explainer."

"I wish I had a transcript of what you said, in case they ask me any more questions."

Rawls removed a small recorder from his shirt pocket. "I'll send you a transcript," he said. He got up, went to a drawer, and came back with a thick envelope. "And speaking of manuscripts, here's mine. There are letters from three publishers inside. They saw one of the earlier ones we disseminated a while back. Will you call them and get me a deal?"

Stone picked up the envelope and weighed it. "It seems to have grown a bit."

"I added a few things."

"Sure, Ed, I'll get it done. Now, I've got some calls to make and then do you mind if I borrow a bed? I need a few hours of sleep."

"Top of the stairs, to your left," Ed said. "In fact, I'm headed up to my bed now." He got up and headed for the stairs.

Stone conferenced in Mike Freeman and Charley Fox and gave them an abbreviated version of Ed's account to the police. "It's okay to pull all your people out of the Carlsson Clinic, Mike," Stone said. "I'll let them know."

"Done," Mike said, "and congratulations on a good outcome."

Stone called Paul Carlsson and told him he would shortly be free of security guards.

Carlsson seemed to speak a little hesitantly. "Ah, Stone, have you, ah, read your e-mails this morning?"

"No, Paul, I've been kind of busy."

"Well, Marisa has decided to stay on in Stockholm and run our clinic there. She'll explain everything in her e-mail."

"Thank you, Paul," Stone said, because he couldn't think of anything else to say.

"And thank you, Stone, for everything you've done for us."

The two men hung up, and Stone went to his e-mail: there it was.

Dear Stone,

I have to tell you I'm staying on in Stockholm for the foreseeable future. I'm needed to run the clinic here. I have to tell you, too, that I've hired a child-hood friend, a brilliant surgeon, to come aboard as chief of surgery. He and I have rekindled an old romance, and we will be married here in a few weeks. I'm sorry not to have been able to tell you this in person, but you weren't answering your phone. I'll treasure the memory of our time together.

Fondly,
Marisa

HIS SHOULDERS SLUMPED, and he realized he had been half expecting this. He'd just have to get over it. He was about to call Joan when his phone rang; private call.

"Hello?"

"Hi, it's Holly."

Stone brightened. "Hi, there, how are you?"

"Very well, thanks. Listen, I know this is short notice, but Kate is in town overnight from the campaign trail, and she and Will want to talk to you about something. Can you fly down here and stay the night in the family quarters?"

"As it happens, I'm down here already, at Ed Rawls's house, near Langley, and I'd love to."

"Wonderful. I've gotta run right now, but we'll catch up later. Use the West Wing entrance, and they'd like you there around six o'clock."

"See you then." He hung up, feeling much better, and called Joan.

"The Barrington Practice."

"Hi, I'm going to be in D.C. overnight. I should be home around midday tomorrow. I'll give Fred an ETA in the morning, and he can meet me at Teterboro."

"Okeydoke."

"Anything going on there?"

"Dino called and said he talked to the Virginia police, and not to call him until tomorrow. He's in meetings all day today."

"Okay. See you tomorrow." He hung up, then trudged upstairs and found the guest room. He stretched out on the bed, fully clothed, and pulled a quilt over him. As he did, his phone rang again.

"Hello?"

"Stone, it's Ed Eagle. How are you?"

"Just fine, Ed."

"There's something you need to think about."

"What's that?"

"You know the Dudleys, from Dallas, who have a place next door to you?"

"Never met them."

"Well, they have three acres, a beautiful piece of land, with a house on it that's smaller than yours. They want to sell, and the price is right. If you combine the two, you'd have five gorgeous acres and a big guesthouse. Interested?"

"Ed, I don't have room in my brain for that right now, but I'll think about it. Can I call you tomorrow?"

"Okay, but don't wait any longer or they'll give it to an agent to sell."

"Thanks, Ed. Talk to you tomorrow."

Stone stared at the ceiling. He felt relief at having Macher out of his way, and regret over Marisa's decision. It didn't take long for him to convince himself that it was better this way.

He drifted off into an untroubled sleep.

59

Stone entered the White House through the West Wing, was escorted upstairs to the family quarters by a Secret Service agent and installed in the Lincoln Bedroom. He freshened up, shook the wrinkles out of his blue blazer, and presented himself in the living room, where Kate and Will Lee and Holly were already on their first drink. A little boy was playing in front of the fireplace, and a glass of ice and a bottle of Knob Creek bourbon sat on the coffee table. All the domestic comforts.

Will shook his hand, and Kate and Holly offered warm hugs and kisses, then Will poured his drink. "Good God," he said, "is that your tiny baby?"

"Bill is three and a half now," Kate said.

Stone had never picked up a child, so he just tousled his hair. "Hello, Bill," he said. Bill ignored him.

"What have you been up to, Stone?" Kate asked.

"It would take me at least an hour to explain that," Stone said, "so I'll spare you."

"I assume you've heard about Holly's new job to come," she said.

"I heard a very interesting rumor," Stone replied.

"Well, it's true, but not for spreading around just yet. Even though we're ahead by double digits everywhere that matters, I don't want to appear overconfident by making new cabinet appointments before the election."

"I understand perfectly," he said.

Will spoke up. "Before we get any drunker," he said, "there's something we want to talk to you about."

"Please do."

"The next four years are going to bring some important changes in our lives—in fact, they've already started. To begin with, our personal attorney, Kerwin Smith, is retiring, and his firm is merging with another, and we're not really going to know the people there anymore. Kate and I would be very pleased if you would become our personal attorney."

"Why, thank you, Will, I'd be delighted. You don't feel the need of a Washington lawyer?"

"In the long run, we won't be spending a lot of time in Washington after Kate's second term. We'll be making some big changes."

"What sort of changes?"

"To begin with, my mother died a few months ago."

"I saw the obituary, and I was sorry to hear it."

"Thank you for your kind note. As a result, we've sold about five hundred acres of her land and her herd of cattle, along with the mail-order steak business. We're auctioning her bulls, not wishing to stay in the bull semen business, and they're bringing big prices on the market. We're keeping the house and about a hundred acres, and mine and Kate's presidential libraries will be built there. I've also sold Dad's and my law practice in Delano to our other partner."

"Where are you going to live when you're free people again?"

"We've got the apartment at the Carlyle in New York, and we'll probably sell that and buy something on Fifth Avenue, with a view of the park. Also, we want to buy a house in Santa Fe and spend a lot of time there."

"As you say, lots of changes."

"Kate's son, Peter Rule, has moved back from London and he's working for New York's Senator Saltonstall as his chief of staff. He's thinking of running for the other Senate seat at the midterm elections, as Senator Slade will be retiring."

"Great idea."

"I think he wants to be the new Ted Kennedy," Kate said.

"What will you do with the Georgetown house?" Stone asked.

"Peter seems to think it's too much house for him, so, unless he changes his mind, we'll sell it, I guess."

"May I make a recommendation?"

"Of course."

"Why don't you rent it to Holly, with an option to buy. We can't have a secretary of state living over an antiques shop on Pennsylvania Avenue."

"What a good idea!" Kate enthused.

"I like that, too," Will said.

"Is anybody going to ask me?" Holly said.

They ignored her.

"Maybe later," Stone said, "if Peter doesn't want to live there, I'll buy it and give it to the State Department as a permanent home for the secretary of state."

"I love it!" Kate said. "Actually, Peter already has a Georgetown house. When his father, Simon, died, he inherited that and everything else handed down by Simon's family, including a New York apartment and a place in the Hamptons and a pot of money."

"Lucky boy."

"Smart, too."

"Something else," Stone said, "as you know, I bought a house in Santa Fe a few months ago, and I think I went a house too far, since I can't spend much time there. It might suit your purposes very well. It has a nice master suite, a study, and a library, where you and Will can work on your memoirs, plus four guest bedrooms, two of them in a guesthouse, all on about two acres. And I heard yesterday that the property next door, which is about three acres, with a small house on it, is for sale. It might make a good headquarters for your Secret Service detail."

"Well," Kate said, "we're going to be in Santa Fe next week for a fund-raiser. Why don't we take a look at it?"

"Better yet," Stone said, "why don't you stay at the house? Ed Eagle can arrange for you to discreetly see the property next door."

"Perhaps," Will said, "we could do some sort of property swap—your Santa Fe place for our Georgetown house."

"That's an interesting idea," Stone said. "I know your

house, of course, but after you've been to Santa Fe we can talk more about that. Also, a client of mine, Laurence Hayward, bought a magnificent penthouse on Park Avenue, with Central Park views, and I think he's bitten off more than he can chew. He has houses in Santa Fe, Palm Beach, and in England. Perhaps you could take a look at his penthouse."

"Why not?" Will said, and Kate was nodding furiously.

"Something else you can do for us," Will said, reaching into a pocket and retrieving a loop-shaped piece of metal with a USB plug on one end. He handed it to Stone.

"What's this?" Stone asked.

"It's a thumb drive containing volume one of my memoirs, which runs from my birth in Georgia to Kate's election as President. I've been working on it for three years, and I'd like you to find me a publisher and make a deal."

"I'll look forward to reading it," Stone said, slipping the device into his pocket. "We could make the deal even more attractive if we include Kate's memoirs."

"What a good idea!" Kate said.

"And, of course, I could also offer Holly's book."

Holly looked startled. "What book?"

"Your memoirs, dummy," Kate said.

"I'm writing my memoirs?"

"Trust me," Stone said, "it will be a great read."

Holly shrugged. "Okay, I'm in."

"Suddenly, I'm a literary agent," Stone said.

"You'll be a great one," Will replied.

"I'll bring in my team at Woodman & Weld to handle your legal matters," Stone said. "I already have sort of a firm within the firm that handles a couple of other clients' accounts."

A butler appeared and called them to dinner.

"This is wonderful," Kate said. "All our problems solved before dinner!"

"We do what we can," Stone said.

60

Stone and Holly lay entwined in Lincoln's bed, or at least a reasonable facsimile.

"Things are moving fast, aren't they?" she said.

"Blindingly fast," Stone replied.

"Thank you for suggesting I rent Will and Kate's house. It's a wonderful place, and I'll have space to entertain after I take office."

"We'll find a way for you to live there as long as you're in Washington."

"Am I going somewhere else, after I'm booted out of Foggy Bottom?"

"We can think about that some more. We've talked about it, if you remember."

"I can't make any decisions now, there's too much ahead."

"Neither can I, so we'll both have lots of time to think about it."

"You'll come and visit, won't you?"

"Do you think we can get away with shacking up in Georgetown while you're secretary of state?"

"I think we should find out," she said.

"I think we should run that by Will and Kate, but not until after the election."

"Fair enough."

"Are you sleepy yet?"

"No, do you want to do it again so soon?"

"Well, sure, but I want to tell you about the past few weeks—a lot has happened."

"Shoot."

Stone began with St. Clair's attempted takeover of the Carlsson Clinic, omitting details of Marisa, and continued until the present day. "There," he said. "Now you're all caught up with me."

Holly replied with a small snore.

"Holly?"

Nothing.

Stone freed his arm, which was getting numb, turned over, and fell asleep himself.

AUTHOR'S NOTE

I am happy to hear from readers, but you should know that if you write to me in care of my publisher, three to six months will pass before I receive your letter, and when it finally arrives it will be one among many, and I will not be able to reply.

However, if you have access to the Internet, you may visit my website at www.stuartwoods.com, where there is a button for sending me e-mail. So far, I have been able to reply to all my e-mail, and I will continue to try to do so.

If you send me an e-mail and do not receive a reply, it is probably because you are among an alarming number of people who have entered their e-mail address incorrectly in their mail software. I have many of my replies returned as undeliverable.

Remember: e-mail, reply; snail mail, no reply.

When you e-mail, please do not send attachments, as I never open these. They can take twenty minutes to download, and they often contain viruses.

Please do not place me on your mailing lists for funny stories, prayers, political causes, charitable fund-raising, petitions, or sentimental claptrap. I get enough of that from people I already know. Generally speaking, when I get e-mail addressed to a large number of people, I immediately delete it without reading it.

Please do not send me your ideas for a book, as I have a policy of writing only what I myself invent. If you send me story ideas, I will immediately delete them without reading them. If you have a good idea for a book, write it yourself, but I will not be able to advise you on how to get it published. Buy a copy of *Writer's Market* at any bookstore; that will tell you how.

Anyone with a request concerning events or appearances may e-mail it to me or send it to: Publicity Department, Penguin Random House LLC, 375 Hudson Street, New York, NY 10014.

Those ambitious folk who wish to buy film, dramatic, or television rights to my books should contact Matthew Snyder, Creative Artists Agency, 9830 Wilshire Boulevard, Beverly Hills, CA 98212-1825.

Those who wish to make offers for rights of a literary nature should contact Anne Sibbald, Janklow & Nesbit, 445 Park Avenue, New York, NY 10022. (Note: This is not an invitation for you to send her your manuscript or to solicit her to be your agent.)

If you want to know if I will be signing books in your city, please visit my website, www.stuartwoods.com, where the tour schedule will be published a month or so in advance. If you wish me to do a book signing in your locality, ask your favorite bookseller to contact his Penguin representative or the Penguin publicity department with the request.

If you find typographical or editorial errors in my

book and feel an irresistible urge to tell someone, please write to Sara Minnich at Penguin's address above. Do not e-mail your discoveries to me, as I will already have learned about them from others.

A list of my published works appears in the front of this book and on my website. All the novels are still in print in paperback and can be found at or ordered from any bookstore. If you wish to obtain hardcover copies of earlier novels or of the two nonfiction books, a good used-book store or one of the online bookstores can help you find them. Otherwise, you will have to go to a great many garage sales.

When Stone Barrington is unwittingly thrust into the limelight, he finds himself scrambling to take cover. Fending off nuisances left and right, Stone soon discovers these efforts only increase the persistence of the most troublesome pests . . . and when he runs afoul of a particularly tenacious lady, he'll be struggling to protect not just his reputation, but his life.

Penguin
Random
House

1

Stone Barrington landed the Citation CJ3 Plus smoothly at Manassas Airport, in Virginia. As he taxied to the FBO he noticed a large black SUV parked on the ramp. To his eye it looked government and armored, and he wondered what VIP could be landing at the small, general aviation airport. His curiosity was soon satisfied: as he parked and cut his engines the vehicle began to move, and it stopped off his wingtip.

Stone ran through his shutdown checklist, then withdrew from the cockpit and opened the cabin door. A man in a blue suit with a shiny button in his lapel stood there.

"Mr. Barrington?"

"Yes," Stone replied, still mystified.

"Secretary Barker asked us to meet you."

Stone then noticed a second, similarly dressed man standing by the SUV and surveying the ramp, and he realized that Holly Barker had been sworn in as secretary of state. It was Election Day, and President Katharine Lee had, apparently, jumped the gun on her appointment, since she was the once and, if things went as they were supposed to, future President.

Stone handed the man a key. "Front luggage compartment," he said. "Take everything."

THE CAR STOPPED in front of the elegant double-width town house in Georgetown. Stone had not seen the place for some years, but he now owned it, having come to an arrangement with the Lees by which he had exchanged his Santa Fe house, plus an adjoining property and some cash, for this house, which former president Will Lee had owned with his late father since he was an aide to a United States senator.

The driver pressed a button on the sun visor and a garage door opened. The vehicle drove into the basement garage, and the security man opened the door for him. "The elevator is straight ahead," he said. "We'll get your luggage upstairs."

Stone thanked him, got into the elevator, and pressed the G button. A moment later he emerged into the main floor central hallway, where there was a buzz of people and voices. Caterers were arranging the living room for a party, and Holly Barker stood in the center of the room, directing traffic. She saw Stone and ran to him, throwing her arms around his neck. "Here you are!" she sang out in a happy voice.

"Here I am, indeed," he replied, joining her in the hug. As always, she felt just wonderful. "I thought you were expecting just a few friends," he said.

"It got out of hand," she replied. "We're at fifty and

counting. I'm learning that nobody declines an invitation from a high cabinet member. The caterers are felling another ox."

"So, you're already a cabinet member?"

"I was sworn in this morning."

"My congratulations," he said, kissing her.

"Come on upstairs, I'll show you your room."

Stone followed her into the elevator and took advantage of their momentary privacy to kiss her and pull her closer with his hand on her ass. They broke before the door opened.

She led him into what was, obviously, the master bedroom, which had two dressing rooms and two baths. "By tomorrow, all of Washington will know we're sharing a bed," she said. "I talked it over with Kate, and we agreed that it was better not to bother with a nod to convention, just to go ahead and let the world get used to the idea of a single woman with a sex life as a cabinet secretary—no fuss, no bother."

"I'm fine with that," Stone said. "It will do wonders for my reputation."

"Your bags are in that dressing room." She pointed. "You get unpacked, and by the way, we've upgraded to black tie. I knew you would bring a dinner jacket."

"You know me too well. What time do we make an appearance downstairs?"

"Seven o'clock," she replied. "I've rented three big-screen TVs, and that's when the action begins. Would you like a drink now?"

"I'd like a nap now, if that's all right. I was out with Dino and Viv until late last night. They were sorry they couldn't come, but the mayor stole them for his party."

"Apparently, my social magnet doesn't reach as far as New York," she said.

"It does, it just can't compete with the mayor's social magnet."

"I'll wake you at six," she said, pushing him onto the bed and pulling off his shoes. She threw a light blanket over him and kissed him on the forehead.

Stone sank into the soft bed and closed his eyes.

At six, Holly, already half-dressed, woke him, and he got into a shave and a shower and his dinner suit. At five minutes before seven, they got on the elevator.

"You are gorgeous," he said, looking her up and down.

"I'm afraid I've infringed on your generosity for a whole new wardrobe," she said. "The new job requires a lot more dressing up than national security advisor to the President. Your credit card is smoking."

"That's what it's for," Stone replied. "Keep the credit card and use it as you will."

The door opened, and they spilled into the hallway. There were already many voices coming from the living room.

The first person Stone recognized was Senator Saltonstall of New York. They shook hands warmly. "Stone, may I introduce my daughter Celeste, and her beau, Peter Rule?"

It was the first time Stone had met Kate Lee's son by her first marriage. He was a handsome young man of around thirty, and Ms. Saltonstall was a genuine beauty. "I'm delighted you're here," Stone said to Peter. Your mother has told me about you."

"Uh-oh," Peter said. "I hope she hasn't blown our secret."

"She has not," Stone replied, "but I think you just did."

"He has a big mouth," Celeste said, kissing him on the cheek, thereby displaying her left hand, revealing about eight carats of glittering, emerald-cut stone.

"And you have a big diamond," Stone said, "so it must not be too much of a secret."

"Dad wants to announce it tonight," Celeste said, "before we adjourn to the White House for the latter part of the evening. Mom and Will have to touch a few bases, including campaign headquarters."

Stone knew from his mother that Peter was planning a run for New York's other senatorial seat at the midterm. Stone leaned forward and whispered into Celeste's ear, "You'd better get something smaller for campaigning."

"I hadn't thought of that," she said, "but you're right."

HOLLY PULLED HIM away and began introducing him to all the others, a few of whom he'd met before. Then the TV sets were fired up, everybody got some dinner from the buffet, and the evening began.

Everyone was cheerful and happy, looking forward to Kate's second term.

2

It was after midnight, and the polls were now closed in the continental USA. The crowd was lighter by half and what little conversation there was was subdued. Everyone was glued to the TVs.

Kate had gone into the election with a nine-point lead in the polls and was predicted to get more than 400 electoral votes. Instead, she was struggling toward 270. That morning's newspapers had headlined a story that Will Lee had taken a fifty-million-dollar bribe from a Saudi prince, to get a huge arms deal with the USA. The Lee campaign had flooded the airwaves with her surrogates, denying everything and blaming the lie on her opponent. From what Stone could see on the TV screens, especially the jubilant reporting on Fox News, Kate's campaign had taken on water, and with very little time to right the ship.

Holly stared at the screen. "I'm going to be the shortest-serving secretary of state in history."

"It's going to come down to Florida," Stone said. "How is Kate feeling about Florida?"

"Just great, until today," Holly replied.

A waiter passed among them with a frosty champagne bottle, topping off glasses.

An anchorman came back from commercial, holding a sheet of paper in one hand and a microphone in the other.

"Here it comes," Holly said.

"Some incredible news has just come in," the man said. "Let's go to Cassie Crane outside Republican campaign headquarters in New York."

A young woman with a microphone stood on the sidewalk in a light rain, next to a geeky young man wearing a dark suit and heavy glasses. "Chris, I'm here with Jason Foxworthy, who is a poll analyst with the Jack Marion campaign. Jason, I think it's best for you to tell your own story, then we'll have some questions."

"Thank you, Cassie," the young man said in a surprisingly deep voice. "Late last night I picked up a phone in our office and overheard a conversation between James Heckley, a speechwriter for Senator Marion, and Eliot Wafford, the owner of the *Washington Debater*, a conservative newspaper. I know it was Heckley because I could see him across the room as he spoke, and I recognized Wafford's voice from seeing him on TV shows. Also, Heckley called him Eliot, twice, during the conversation. They were confirming details of the big story that broke today about the alleged bribe taken by Will Lee. In fact, it might be more accurate to say that they were getting their stories straight, because Heckley was reading a draft of the story, and Wafford was suggesting changes to make it stronger and more damning. When they had finished their conversation, Wafford said that he was holding the *Debater*'s presses to get it into the early-morning edition. They both seemed very pleased with themselves."

"Let's be clear, Jason," Cassie said. "You are saying that you overheard James Heckley and Eliot Wafford contriving this story?"

"That's exactly what I'm saying," Foxworthy replied. "The story is a lie, a complete fabrication." He held up an iPhone. "And I recorded all but ten or fifteen seconds of their phone conversation." He held up a wrinkled sheet of paper. "And I retrieved the draft from the wastebasket beside James Heckley's desk."

Cassie addressed the camera. "Chris, I have to get Jason to a secure location right away, and we've got a car standing by for him. There's one more revelation in the story, though—I've heard from two campaign staffers that James Heckley left campaign headquarters nearly two hours ago for Teterboro Airport, where a private jet was waiting to fly him out of New York. First reports say that the airplane had filed a flight plan for Caracas, Venezuela, but of course that destination could be changed en route. Back to you, Chris."

The anchor stared gravely into the camera. "Cassie, that was a brilliant piece of reportage, and we here all thank you for it. Unfortunately, the polls have already closed."

It was as though lightning had struck the living room—everyone was talking at once, some happy, others in tears. Two people were shouting into their cell phones.

Stone stood up and pointed at the TV set. "Everybody shut up!" he shouted.

The anchorman was now standing next to the campaign map. "We have just heard that Florida has reported its election results, and by a margin of less than four thousand votes, Katharine Lee has carried the state, and with Florida's twenty-nine electoral votes, has been reelected President of the United States, winning three hundred and three electoral votes. I think it's fair to say that a national catastrophe has been averted."

Cheering erupted in the room, and Holly fell into Stone's arms.

STONE AWOKE A little after seven AM to the sound of Holly talking on the phone. She hung up. "Big news," she said. "Eliot Wafford has been arrested by the FBI on a charge of election tampering. They're still looking for James Heckley, but his flight diverted to Mexico City and landed there early this morning."

Stone switched on the TV, and every news station was reporting its version of the Heckley/Wafford story. Kate's victory in the election seemed almost like an afterthought. He switched it off. "I don't think I can take this on an empty stomach."

As if on cue, a maid knocked and pushed a cart into the room. Moments later, Stone and Holly were sitting up in bed eating scrambled eggs and bacon. The TV was back on.

"And what does your day hold?" Stone asked.

"I'm visiting the State Department and being introduced to my staff, or at least, those I don't already know from working with them on the National Security Council. Stan Adamson is going to be there to introduce me. And you?"

"I'm due for a drink with Kate and Will in the family quarters at six. So are you."

"Oh, yes."

"Since they appointed me their personal attorney, I've put together a team at Woodman & Weld, which will be known as The Barrington Group. There's a thick envelope on the table across the room containing a document I put together explaining everything. I'll deliver a copy to them this evening."

"I'll look forward to reading it."

"There's something else I want to discuss with you, but I don't want to talk about it here." He tapped an ear with his forefinger.

Holly looked shocked. "Really? Not here?"

"That's correct," Stone said. "We'll talk about it later, when the circumstances are more favorable."

"Whatever you say," Holly replied. She jumped out of bed. "I've got to get myself together."

3

That evening they took the elevator to the basement garage, where Holly's SUV awaited them. The street door was open, and Stone pulled her up the ramp with him.

"I'll be just a minute," Holly called to her security team.

Stone put his briefcase into the SUV, then they turned down the block.

"Okay, shoot," Holly said, taking Stone's arm.

Stone didn't hesitate. "I want you to have the house swept by your security team for listening devices, and I want them to do this at least every three or four days, but not on a regular schedule. Your car, too."

"Are you coming over all paranoid on me, Stone?"

"I don't think that the political opposition is going to cheerfully accept the election results," he said, "and we've already seen how far they're willing to go."

"But Wafford is already in jail, and Heckley is a fugitive."

"Wafford has certainly already been bailed out, and being a fugitive won't keep Heckley from operating for long. Even if I'm wrong about this, it won't hurt to be a little paranoid."

"All right, whatever you say."

"Also, you have to start being more careful in how you proceed with your life."

"What do you mean?"

"For instance, you had your car meet me at the Manassas Airport yesterday. That's personal use of an official vehicle, and that could come back to bite you on the ass."

"I suppose," Holly said.

"When you get to the office tomorrow, I want you to report that to your chief administrative officer, have him give you a bill for the cost of that service, and reimburse the State Department with a personal check. Thereafter, anytime you make personal use of any government property or service, do the same thing. You want to establish a consistent paper trail."

"Oh, all right."

They reached the next corner, and Stone turned them back toward the house. "The other thing is, we're probably being photographed while we're on this little stroll, so you'd better get ready to see the photographs in the *National Inquisitor*, because that little rag is one of Eliot Wafford's properties."

"I told you, I've already discussed this with Kate, and she's fine with me being a single woman with a sex life."

"Tomorrow morning I want you to meet with your public affairs officer at State and discuss me with him or her."

"Her."

"Have her prepare a few statements to the press, to be distributed as soon as such an article runs. We'll be mentioned in the more prestigious papers, too—you can count on that, so be ready for an instant response."

"Okay."

"And don't mention a sex life—make it a personal life. They won't need any help from you in bringing sex into the story."

"Well, the good news is they won't be able to call me a lesbian."

"No, they'll probably hint that you're bisexual. Don't let yourself be photographed hugging or kissing a woman. And, apart from the statements that you and your public affairs officer are going to write, don't make any statements or answer any questions on your personal life. You'll want to establish that rule immediately and stick to it."

"All right. Anything else?"

"Yes. Do you recall an occasion in your personal life, many years back, when you were chief of police at Orchid Beach, when you liberated a suitcase full of cash before, during, or after a major drug bust?"

"I seem to recall such an incident," Holly said.

"And you may recall opening a numbered account in a Cayman Islands bank, which issued you a credit card for your surreptitious use."

"Yes."

"I've given a great deal of thought as to how you might legitimize these funds, which now amount to, what, seven million dollars?"

"Eight and a half."

"I've come to the conclusion that any action we might take with regard to laundering that money would be far too dangerous to contemplate, so you must immediately stop drawing on those funds with your credit card or depositing or withdrawing further funds. Do you have a legitimate investment account?"

"Yes, with a brokerage house."

"Good. For as long as you're secretary of state, and maybe for some time after that, don't go near any of the Cayman funds."

Holly nodded. "You're right."

"And avoid any trips—official or unofficial—to the Cayman Islands. When you opened the account, was your passport stamped on entering that country?"

"No. I'm not that stupid."

"You're going to be issued a diplomatic passport, so shred your old one and lock your credit card in your safe at home." He paused. "On second thought, give the card to me, and I'll secure it."

"All right, I'll give it to you tonight."

"And I hope I don't have to tell you not to use a personal e-mail server?"

Holly laughed. "Of course not."

"And close any personal e-mail accounts you already have. Have you usually done your personal e-mail on your own computer?"

"Yes, it's at home."

"Then remove the hard drive from it and give it to me, along with your credit card, and install a new hard drive."

"I know how to do that."

"The State Department will issue you a new phone, perhaps more than one. Give me the old one and buy a new iPhone for strictly personal use, as in e-mails to your father and his wife or to me. Even then, be very circumspect about what you say in any e-mail and use that phone as little as possible."

"Why not just destroy the old hard drive and the phone?"

"Because you may find yourself in circumstances where it's to your advantage to turn over old devices. That way, no one can say you've destroyed them to hide something."

"I see."

"You're also going to have to be circumspect in your personal life, especially with what invitations you accept, even to dinner parties. In those cases, always ask your hostess to send you a guest list. You don't want to find yourself backed into a corner by a journalist who demands some background or a quote."

"Can I see men other than you?" she asked slyly.

"Of course not!"

"I thought not."

"Oh, all right, but before you make any dates, ask your people to run a background check on the men."

"You're serious?"

"Do you want to find out later that somebody you've slept with is an unregistered lobbyist for some creepy foreign regime? Or that he has two wives and families in different cities?"

Holly sighed. "You know what I'm really happy about?" she asked.

"What?"

"I'm just delighted that I don't have an ex-husband out there, spreading lies about me, or even worse, the truth!"

Laughing, they got into the car and left for the White House.

STUART WOODS

"Addictive . . . Pick it up at your peril.
You can get hooked."
—*Lincoln Journal Star*